Where is God? Wherever human beings let God in.
We must let God in even as Job did in the depths of his bewilderment.

—Rabbi Menachem Mendel of Kotzk

Disturbance
of the
Inner Ear

....

JOYCE HACKETT

CARROLL & GRAF PUBLISHERS
NEW YORK

In addition to my wonderful agent and editor, Tina Bennett and Tina Pohlman, I wish to thank the Blue Mountain Center, the Czech Music Fund (and Miroslav Drozd), the Ruth Ingersoll Goldmark Fund, the MacDowell Colony, the Ireneaus Trust, the Pennsylvania Council on the Arts, the Ragsdale Foundation, the Puffin Foundation, the Virginia Center for the Creative Arts, and the Claire Woolrich Foundation, as well as the fine staffs at the Leo Baeck Institute and at the United States Memorial Holocaust Museum. I am also grateful to the many first and second generation survivors of Theresienstadt who shared their experiences.

DISTURBANCE OF THE INNER EAR

Carroll & Graf Publishers
An Imprint of Avalon Publishing Group Inc.
161 William St., 16th Floor
New York, NY 10038

First Carroll & Graf edition 2002

Interior design by Sue Canavan

Library of Congress Cataloging-in-Publication Data is available.

ISBN: 0-7867-1046-2

Printed in the United States of America
Distributed by Publishers Group West

I

(falling, as a body falls)

Signor Perso was the last person who knew who I'd been, and what I'd done, and when I awoke to the silent absence of his breathing, my stomach fluttered with giddy, untethered possibility. I set my passport in the hotel ashtray and lit its pages on fire; before the flames withered, I had thrown on my clothes. But when I opened the door a flurry of ashes swirled up into the restive air, and instead of leaving, I rushed back to try and catch them before they could drift down onto his body. His utter stillness ridiculed my frantic, stupid groping until I quietly stood over him amid the black snow. After a while, though I knew I shouldn't, I touched his face. My finger scudded against his dead cheek, and there I was, sitting on the bed in our pension room, stuck behind a wall he had sailed over effortlessly, without me, in his sleep.

I turned off the light and sat down. Unbuttoned my coat. There was no point, really, in fleeing. With my history it would only be quixotic not to expect this sort of thing, wherever I went. I'd been waiting for this to happen since our last night in Milwaukee: even at the Milan airport, as Signor Perso breezed through the customs line for Italian nationals, I'd gotten stuck in a line of Americans so long and stagnant it curled back onto itself like a tangled fly strip, and when I suddenly couldn't see him, I was sure he was dead. So that now, a week later, I was not terribly surprised. I emptied the ashtray in the toilet. With a wet washcloth, I dabbed the dark fingerprint I'd left on Signor Perso's cheek and proceeded to lift the flecks of ash from his perfectly groomed white mustache, his tissue-thin eyelids, from his dressing gown, from the hands folded over the little volume on his chest as if he'd laid himself out for the occasion. Then I started on the bed and carpet. Once all visible evidence of ash had been removed, I confirmed the pronunciations of *cadavere* and *coffina* in my handy plastic-coated dictionary and compiled a short list of new words I might now need. And while the Italian police put me on hold, I practiced his signature, over and over, until my scrawl matched the top of his traveler's checks.

There was one minor problem. I'd found Signor Perso in the middle of the night, and towards dawn, I got horribly hungry. There were two eggs in the tiny kitchenette refrigerator. I thought I should probably eat them. But I had never actually cooked breakfast: I had lived in hotels with my father, Yuri, since I was seven; when I wasn't touring, my mother cooked; and later Signor Perso had insisted on making me breakfast in bed, every morning, because he had stroke-induced aphasia, kept losing the words for things, and the ritual of breakfast was a firth flowing surely back towards memory. Still, I got out a spoon, determined to scramble the eggs. But something was wrong: no matter how hard I stirred, stubborn gobs floated up to the surface. I thought I remembered from TV that you put milk in scrambled eggs, but there wasn't any milk, and now the eggs were gooey and ruined and I couldn't even boil them. For a minute everything started closing in, how little I knew about anything. But then a notation came into my ear, in my father's cutting basso, about how to handle the passage: *(as if for the hundredth time)*. Yuri's standard refrain, if I complained about a difficulty in a passage I was practicing, was to tell me that boot leather tastes like steak once you eat it for the hundredth time. The fact was, this death was not my first.

(as if for the hundredth time) I held my breath to slow down my heart, the way I used to do before I went onstage, and counted the number of minutes Signor Perso had now been dead. Once I had a number, I could breathe again. It was proof that time was passing, was a current that would slowly tow this latest death downstream. I turned on the spigot, poured the egg goo down the drain, took a shower, thoroughly cleaned the bathtub behind me, and dressed. Beneath the thin silk fabric of his gown, Signor Perso seemed too naked, so I wrestled him into a suit and tie. And as a flat slate light diffused the dark, I played to him.

No one heard me. For years now I have muted my cello by wrapping a thick silk sash around the bridge and wedging its ends firmly into the *f* holes. To save my ear from being dulled by too much sound. That was how it started, anyway: I used it on tour, to warm up for performances. The silence forced me inside, forced the music back up into my nervous system until I walked onstage with all the notes of a perfect performance streaming through my flesh at once, the sound bursting from my bow's first slice like the flesh of an overripe plum.

In any case: I was not arrested. At dusk, after fourteen hours —luckily Signor Perso had just bathed—a *commedia buffa* traipsed in. The bumbling carabinieri in their tricornered hats were surprisingly manageable; they seemed to feel that Signor Perso's Italian passport simplified his death. The interrogation was of limited duration. Once they understood that I was neither the wife nor the granddaughter, they let the matter drop and took a protective, tactful stance. Their only direct question was the captain's greasy, expectant *Looks like my size?* as he fingered the hem of Signor Perso's pants, prompted by the detective's astute observation that pleats that looked that good on a dead guy had to be Italian tailoring. The detective mentioned his cousin, a mortician; I understood the deal that was being cut and asked about the price. He said that depended. Presumably, he said, the body would be cremated? My voice stuck in my throat at the thought of burning him in an oven. The detective said they'd give me the day to decide. Though the deposit he requested was six out of my seven traveler's checks, I signed them over. And avoided further discussion when, after several unsuccessful attempts to upend Signor Perso's body into the pension's tiny elevator, they dropped him on the carpet and lit up. After a suitable caesura I simply walked out into the hall, retrieved the cuff link that had fallen from Signor Perso's wrist, and set it atop the ashtray's tiny, pristine dune, thus forcing them to extinguish their cigarettes between their fingertips before carrying him down the eight flights of stairs.

At the memorial, though, something happened that I could not have expected. The basilica's acoustics were abysmal, the organist's junky spinet piano a joke, the world-famous cello, not in great shape. There was no rosin in the case, and I had to make due with a stub of chalk from a blackboard in the basement. The ancient bridge was parched and shrunken, the action far too low, and the strings buzzed when I shifted. They were unwrapped steel and cut into the pads of my fingers. It felt like the bass board was coming unglued. I had been playing muted for nearly a decade, and as I rocked the bow over the strings in a balance exercise, the precision of movement needed to bring out a decent tone was wildly beyond my muscles' atrophy. Right away I cramped my hand trying to bow hard enough to fill the damp Romanesque basilica. The Savant had nowhere near the attack of a Strad or a Montagnana. The mousy sound stayed muffled within its body, like a cello wrapped in a cocoon. What a joke, I thought, the old saw about instruments picking up the tone and pattern of their former owners—if the Savant had absorbed anything from its years of being played by Vrashkansova, its wood had long since ceased to resonate at her frequency.

I was having so much trouble manipulating the belly that I was practically leg wrestling the thing. But then I somehow pulled off a phrase a bit like the way Vrashkansova did it on that old Victor 78 of her last public recital, in Prague, in '37. It slid out without my doing, as if she had reached up from the dead to grasp my bowing hand. Everything became different then, the way someone's looks change when you fall in love with them. I stopped trying. Suddenly the Savant's laryngitis took on texture and mystery, and we saturated the dome. A long still spell opened where each note came in slow motion. Phrases fell like ribbons. I was playing the Fauré *Elégie,* and for a second, for literally an instant, I shut my eyes and forgot the death.

Vrashkansova was Signor Perso's idol. In Paris, before the war, he had taken a master class with her that he said had changed his life. In photos she wore dark mourning dresses; she was tiny, always slightly hunched; you had the feeling she carried the weight of the world on the small hump that peeked out between her shoulders. On the recordings her low voice hovers behind the Savant, like a mourner at a wake, quietly chanting a ritual lament. Music resonated through her body, took physical control. She was, herself, an instrument, and Signor Perso had lived for the moment when I would take her place. His leftover confidence, his huge memory of hearing me as a child, had been crushing me for years. By the time we met, six months after my parents died, my talent was unraveling like a string stuck to their heels, but Signor Perso straightened his tie and cleared his throat as if I were his arranged-marriage bride. Someone like yourself, he said nervously, ought to go down to Chicago? Then I started sawing away, and he understood. He'd tried to help me for nearly a decade, taught me piano, played duets with me for hours, played me poetry records late into evening, but the longer he held fast to his faith in me, the more ashamed I was to make a sound. Until finally I just stopped making them.

What I heard now was a sound beyond Vrashkansova, a voice so sacred and whole that it occurred to me to wonder whether an inanimate object could possess the spirit of God. When I drew back my bow I felt it tugging the breath of the mourners. A frisson of excitement jolted through me. I wondered what he would say.

It had not really occurred to me until that moment how enormously *dead* Signor Perso actually was. Like a plane door blown open my pretence of surviving exploded, and then I was spiraling, the piece nearly over, I was outside the cello and outside my playing, the music devoid of breath, the sound flat and hard and too correct. What followed was the usual pillar-of-salt disaster: my hands rushing through, dying to get it over with, my heart sitting by the roadside, begging to go back and start again. And the music was gone, shriveled back into its score, to clusters of spots as still and lifeless as the dark-veiled widows dotting the wooden pews.

Performance is final, final the way things are that burn up time. A great performance is precious for the same reason an awful one grows tumorous in memory, because it can never be repeated.

I had thought that someone at the funeral might offer me a ride after I performed. As I was leaving I carried the cello awkwardly, with the bulge facing in, like a TV actor playing a cellist. I've been lugging around a cello since I was four, so I have to do this to seem at all helpless. But Signor Perso had come back to Italy to retire after forty-some years abroad, so besides the pock-marked mortician I was avoiding—I had promised to pay the balance at the funeral—only a few people had shown up. I didn't know any of them, and none of them knew me; in Italy, intro-ductions count for a lot. Also, as the church-mouse organist drooled out the end of the *Elégié* on his abysmal spinet piano, I had stopped playing, midphrase, and walked off the platform. This may have been a factor.

Outside the basilica, there were no taxis. It was a Saturday evening, but other than the triumphal statue of Augustus pre-siding over the piazza, the street was empty, the shabby shops behind the monumental colonnade, dark. Fog curdled above the gray heaps of snow. Signor Perso and I had arrived in Milan at the end of the coldest November on record; but that afternoon, as I was leaving for my interview at Mr. Pettyward's, the owner of the pension near the Brera where Signor Perso and I were staying had banged on the door and demanded money; so I had put on my best black dress, because I knew that no matter what happened at the interview, I could not come back to the pension before the service, or indeed, ever again.

A light snow had begun to fall. In my thin wool dress and coat, I was freezing. I stood awhile in the deserted piazza, deciding what to do, while not deciding anything. Before my eye I saw Signor Perso, after our first time together, saw his hands falling, fingers wiggling, as he searched for the word for snow. After the stroke, the aphasia had eaten into the farthest recesses of his mind; that morning he'd gone out without a shirt. When he got home and saw me looking at him, he looked down and saw his naked chest, and lay down and wept. We both understood then that it was the beginning of the end, that he would not recover. I'd put on the radio and sat down beside him and rested my head on his chest. The skin was leathery, but his flesh surprised me. It wasn't old. It was hard with experience. I raked the long white hairs with my fingers, liking his safe smell, the way age had muted his chest into something neither male nor female. And I'd kissed it.

But, us, why, he asked. I'd assumed all along that he was waiting for me: why else had he settled my aunt's debts, and asked me to move in, and never mentioned my parents? Why else would someone read you the Bible and Shakespeare and Dante, or take you on a boat across the Great Lakes for your twenty-first birthday, just to hear the falls? But then he asked again, *Why now, you with me?* On the radio, Christa Ludwig was coming into the slow, luminous rise towards the end of the *Alto Rhapsody.* I lay my head down on his chest, and for a while I lay listening, under his slow wheeze. Finally I asked him why, why he'd kept on teaching me for so long, when we both knew I couldn't perform. That was when he told me about the old piano teacher in *Doctor Faustus* who gave his incomprehensible lectures on Beethoven. What mattered was not whether the people in his village had understood his ideas. It was Important Simply to Hear Them. Then the music ended, and Signor Perso lost his words again, but he got urgent to finish. He raised his arms, and then his hands floated down, fingers wiggling, as if playing a falling piano. *What is the notes,* he said, *the white notes falling? Snow?* I said. He nodded. *In a garden, the snow, it wets,* he said. *Not asking where the seeds are hiding.*

On our last night in Milwaukee, our last night in his big oak bed, a gap had opened inside me as we were making love: all at once I looked at the packed suitcases, the travel clothes he'd laid out for me on top of my trunk, and knew, as I hadn't before, that we were moving to Italy to end his life. I *missed* him. Signor Perso saw the wanting in my eyes, had tried, again, but in the end it was the same as every other time. I'd been watchful, while he cried out. Afterwards I lay awake, my years of failing grinding against his empty mortar-bowl of waiting. Once his breathing steadied, I disentangled my limbs and sneaked down to the basement to try and play for him, one last time. A while later he'd found me laboring over Bach, playing muted. With the bottom of his nightshirt he blotted the sweat on my temples. His eyes saw the frantic overtrying, saw my hands toiling like blind, frantic ants. And did not speak. When I looked again, his eyes had cohered into grief.

A grimy orange streetcar squealed up in front of the colonnade like a cattle car. The piazza was now blanketed in white. I realized I had been standing outside the basilica for nearly an hour; I could not feel my feet. I had never been on a tram; it would cost money; this was not the time to waste what little I had getting caught and fined for traveling without a ticket. Besides, the tram was headed out through a huge arch in the ancient city wall, which seemed like the wrong direction, because the Pettywards lived near the *centro*.

As it hurtled into the dark, a spark ignited a vast overhead web of wires I hadn't noticed. I hoisted up the cello and headed in the other direction. It did occur to me, as I stumbled forward, that someone might try to steal the instrument. One of the doughy, well-meaning librarians at the Milwaukee Public Library had cautioned that in Italy, everybody steals everything. But *(as if for the hundredth time)* seemed to indicate that this passage ought to be played out without precautions, that precautions might actually bring on what was dreaded. If I had learned anything from Yuri, it was how to remain innocuous. Carrying the Savant on foot, I reasoned, I would look like a student. I had not slept in days, and though my hair was pinned in a bun, I looked scruffy, a bit unkempt; no one would speculate long about the instrument in my scuffed brown case. For Italians, the notion that a young woman with puffy eyes and a boxy American coat could be carrying a rare sixteenth-century cello, let alone one of the thirty-eight instruments that Charles IX ordered from Andrea Amati in the early 1560s, was not within the realm of possibility. That I would have *the* Amati, the *freak* Amati, sized smaller and completed in error, the only one he made that not only swelled with the warmth and complexity of the best cognac in France— Amati's signature tone—but also had the burn of it, the acoustics for a modern hall, the caterwaul of a Strad: to a bunch of people so steeped in style and beauty that they seemed to have lost the gene for depth perception, the notion would seem absurd.

I suppose I was under the spell of the kind of insane yet practical thinking that subtly undermines everything during a crisis. I remember spot-calculating that I had passed the three-day anniversary of Signor Perso's death and taking it as a sign that I was surviving. It was the first winter night, ever, that I had gone out without wearing gloves—I had decided I no longer needed them. And so in spite of the bitter cold, despite the instrument I was carrying, though I was wearing stockings and pumps and everything was icy, I thought I should save the last of Signor Perso's money, my last traveler's check, and try and walk.

I wandered for hours. At some point, a lovely postperformance coda, the theme from Schubert's *Unfinished Symphony*, drifted into my ear. That afternoon, at my interview in Mr. Pettyward's palatial living room, I had gradually tuned in to someone humming it behind the door. When I finally tipped my head in the direction of the humming, Mr. Pettyward announced, *My son*

Clayton, as if he were presenting a fancy car or an antique. As if on cue, a tall, gangly kid with curly red hair walked in, his finger in a book. He looked me over defeatedly—either this had happened many times before, or he saw right away that something about me was terribly off—but then he said, *Yeah, fine,* and picked up the Schubert again. Under his corduroy shirttails, what seemed an unnatural lump bulged in his pants. He caught me staring, and his lips curled upward, watching me blush. Then he reached in his pocket—the Schubert gathering momentum—and wriggled out a green rubber fish. Flashing me a happy-face, he swam it out of the room.

The Schubert kept up, from the hall. As quietly as I could, I asked about the bandage on Clayton's scalp. Mr. Pettyward got up and flipped a switch on the wall, and a thick blanket of white noise drowned out the humming. There seemed to be machines in every corner, their sounds settling over us like layers of Vesuvian ash. He sat back down and cleared his throat defensively. In a low voice, he said that Clayton lisped. That he was left-handed. That he tripped frequently. That for the last set of stitches he'd had to wait seven hours in the *polyclinico.* This time he'd taken Clayton to an absurdly expensive private clinic in San Pretorese. Without the slightest trace of humor he said he thought the time differential just about made up the cost. He said he was banking on the fact that Clayton's head was worth it. Or at least it would be after I taught him to play.

At the very least, Mr. Pettyward added, his son seemed to have quite a *durable* head.

For as long as I can remember, exposure to cold has pitched me over the edge. That pain's petty tyranny, the tiny focus it exacts, exceeds my interest in the quotidian. But I didn't panic immediately. The blocky neoclassical facades looked familiar, and the Schubert was a trusted companion. Mr. Pettyward had sent his driver to pick me up that morning; through the tinted glass windows, I had not noticed the route we were taking; and after the interview I hurried off to the funeral, without taking note of the address. Still, I wandered Milan's twisting streets, hiking over heaps of plowed snow, confidently expecting the building to appear at any moment. Mr. Pettyward and his son lived across from a church, so whenever I spotted a spire, I headed towards it. At some point I glanced across the street and saw an arrow-topped gate undulating beneath four small archways. Behind the tiny courtyard it guarded sat the fat square brick tower of the old Roman circus that Signor Perso had pointed out when we visited the home of his acquaintance, Marie-Antoinette de Something. Her home was nowhere near Mr. Pettyward's. It suddenly got much colder. I sprinted out into the cross-street, to try and find somewhere to go, but my heel caught in some tram tracks. I slipped. And once I knew I was falling I let go and I fell like a dead body falls.

I couldn't move.

Not because I was hurt, but because I was trapped in a dream I'd had when I was fourteen, on the eve of my Carnegie Hall debut. In it I am sitting on a sidewalk with my cello, on a winter night, in a deathly silent city with no one in it but me.

Throughout my body, my heartbeat hammered out bruises. But there was also a comfort in having hit ground, in having nowhere left to fall, in having the skin of my cheek stuck to the icy concrete. My body's shudder finally quieted. It had been the vertigo, I realized, of free fall.

Then I heard a sniffle. Breathing. And I knew I would have to get up. A low voice asked if I was all right. Something was tugging at my arm from behind, pulling off a hard, heavy weight. Someone was taking the Savant. I grabbed it down again.

—*Lasciami star*, I barked. Leave me be. Signor Perso and I had met as teacher and student, when I was fifteen and he was sixty-six, so we had never stopped using the formal. I was glad it came out, now, instinctively, to draw the line between me and this man.

—Let me help you, he said at the same time, and tried again

to take the Savant. But I was holding it by the neck, so he hauled me with it. Halfway up, I said, —I'm fine. His eyes locked onto mine and he let go. I thudded back onto the sidewalk, the cello on top of me.

This second fall knocked the wind out of me. For a long while he stood there, his arms folded, as vague versions of faraway cars rolled in and out like waves. Though a whole trapped universe sparkled in the mica sidewalk, the streets were deserted, the sky starless and empty. In the ice-cold air our breaths hung like clouds before they disappeared. I held my breath so I could see him. Turned out my mugger was a man in a salmon silk shirt and a navy blazer with gold buttons that glistered in the streetlight: a fireplug body, dressed casually patrician, gloves but no coat, in his early thirties. His early baldness made it hard to tell.

—I wouldn't want to be the one who tried to take that thing away from you, he said softly.

A thick mass of pain crammed itself inside my head. My hands stung and my left knee was throbbing. I handed up the Savant—the fall, in this cold, had probably cracked it—and pushed myself up. A dimpled knee bulged out of a rip in my stockings. I wear control tops—they squeeze you in—so a pudge blobbed out of the hole, scraped and bloody, and when I tried to shove it back in, to pull the hole together, I teetered and began to slip. As I went down, a gentle hold rose up against my elbow. I had not cried when Signor Perso died, had kept my breathing steady, and played to him instead. Now, just this man's hand cradling my elbow made me shudder and start to break down.

—Don't help me, I said quietly.

One thing you learn with a father like Yuri is that to allow yourself to be pitied is the beginning of the end. I concentrated on stopping my body's shivering, on relaxing, on not appearing cold. It seemed crucial to handle the encounter as *moderato*, crucial not to appear desperate. The man seemed genuinely concerned; but on the other hand, if he was a detective sent out to arrest me, concern would be the right tone for his performance.

—Let me help you, he said, almost annoyed. I'm a doctor.

He was a short man—with heels, I came almost to his nose—and his presence was quiet. He pulled off his glove, softly brushed some grains of ice from my cheek, then studied me closely.

Reaching around under my chignon he cradled the back of my neck with a gentle, steady pressure, and I felt myself unraveling in the kindness of the gesture. Most people touch to take, but this man's hands listened—it was almost frightening for how long—until the muscles in my neck gave way. His features blurred. I forced my eyes to focus. We were standing in front of an eyeglass store with a huge lit eyeball in the *vetrine*. Its light gouged out the hollows under his eyes. He was actually only bald in front; on the sides and back he had wavy black hair that, by compensation, was a little too long. He had dark eyes, dark, thick lips, and a gnarled, ugly, crooked nose that looked like it'd been broken. But his voice had a muscular grace that felt familiar, the broken strength of a scar.

He eased my head back until he had me looking straight up into the streetlight. Beyond its hazy aura, the sky glowed a heavy, chalky rose. He probed my forehead gingerly, pulling down my lower lids one at a time.

—You have an accent, he said, passing his hand back and forth in front of my eyes.

—Foreigners often do.

—That would explain it, he said. Did you lose consciousness?

—Not really. I think I wanted him to think I had but wouldn't admit it.

—Can I take you where you're going?

—That's all right, I said, relieved to have someplace to go.

He passed me my cello. —*Sicura?* he said, as if he could see that what I really wanted was for him to pick me up and carry me.

I thanked him again. He turned and ran towards a *tabacchaio* on the corner.

Marie-Antoinette's apartment number, 21, was the date of Signor Perso's birthday. That I remembered. Though by now it was far past dinnertime, I rang her bell. Signor Perso had taught Marie-Antoinette's mother at the Paris Conservatoire; her grandfather had been a patron of Casals. We had run into her at the Scala, and she'd invited us back for a drink. Two days later, as the police were carrying him out, she called wanting to talk to Signor Perso about some job teaching the fifteen-year-old son of some rich man named Pettyward. I could not bring myself to say it, to say the word for what he was, so instead I said he was *retired*. As an afterthought, Marie-Antoinette asked if I'd be interested. Our one meeting had been enough for me to see that she was the kind of person who held perpetual auditions for the play that was her life, who would bring in an understudy at the first sign of trouble. Still, I took the number.

She buzzed me in through the small, human-size cutout in the tall wooden *portone,* and then released the lift without asking who I was. I wondered whether she was having a party. The wooden elevator was cocooned in a fuzzy, surreal silence, like a room in a dream. I reached down to pick some of the granules out of my bleeding leg. Just when I began to think the elevator wasn't moving, the doors slid open onto the lavish apartment.

Marie-Antoinette's maid was a hunched, white-haired woman who clearly did not want to be up at this hour. She cringed at the sight of me—clearly, I looked like a refugee. I took off my coat myself, so she wouldn't have to touch me. At least my leg and face were proof I'd fallen; they gave me an excuse to drop by.

(con brio) I bent down and petted Marie-Antoinette's aging Afghan hound. I dislike dogs, dislike the way they sniff you and lick you and deposit their saliva between your legs as if they weren't the sort of obedient brownshirts who would dutifully sink their teeth into your calf upon command. The one time I'd been here with Signor Perso, I had particularly disliked Rudolph's skinny face and the minuscule brain it contained. That said, I hugged the thing. Marie-Antoinette had stated outright that she never invited anyone back who didn't adore her dog.

—Lovely, Marie-Antoinette said, as she relocked the elevator. Marie-Antoinette was a small, perfectly coifed blonde. —You went like that to your interview?

Before I could explain, she walked away. Probably it didn't matter: already the last time, when she had invited us back for drinks, Marie-Antoinette had let me know that my ensemble fell far below a passable level of Italian sartorial elegance. Onstage, my mother's taste had prevailed, but in life Yuri's peasant utilitarianism domineered my wardrobe. In Milwaukee I had fit in, but here in Italy, I simply couldn't pass.

Though I wanted to check the Savant, I followed her into the sitting room, where a tanned man with big white teeth, who looked like a game-show host, was pouring a drink for a tall blond middle-aged Barbie.

—Fabio, meet my little friend *La Boheme,* Marie-Antoinette said dryly.

—Mimi, I jokingly introduced myself, and we exchanged nods. The tanned man turned to introduce the blonde by his side. In the middle of saying that she was a former Miss Czechoslovakia, his eyes dropped to my scraped, bloody knee. Before long I found myself enmeshed in an elaborate lie about someone knocking me down and trying to steal my cello. It had only been luck, I said, that I'd found myself around the corner. It was going well: Fabio asked the maid to find some gauze, and was translating for the beauty queen, who expressed her concern with swishing noises, alternating with clucking noises. But just as I was about to bring the story around to the Pettywards' address, the bell rang. Marie-Antoinette jumped up to unlock the elevator again. I stood up.

—No no no, stay, she said. It's just somebody I sent out for cigarettes. Giulio! I'd forgotten you were visiting. Know someone in the neighborhood?

—I wasn't gone that long. *Good evening,* he said in English.

I froze, not just because I was caught, but because he already knew, just from our few words in Italian on the street, where I was from.

—You know each other? Marie-Antoinette asked.

Giulio handed her two packs of cigarettes. —We've met, he said, as he lit two in his mouth.

—Via whom? she said, as if trying to reel in the net of people who had connected us, behind her back, without her permission.

Giulio passed her a cigarette without answering.

—Isabel's just been mugged and almost raped, she whispered urgently.

—Just now? Down on the street? asked Giulio.

The blood began to drain from my head. I nodded.

—Really, Giulio said, his eyes boring into me. I wish I'd known at the time. I might have *done* something. Do you need a doctor? he asked solemnly.

The idea of my needing a doctor, now that everyone I'd ever loved was dead, was so absurd that I began to choke. Everyone stared. I hiccuped abruptly and tried to salvage my pathetic tale. For obvious reasons I glossed over the earlier part of the evening—the notation I came up with for Signor Perso's state, now, was *resting*—and continued with how I'd barely escaped. I described a struggle, begging Giulio with my eyes to keep quiet.

—Milan's chock-full of miscreants and reprobates, Giulio said, shaking his head.

Marie-Antoinette frowned. —But excuse me, from the Basilica of San Lorenzo, in this weather, I mean, why not take a taxi?

I opened my mouth, then slowly closed it to avoid triggering the avalanche of sobbing gathering behind my face. Luckily, Giulio interrupted, —Because then we'd never have met.

Giulio seemed to intuit right away that I didn't have money, or that money was somehow a factor, because he smiled reassuringly and changed the subject. As he cleaned my knee, his measured Italian gave way to a burbling, melodious French. He went off on a long riff about noses in Milan versus noses in Paris, where he had been to see his fiancée, Daphne, who was a friend of Marie-Antoinette and an heiress of something. From his breast pocket, Fabio pulled out what looked like a sterling silver cigarette case. He lay two tiny white plastic cups on his eyes, tucked in his collar, and flicked a switch. A bright purplish glow lit up his face. He was tanning it.

As they talked I fell in and out of dozing. I suppose I was hoping that Marie-Antoinette might invite me to stay the night. But Marie-Antoinette, it turned out, was going in for minor surgery in the morning, then flying to Paris. Besides the Pettywards, whom I had met that morning—and my new friends Fabio and Giulio and Miss Czechoslovakia—she was the only person I knew in Milan. Giulio must have noticed my face fall, because suddenly he asked whether we ought to speak in English. Marie-Antoinette pronounced the idea tedious. Whether she left now, I thought, or six months from now, was immaterial. She'd be as much help in Milan as she would a million miles away.

—Mary Ann's one-quarter American, Giulio said. Though she's in the process of shedding that part of herself.

—Don't call me that, she snapped. She grabbed the silver case out from Fabio's hand, snapped off the ultraviolet light, plopped down next to Miss Czechoslovakia, and smushed her cheek against hers, peering at the two noses in Fabio's mirror.

—What do you think, Isabel? Will hers be too radical on me?

The old maid carried in a silver tray with more bottles on it. Fabio pulled up Miss Czechoslovakia, slipped some cash into her jacket pocket, and dismissed her towards the elevator with a little pat on her ass. Clearly she was another disposable, like me. He took back his case from Marie-Antoinette, peered into the small mirror, and began jabbing at the flesh on his cheek to see if he was sunburned.

Giulio shook his head. —Fine example you, *Professore,* he said. In the health field and all.

—I've got a healthy glow, Fabio said.

—Like from *il big bang*, Giulio said scornfully.

I thought I was understanding the conversation in Italian, but then I did not understand. —What big bang was that?

—*Il big bang*, he said, as if everyone knew what it was.

—I'm not sure I follow.

—The big bang, Giulio said in English.

—Of the universe, Fabio said in English.

Still I thought they were making fun of my fall, that they knew my story had been a lie. But then Giulio and Fabio glanced at each other, their faces ashen with worry. They swarmed around me. Giulio began poking at my skull. The tip of his right pinkie, I noticed, had been chopped off at the joint. I wondered what sort of life these people were leading.

(molto allegro) —Just kidding, I said.

—I *am* relieved, sighed Marie-Antoinette, pointing at the hole in my stockings.

The hunched maid served hot chocolate on an absurd Rococo tray covered in absurd Rococo doilies, and Rudolph lay down at my feet. Though the big bang thing upset me—why had Signor Perso never told me about it?—I slipped off my pumps and sandwiched my feet beneath the dog's body. Gradually the calm of being weighted down by another being took hold. Marie-Antoinette asked the maid where Fabio hid his wonderful Armagnac, and she went to get it. I wondered if they were living together here, if he brought his girlfriends home in front of her. The conversation went excruciatingly slowly, like the slow movement of a Boccherini trio. These people are talking for the sake of talking, I thought, as if time were an infinite mansion waiting to be filled. I shut my eyes and wondered whether the largesse that enveloped us was what it was to live in an ancient culture, a mass resignation that the important things had already occurred, or simply the bodily feeling of wealth. Then Giulio turned to me again and, with a straight face, asked why, if I lived here in Milan, I still had such a *putan d'accento Americano,* which must make me anathema to half-Parisian purists like Marie-Antoinette.

—You might want to avoid the word *whore,* Marie-Antoinette said to Giulio, as she set down a tray. Then she giggled, as if to cancel what she'd just said, and pecked him on the cheek. —Did you know that Isabel is a brilliant cellist? she asked, though of course she'd never heard me play.

Giulio turned to me again. —To a Parisian, he continued, lighting her a new cigarette, anyone below the Alps is a Macaroni.

—Please, said Marie-Antoinette. The Romans are a clan of well-dressed provincial snobs. Agoraphobic. If one of them should drive out farther than the beach at Ostia, and discovers the empire has fallen, he immediately rushes back in town to the Via Condotti for a gelato sedative.

—Well, Giulio conceded, maybe it's just southerners the Parisians hate. For them Africa begins at Naples. But we Milanese have a more broadly continental weltanschauung, he said, affecting a German accent. He leaned in her face. —Don't we, princess?

—*Je suppose,* sighed Marie-Antoinette, blowing smoke in his face.

Giulio looked me straight in the eye and asked if I wouldn't break up the monotony by playing.

—Yes, do, said Marie-Antoinette. Like a salon.

I sat staring at them, frozen, all of us trapped now in my awful, mute *retard*. As the interval grew awkward Giulio spewed out another broad, rushing stream of speech. I floated out into his flood of language, grabbing at branches, but not understanding much. He told me, later, that he'd been trying to entertain me. But at the time it was like watching a foreign movie where the characters babble and everybody laughs, but the subtitles are completely unfunny. They began picking apart the production of *Bluebeard* we'd all seen at the Scala. As a joke, Marie-Antoinette began playing Judith, Bluebeard's bride, and demanding the keys to the forbidden doors, in this case Fabio's country house, where she wanted to go to recover after her surgery. The chatter and laughter dissolved into an impenetrable roar. At room temperature, air molecules are agitated enough that their banging together generates a terrific din just barely outside the audible range: now, feverish, I thought I could start to hear them, as if someone was turning up the dial on my already hideous hearing. I thought of the vast expanse of tears Judith found when, after finding the bloody torture chamber, the bloody weapons, the bloody treasure chest, and the bloody whatever else, she opened Bluebeard's fifth forbidden door. At the Scala I'd shuddered, imagining the vast emptiness of life without Signor Perso. And he'd taken my hand, as if he'd known.

A tiny tapping at my feet brought me back to Marie-Antoinette's. Rudolph seemed to be having a seizure. The dog was dreaming, its paws jittering as it ran. A growl issued from its twitching lips as it bared its teeth against the prey it was hunting inside its head. Why was my life an endless series of discoveries like Judith's? I'd never asked questions, had never asked why my talent had to be honed as a weapon; not once, hiding in the shrubbery of Czech houses and Argentinean villas and alleys in Tel Aviv, not once did I ask Yuri who the strangers were that he needed to track down, but could never speak to. After my parents were gone and my aunt Carmela was dying, I'd believed her when she said she'd taken care of me—because she believed herself, because I could not imagine what would become of me if she hadn't. Just as I could not possibly imagine what would become of me now. When she died, and I had nothing, Signor Perso had dropped by the house and invited me to come live with him. Now there was no Signor Perso. It was all I wanted to bury my face in his chest, but now that I had skipped the pension without paying, and skipped on the mortician, I would never find out where he was.

As the confusion began dissolving into panic, I heard Marie-Antoinette's voice say, *The warm blue eyes he has!* I realized she was talking about Signor Perso, whose gray-blue eyes were flecked with gold, and I suddenly saw them again, glazed with confusion after our first time together, when he could not remember my name. She launched into a story about her mother never being able to concentrate during her cello lessons because of her crush on Signor Perso. I wanted to shut her up, to tell her he was dead, but I hadn't come out with it to begin with; now there was no way to say it without it looking very, very odd. I closed my eyes and pinched their corners into the bridge of my nose, like I was thinking hard about some hard mathematical equation, in order not to cry. Luckily, Fabio's cell phone piped up with a double opening bar of *Für Elise*.

He dropped the silver tanner into his breast pocket. —Well. My wife will be getting out.

—*Il Professore* happens to be married to the fattest mezzo-soprano in the world, Giulio whispered loudly.

—She's also the greatest mezzo of her generation, Fabio snapped as he answered his mobile phone. He conducted a curt, monosyllabic conversation, then beeped off.

—So, tailors, Marie-Antoinette said, will it be the drawing or the fragment?

—You're a tailor? I asked Giulio, hoping I'd caught him, too, in a lie.

—Of flesh, Giulio said.

Giulio and his professor, it seemed, were endowing Marie-Antoinette with Miss Czechoslovakia's perfect Roman nose.

—So what do I take? Fabio asked Giulio.

—The Bellini sketch is the obvious choice, Giulio said, and

worth more at the moment, but I'd take the fresco fragment. It's a piece you come across once a century. In a few years, it'll skyrocket. It's sheer disgusting luck that that little gem fell into her hands.

—So be it, Fabio said. You take it along.

Marie-Antoinette stood up and stretched. Fabio turned to me and said it had been a pleasure. I asked if he was returning with his wife. He laughed and said that they lived at her place. It dawned on me that the apartment we were in was his, that Marie-Antoinette was staying here temporarily, that I did not even know where she lived.

—So what brings you to Italy, Giulio said in a low voice, once Marie-Antoinette had gone to show him out.

I stared at the ceiling. We had come to Italy to take Signor Perso home to die.

—Basilicas.

—Basilicas? he said skeptically. I mean, you've seen one, you've seen them all.

—I find repetition relaxing.

He pursed his lips, and his chin went up, then down, a compact Italian shrug. —You can't fuck in them. I mean, if you're not a priest.

—You'd be surprised, I said, though Signor Perso and I had never made love anywhere but in his big oak bed.

—You don't seem the religious type.

—You don't believe in God?

He smiled wryly. —I come from a long line of communist atheists. My paternal grandmother wrote pamphlets for the party into her eighties. We tend to avoid churches.

—So it's a tradition.

—I'm not an atheist because my father's an atheist, he said. It's

just, the idea of God is ridiculous. Nothing could be more unsci-
entific. We Italians—

—My teacher's Italian, I interrupted, before he could say
any more.

Giulio took a sip of wine, then nodded slowly. —I've never
tried it in a basilica.

Marie-Antoinette pranced back in her little ballet steps. I
stood up and started thanking her. I was hoping to move the
conversation around to the Pettywards, to the address of their
apartment, to find the neighborhood of the church with *The
Last Supper*. But she got flustered—for some reason the Pettywards seemed off-limits as a subject—and she jumped up and
tried to give me a pair of her snow boots, saying she was getting
rid of some things before leaving town.

My throat closed. I'd thought she was going to Paris temporarily. I shook my head, said I had my own pair.

—Warm ones? she asked, as if my feet were suddenly her para-
mount concern.

Giulio stood up.

—You're deserting me? she whined.

—You're deserting us, Giulio said, picking up the cover to his
car radio.

—I muss guh unzaground, she drawled in a thick vulgar
German accent, like Giulio had done not so long before.

Why is anyone surprised that the way to kill a moth is to light
a candle? That a creature trapped in darkness seeks a sun? That
after 1939 people like my grandparents could still believe a pub-
licity brochure—the idyllic lake, the majestic mountains with
sun rays brimming up from behind—and hand over their entire
fortune to buy a safe lakefront villa at the Terezin Spa? I then did

something very stupid, out of sheer weakness, that I immediately regretted. I already had snow boots, I had very practical rubber boots from Milwaukee that are actually warmer than anything Marie-Antoinette, with her limo and her driver, has ever owned or ever will own. But of course my snow boots were back at the pension, along with everything else I owned, and the pumps I had on were soaked through and ruined, which may be why I lost control of my thinking: having already rejected them twice, knowing that Marie-Antoinette would use them as she used everything else, just as she had waited until Giulio came out of the bathroom to peacock her feathers and press them into my hands—as if she and I sat on two trays of a balance, so that the more she heaped upon my plate, the higher she'd ascend—my thinking was this. After Marie-Antoinette went to Paris and I never saw her again, after she died, or simply used this trip to jettison me, I would be better off wearing boots that gave off an air of not needing help. I was pretending to myself that I might meet people, new people who would conclude from my nice boots that I had only recently found myself in dire straits. But if I was going to take them, I thought, I should have taken them right away, as if I could take them or leave them, but as it happened I had decided to take them but could easily decide to throw them out. Instead I asked for them after her paranoia about my health had subsided, and then I was too grateful, as if thanking her for sparing my life. She'd tossed the Pettyward job my way without having any idea of how desperate I was. But when I asked for the snow boots the way I did, and put them on in front of her and Giulio, I might as well have sewn a yellow star on my coat.

The elevator door shut on Fabio's apartment and I left without the Pettywards' address. As we began our silent descent Giulio turned to me and said, very quietly, *Giulio Romano Salvagente.* He held out his hand, then saw that I was laden down. —Oh, he said awkwardly. He took my ruined pumps from my hand, and I shifted the Savant, and we shook hands with exaggerated formality. Like his glove, his hand was buttery soft. I did not offer my last name.

We turned to stare at the descending floor numbers. It had been a mistake to assume she could help me; a mistake to take the snow boots; a mistake to take the job teaching Mr. Petty-ward's son. When she'd offered it, it had seemed generous. But from the way she'd avoided talking about it, it seemed like some-thing about the setup wasn't right.

—Now I insist you let me take you where you're going, Giulio said, as the elevator opened. So you don't get mugged and almost raped.

We slid the cello in the back seat—Giulio lifted up a giant pile of dirty laundry, then plopped it back on top of the Savant—and I got in. My seat felt strangely warm. Giulio's Lancia was large and plush, and dark and deep; it felt foreign and luxuriant, like stepping onto an Egyptian barge. I cringed a little at its opulence, at being so surrounded and enclosed by him. Though I was grateful to be in his car, its strong odor—the odor of him—girdled me in claustrophobia. A car makes you an armadillo; you drag a big, clunking hull of a self along, wherever you go; whereas the part of traveling I like is the leaving your-self behind. As a child, though I knew I wasn't supposed to, I loved trains—loved their anonymous plainness, their generic design, the indifferent way they shrugged people off on the plat-form. Yuri never let me have my picture taken, ever; when he'd been rounded up in Prague, they'd identified him from a photo. He'd nearly strangled one photographer who tried to snap my photo, had nearly been locked up more than once and more than once had had to buy his way out after a brawl. But nobody expected me to take trains; there we had a safe anonymity of movement. And trains kept Yuri in check. He was too busy triple-checking timetables and platforms to become enraged. However he critiqued my performance, in the cabin I was just another passenger, shutting my eyes amid the chatter and imagining a landscape to correspond to the languages spoken, to the rise and fall, the ticks and glottal stops of the cabin's vocal terrain. My most memorable meals, my clearest musical ideas, my best debates with Yuri came on trains shuddering into motion, taking me somewhere else.

While Giulio brushed the snow off the windshield, I racked my brain for a place to tell him to take me. Then the thinking dissolved. I slipped into a new calculation of the number of minutes I had passed through since the death. Perhaps there is some truth to Leibnitz's saying that the pleasure we take from music comes from counting, for my only steady moments, now, were when I had already arrived at a figure and could add each additional minute as it passed. How different Signor Perso's death was from my parents'—how relentlessly it pressed on my chest. When my parents' car crashed, I was onstage at Carnegie Hall, inviting the disaster; when I saw their seats were empty I had stepped outside Yuri's web of precautions, had left him alone, there in his past, and simply let go and played. Now, I knew the stabbing revelation people talk about: I'd had it the moment I woke and heard the absence of Signor Perso's breathing, and I kept having it, again and again. But at Carnegie Hall, while my parents died on the highway, I had utterly forgotten them. I think I was the happiest I've ever been.

By the time Giulio finished brushing off the car, I had a plan. I would casually ask—*(allegro)*—if we might drive by the famous church. Giulio nodded. But instead of driving to the *Last Supper* church, suddenly we turned a corner and came upon the Duomo's towering white rock-face facade at the center of the city, harshly lit by the neon garland that enclosed the icy, deserted piazza. Outside my window I heard the rustling coos of restless pigeons. My face fell, even through the smile I had appliquéd. Perhaps to fill the void, Giulio began explaining how Leonardo had built Milan's canals to transport the huge white blocks of stone for the Duomo into the center of the city. We slowed to a red light, and I looked up and saw that the cross-street was Via Solferino, the street of our pension. I cut him off and asked if we could make a quick stop. Though clearly he wanted an explanation, he clicked down his turn signal, too tactful to ask what I intended.

Outside the pension, the squat, chubby owner was conferring with the police. I sneaked around behind him into the lobby, ran down the hall and up the fire stairs, and slid my key into the lock. Our room had been cleaned; all trace of Signor Perso was gone. I stood staring at a moment in time before Signor Perso's death, at the room as we had entered it together, then quietly shut the door. I tiptoed down the back stairs to the laundry room, where I had delivered some shirts to be washed the day before Signor Perso died. The machines were chugging; the young Yugoslavian girl who had been our maid was lying on a cot in her shorts, smoking and reading a comic book. When she saw me, she motioned down a hall with a naked lightbulb to a janitor's closet. She'd saved everything. She pulled out Signor Perso's garment bag, which I'd stuffed full. Draped over my arm, it hung like a body bag, so I had to drop it. It fell on her foot. She stared at me. She couldn't find the Italian words, but her face said she thought she'd done an enormous favor and risked her job for some lunatic. Like an idiot I reached in my pocket for the cache of Marie-Antoinette's marzipan I'd stolen, wrapped in a napkin, and pressed them into her hand. This only made things worse. I grappled up the metal crate of my scores and said I'd be back for the rest. The lobby was deserted, so I took a risk and charged out through it. But out on the street, I stopped short: I had forgotten Signor Perso's wallet and passport. Then I saw the short, stubby hotelier coming after me.

—*VEDOVA STRONZA! VEDOVA STRONZA!* he screamed. I jumped in the car and slammed the door.

—Friend of yours? Giulio asked, pushing a button that snapped down all the locks. The man was banging on the trunk of the car with his palm. I shut my eyes and willed Giulio's foot to accelerate. He drove through a red light, went a few blocks, and turned onto a deserted cobblestone street. —So you're a widow *and* a scoundrel?

I did not reply. I was paging through the scores, looking for the address of the one bed in the world where I could lie.

—What's in there?

—My life, I said, which closed the discussion. I showed Giulio the Pettywards' address, and he pulled out without further inquiry.

As we rode through the silent, white, abandoned streets, my mind wandered to riding home to New Jersey after my last real concert, my Carnegie Hall debut. My parents had failed to show up after the concert; a violist who had waited with me in the green room had taken me home. Then, too, there had been a blizzard; we had glided along the icy streets, through the quiet white radiance, as if slowly floating. It was as if the clear expanse of silence that had fallen on me, in the moment before the applause, had fallen on the world.

The street approaching the Pettywards' building had waist-high yellow wickets embedded in the curb to prevent parking, so I assumed Giulio would simply drop me off and be done with it. But he spotted the one place they were missing and said, There's my space. I got the sense that he was extraordinarily lucky, that he just expected things to go his way, so I felt a little triumphant when his car didn't fit. There was a big pile of snow in the front and he had to pull in diagonally, with the back end of his car sticking out into the middle of the street.

Milan is a grim, gray, German city. Its few surviving Italian grace notes dim amid chord after heavy chord of industrial postwar morass. In the days I had spent there before my Scala recitals, I had never seen a private building as elegant as the Pettywards', a seventeenth-century palazzo with pink marble columns and a green bronze fountain with dolphins spurting water in the courtyard. It survived the war, Mr. Pettyward told me, because it's across from the church with *The Last Supper*, which the Allies wouldn't bomb. Now, as Giulio stared at the huge, arched, elaborately carved doors of the Pettywards' *portone*, I knew what he was thinking, how unlikely it was that a transient foreigner like me could manage to live in such a beautiful place.

—You're sure this is where you live? Giulio asked, turning off the ignition.

(forte) —Surprise surprise, I said, happy not to seem like such a waif. I opened the door and shoved the metal crate onto the sidewalk.

—Wait. Giulio reached past me and pulled my door shut.

—How long have you been living here?

—A while, I said.

—You live with your maestro?

I bit my lip and slowly shook my head.

—So you live with your parents, he concluded.

—Dead.

He nodded slowly. —So you live alone, he said, after a pause. I shook my head again.

—I see. He looked forward through the windshield and gripped both hands on the wheel. Then he dropped them on his lap again.

For a while we were silent.

—How do you spell your name? I asked.

Giulio printed it on the windshield with his finger. —Like the painter.

I nodded, though I did not know the painter. —Sounds like it should start with a *J.*

—A woman surgeon in America once told me my name sounded like Juliet married to Romeo. She wrote it *Julie-O.*

(con sentimento profondo) —Romantic, I said.

—Tell me—have you always had those bags under your eyes?

—You're bald, I said in English.

He frowned, clutched at the top of his head, and scanned it frantically in the rearview mirror. —Let's go back.

I smiled at the improvisation.

He stroked the top of my head. —You misunderstood, he said. I thought you might have a concussion. I was worrying about the swelling. Really. I like them. They make you look like a depressed Russian countess. And by the way. In English, it's balding.

—*Che?* I continued in Italian.

—Balding, he said in English. I'm not bald. I'm bald*ing*.

When I smiled, Giulio said, —Finally! and apologized for being a tease. And he insisted we speak in English so I could see for myself just how bad he was with languages.

—My parents divorced themselves when I had three, he began. And after that my mother was going on cruises or on safari with some other men. Each year when she is coming back to visit, my mother, she is bringing a new nanny from the different country and is firing the old one. I have began to hate her coming home, because just when I begin to know the before nanny, she was hiring a new one. When I was eight she left me with this old Panzer-tank named Fräulein Edwige, who would weep into her handkerchief whenever I cried over my mother. *Sie hat uns ganz vergessen,* he cried, imitating her falsetto blubbering. Totally forgotten us. My mother picked her up on some cruise ship. I think she was in love with her.

Giulio was laughing. I didn't know what to think.

—My mother hoped I would learn many languages, he said. And I did. I now speak five of them, all at once. I rebelled to learn any of them, and confuse them all in my head. So now I speak no language purely, not even the Italian, maybe only the French because my fiancée is correcting me always.

—Enter the fiancée.

In Italian he said: —She's a blonde, very beautiful, but delicate, not like you.

I wondered if that meant I wasn't beautiful, or wasn't delicate, or that he didn't like my body, which is a short, ample tribute to Russian peasanthood.

—Does she know you see other people? I asked, to find out whether he did or not.

He shook his head. —She'd be crushed. He reached over, lazily fingered a loose button dangling by a thread on my coat, and plucked it off, the gesture almost violent. But then he took out a sewing kit from a compartment in his door and matched the thread color. While he sewed it back on, we talked about his talents at surgery and skiing and sewing, and about my perfect pitch. He asked my last name. I took a breath and said it. He said, Of course, with the black eyes and hair he might have guessed I was Russian. He repeated my name. I flushed, thinking he was about to recognize me. But I recovered, told him my mother had been a singer.

—Knew I'd heard the name, he said, as he knotted the thread and clipped it with a little scissors. He said I looked a little like Callas. When he told me he thought German opera the consummate musical form, I had a desire to grab the needle and poke out an eye. But then he added that in German he understood nothing, less than nothing, making it a good time to think.

—Do you sing?

—I also have perfect pitch, he boasted, flipping open a narrow wooden panel tucked against the steering column, next to my feet. I'm always perfectly pitched one note flat. I try not to sing in my own presence. It gives me a deep headache, he added, very profound, which only absinthe takes away.

He took out a pair of shot glasses, and two flasks, and flipped the panel shut. He held a slotted silver teaspoon over a shot glass, balanced a sugar cube on it, and poured a few drops.

—Add some water, he ordered, when the melted sugar had collapsed through the slits.

Mechanically, in spite of myself, I unscrewed the bottle Giulio had handed me.

—Absinthe is a controlled narcotic, I objected puritanically, as I poured water into the tiny glass. The wanting in my flesh made me dig at everything he said.

—Only if you can't get it, he said, toasting his shot glass towards the streetlight to watch the liquids swirl and couple.

The liqueur swerved my senses. I knew I had to be careful. But I did not bring up his fiancée again, even though, or perhaps because, Giulio reached over and twirled a curl of my hair in his finger. The sleeve of his cashmere blazer nestled my neck, and I felt like one of the silver things I'd seen in a drawer in Fabio's apartment, wrapped in its perfect cloth. A blanket of snow was thickening over us, muffling the sounds of the city, and the windshield glowed dark white, as if we were in an igloo where other people were no longer a factor.

—Really, Giulio was saying, my life consists of limitations, the things I'm unable to accomplish, women who refuse me.

He looked at me steadily. I leaned in. But instead of kissing me he reached past me to put his car phone in the glove compartment, so I pretended I was leaning forward to peer at the cuff links peeking out from his jacket sleeve. Their gold bands were engraved around the edges. I tried to concentrate, to absorb what he was saying, to reconcile it against his fortressed, moneyed confidence. I think I probably knew even then that his modesties were camouflage for a wild gaping appetite. But his mahogany voice was like a cello down in the lower ranges, and instead of thinking, I held my breath and slid down under its warmth.

—You speak English well, I said.

—I had a research fellowship for one year in New York. At the New York Hospital.

—Impressive.

He shrugged. —Let me enlighten you. My uncle's friend is the head of surgery there. I taught him skiing. But once I got there, you know, I did very brilliant. I found in your country that I can adapt to almost anything.

—Helps you survive, I said.

—But sometimes you no longer know the person who survived.

—Did you like New York?

—Have you been there?

(lightly) —Only the airport.

He puffed up his cheeks and blew out. —Here, no one wants to die, but we know we must. There, people expect not to. Americans want you to explain death in terms of science. They always wish to know the exact chain of reaction.

Giulio sighed, blowing a round platter of fog on his side window. —It is difficult to explain people why things end. Because—

—Because they just do.

—Exactly. And of course then there are the women. There are very few beautiful women in New York. They have all seen everything.

He shifted in his seat; I wondered whether he was getting an erection, whether he was insulting me, or telling me I was one of the few. Signor Perso had an intuitive understanding of ambiguous passages; I made a mental note to ask him what Giulio might have meant here. Then the death sunk in again and I realized what a betrayal it was even to be sitting in this car.

Giulio reached over and gently clasped my left wrist. I waited for the inevitable comment on my hands, which are preternaturally large. Also I was afraid he might somehow be able to detect that my two middle fingers were numb. But then he squeezed the wide, fleshy pads at the tips—the fingers of my left hand are square, callused hammerheads from practicing all the time.

—Either pulmonary edema, he said, or you're a cellist.

So there comes a grace, I thought, from dealing in deformity.
—One or the other.

He reached across and took my other hand. —Two wedding rings?

I shrugged. I wear my mother's and Yuri's wedding rings, the only possessions of my parents I have left.

—On the right hand?

—Otherwise they'd get in the way, I said, and played a fingerboard on my chest with my left.

He nodded.

—So they're just rings.

—What else would they be?

Giulio reached over under my hair to stroke my neck. From under his arm, I smelled his scent. I shut my eyes and inhaled long. The burning inside my chest fell away. I was home. In Giulio's smell there was nothing I could make go wrong. Wrapped in his smell, I thought, I could sleep as I had not slept in years.

I leaned over and lay my head on his lap. He stroked my cheek. Then I felt a shift under the fabric of his pants, and I sat up, shocked at what I had done.

—I can't, I burst out, knowing I had to get out.

—Can't what?

—Forget it.

—Can't what?

—I'm in a relationship.

—You are? Giulio whined, softly looping his voice like a disappointed child.

—I'm married, I ventured idiotically.

He nodded. —Is it serious?

—Stop.

—Stop what? What am I doing? Ever since I lifted you off the sidewalk you've been looking at me as if you knew something terrible. Whatever it is, it's probably true. But even so you shouldn't judge. People only hate traits in others that they can't stand in themselves.

—You didn't *lift* me off the sidewalk, I said quietly.

He reached behind my waist and pulled me towards him. But as he looked into my eyes, he frowned and said my name again, as if something was coming back to him. Just then a siren sliced the air, punctured our bubble, and I understood what was happening: Giulio had seen me perform as a child, was connecting who I was now with who I'd been, was a minute from knowing what I'd done. The fire truck hurtling towards the Pettywards' slowed by Giulio's car, its taut impatient warbling seesawed, E, B-flat, E, B-flat, and I got distracted, as I tend to, wondering if the Europeans deliberately used two notes that formed an unresolved fourth to produce an alarm that was particularly grating. Then Giulio said he had to move and started the engine. I realized where the fire truck was headed. I'm not an idiot—in my mind I knew the Pettywards' apartment wasn't burning—but deeper down I knew it was. I grabbed my purse, jumped out of the car, slammed the door, hoisted up the crate, and ran, shoved my key into the cutout doorway in the huge wooden portone, stepped through, and kicked it shut behind me.

Upstairs, though, the hall was startlingly calm. No smoke was seeping out from under the Pettywards' door. After some difficulty with the keys, I managed to unlock the entrance to the little maid's room where I would be staying. No smoke there either. But I knew I would have to be careful, to keep anything from happening, now that I was living there.

Usually I am running and running, running towards my spool, my childhood night table that secretly flipped open, that I fit in, that I would fit in when they came. Where Yuri found me hiding, at six, and reshut me in. A minute later he knocked on the lid. He had returned with my cello and asked me to rest my hand on its belly. Yuri told me then that if I learned to play well enough, my playing would protect me. That bad people crumbled if they heard Beethoven or Bach. That for the rest of my life we would keep the cello by my bed. With tears streaming down he said that if they came while I was sleeping, all I had to do was reach over and touch my cello, and then they'd turn into little anthills of cinnamon sugar we could scoop up in the morning and sprinkle on our toast. But the night I met Giulio, I was running, running, and then Signor Perso opened my cello case, like a waxy undertaker, and stuck out his leg and tripped me. I fell sprawling onto Giulio, a Giulio midget in a tiny tuxedo, lying in a tiny, crimson velvet coffin. In a creepy, wound-up munchkin voice he said, *Guten Tag*. Then he reached out and broke off Signor Perso's leg at the knee, and handed me the drumstick, and I gorged myself.

I tried opening my eyes, but I had wept myself to sleep, and my top and bottom eyelashes were crusted together. I started to gag from the awful taste of the dream in my mouth. To calm myself I ran my inner eye over our bedroom at Signor Perso's in Milwaukee—over my steamer trunk, my framed Yo-Yo letter, my autographed Barber score—the way, as a child, I'd traced over my New Jersey bedroom if I woke up in some creepy place on tour with Yuri. Then I reached out from my side of the bed to touch my cello.

What I felt was the wall. It was the first time since I'd had a cello that it wasn't there. I forced an eye open: the dripping faucet in the corner sink, the slouchy mattress, the chipped iron bedstead, the old black dial phone could have been any one of the hundred creepy places Yuri had dragged us to, in the days after I had given a performance, to look for people he once knew. I tried to remember the performance. I remembered I hadn't performed in years. Then my knee began to throb, and my cheek, and then it slowly came to me, the fall, and funeral, the death, and the Savant, which I had left in the back seat of Giulio's car.

(andante)

I suppose I should say that the Savant was not my cello. The cello I had owned for years is an excellent Montagnana knockoff worth about twenty thousand dollars made by an Italian luthier from Philadelphia. The reason it was not by my bed was that it was sitting in Mr. Pettyward's music room, hidden in the case of the cello I lost.

Though I may have called the Savant my cello, in fact it was owned by Mr. Pettyward. Like all the great instruments owned by Jews before the war, the Savant had dropped out of sight when

Vrashkansova was taken to Theresienstadt. Unlike most of the others, it had never resurfaced. It was the only completely intact Andrea cello, the only one of the eight he sent to the French king that was accidentally made to smaller dimensions, the only original Cremonese cello of that period that was never cut down. The Savant, in other words, is one of the two or three most significant cellos in the world. That it was played by Raya Vrashkansova transports it from one of the two or three most significant cellos in the world into the realm of the immeasurable. It had been ill-considered, at best, to borrow the instrument; to take it out by foot, in that weather, had been madness. But when I'd managed, that morning, to get the job without playing for Mr. Pettyward—by showing him the original label inside the Savant's belly, the famous Latin inscription Vrashkansova had shown Signor Perso fifty years before—a perverse and specious confidence corroded my thinking. And I'd switched the cellos.

Before Mr. Pettyward, the only collectors I had known were nice people, conservatory musicians who were good, but not good enough, who collected out of a love of music they accepted as unrequited. But the combination of him, his name, and his palatial apartment made me think, This man's just the opposite, one of those hoarders who buys instruments and sits on them for decades to drive up the price. My teaching the son was a murderously easy disguise.

Mr. Pettyward seemed both too formal and too friendly. He lacked the tiny edge of awkwardness or curiosity I would have expected from a married man hiring a woman half his age to live in his house. His left arm hung in a silk paisley sling that matched his ascot. He served us two brandies on a tray and said the person he was looking for would be a person of utmost discretion. I nodded, assuming he meant that he might bring home women whom I would pretend not to notice. Then he began probing. When had I come to Italy? How long did I plan to stay? Was there no family who would miss me? I had not prepared a performance, so I lied as close to the truth as I could, said I had been raised by an aunt who died, that I was here indefinitely, that I was the last of my family on either side. And what about in Italy? he said, his big white teeth flashing. Did I know people here? I said there was a teacher I would be working with. Once I made friends, could I be relied upon not to bring them home to parties?

The thought of trying to get to know people, of constructing a new person they could want to get to know, was exhausting. To avoid another question I dipped my finger in my glass and ran my fingerprint around its edge until it sang a G. Luckily Mr. Pettyward got distracted pouring a refill so that he could try it himself. Then he continued his proposition. As soon as his elbow healed, he said, he wanted to take lessons on the cello with Clayton, father and son. Until then I would start Clayton on the viola, without him. Making sure, he joked, that Clayton didn't get too far ahead. Mr. Pettyward said he'd injured himself during the course of Mrs. Pettyward's departure. Which of course was rather painful. I didn't know whether he meant the elbow or the accident, so I said I was sorry and asked how long it would take to heal.

—Heal? he said curiously. His wife had been killed, I suddenly understood, in the accident in which he'd been driving. There were no pictures of her for the same reason I had no pictures of my parents: in some way, he'd done it.

Mr. Pettyward said he'd been looking for a Strad but had settled on an Amati. Better the teacher than the student, I said, playing it safe. It was Nicolo Amati, Andrea's grandson, who taught Stradivari; if his cello wasn't the Savant or the King—the only two Andrea Amatis worth mentioning—then this was the polite way to go. The Nicolos are known for their silky sound, whereas the Andreas are mostly showpieces, smaller, chamber instruments that can't be strung tightly enough to project. If you were looking for a decent cello for under a million, a Nicolo would be the logical choice. But Mr. Pettyward smiled and replied that his was an Andrea. That Andrea was our first known cello maker. Our, he actually said.

Mr. Pettyward said that the Amati—for that was what he called the Savant—had come down to him through his family. He was vague about how long ago that had been. He let it be known that the instrument had not been played in some time. At the same time he joked anxiously about the cello losing its voice. Gradually it came out that one of the brothers at Hill and Sons had called to ask him to lend it for a benefit. Given the climate of thieving in Italy, Mr. Pettyward said, he had followed his policy of denying ownership. But whoever he spoke to had joked that an unplayed cello loses its voice. Mr. Pettyward seemed not to know that a cello gets its voice back after a few months, especially if it happens to be not an Andrea but *the* Andrea, the Andrea Amati ex-Giardino Savant. Either the person assumed Mr. Pettyward knew that, or Mr. Pettyward panicked and didn't listen, because an hour after I called about the position, he had sent his driver to pick me up.

I'd never been on a job interview. Since I knew my playing would surely falter—and since there are not many cellos in the strata of what Mr. Pettyward was coyly hinting at on the phone, I brought along the little dental mirror Signor Perso used to check his gum disease. Just in case. It seemed impossible that Mr. Pettyward could not know what he had on his hands, but not once did he mention the tone, or Vrashkansova. He swooned over the instrument as if it were an antique. The faded paintings over the *f* holes, the translucent folds of the toga of the figure of Justice, the faint blue arm of the figure of Piety. As he was upending its bottom to show me the tiny sets of dotted tracks—from the days before endpins, when Napoleon had demanded to try it and set it down on his boot spurs—I pulled out the little dental mirror, slipped it in an *f* hole. For a moment we both stopped dead. *ARBOR VIVA TACUI. MORTUA CANO. AS A LIVE TREE I WAS SILENT. DEAD, I SING.*

Mr. Pettyward pulled back, bristling, and said that of course the label was a facsimile that had been affixed later. It was a patent lie. I thought I had ruined my chances by showing him up. But then he asked me to try it out, and a miracle happened. I looked in the Savant's case for rosin. I saw now what I had not noticed in the somber light of the basilica, that though the faded purple velvet lining of the case was clearly original, it was curiously pristine and dust-free. Mr. Pettyward searched with me, in the cases of his viola and his violins, but it was the oddest thing, there was not a piece of rosin to be found. Yours is the first music room I have ever come upon, I joked gently, that is entirely rosin-free. Mr. Pettyward simply looked uncomfortable. Then he almost barked an order at me, to buy some and save the receipt. The phone rang, and he signaled me to follow him to his study. As we walked down a long marble hall I wondered if his son had taken the rosins for spite, if they were in the back of his closet in a box, and then I remembered the brown cardboard case of used rosins I had stumbled upon in the janitor's closet of

Paul Tortelier's Paris luthier, the German word *Rosinen* penciled on the side in old Gothic script, remembered the blood draining from Yuri's face as the luthier remarked that he had picked up the carton cheap from the son of an ex-guard at the Austerlitz-Tolbiac depot, the central French storage area for confiscated items to be appraised, distributed to officers, or shipped back to the Reich. The Nazis had ordered the rosins removed from the cases of confiscated instruments, the luthier explained, for the sake of cleanliness. As we approached Mr. Pettyward's desk I took a risk and blurted out that I was late for a funeral. It was like improvising some radical tempo shift and having von Karajan pick up on it, exactly. He unlocked a drawer and tossed me a set of keys.

With that, I'd gotten overconfident. Alone in the music room, surrounded by the gleaming rosewood walls, it was literally as if I were standing inside the instrument itself. I reached down and plucked its C string: the out-of-tune B that came out resonated so radiantly that for a moment I déjà vued into the concert hall of the Sydney Opera House, which is paneled in white Australian birch and has the best acoustics of any house, ever. The note was impossibly rich and graceful, like one of my mother's low notes. What else can possibly happen? I thought. Like the talent, I told myself, the tzuris has burned itself out. Then both thumbs were snapping open the latches of my case, the knockoff out, replaced by the impossibly real. Because Signor Perso would have loved more than anything to hear me on the Savant, in possession of myself.

I rolled over in the slouchy single bed in the Pettywards' maid's room. The springs poked at my ribs and there were not enough covers. I laid my coat over the blanket, but I was still freezing. The faucet in the corner sink was dripping. The transcendent sound that came from my bow at the funeral, the perversity of its perfection, haunted my inner ear. The past is prologue, Signor Perso had said, holding me in his arms the night before we left. I could not just lie there while Giulio walked away with the Savant. I picked up the heavy receiver of Mr. Pettyward's old black rotary phone, dialed a zero, and asked for information. There was an unlisted Giulio, and one G. The G. turned out to be an old lady who screeched at me for waking her up. I called again, to try to get them to give me the unlisted one, and got turned over to a supervisor. The supervisor hung up on me.

Down on the street, a car alarm squealed. It came to me that the thing to do was to take my cello from the music room and sell it. I couldn't travel with it anyway; as soon as Mr. Pettyward called the police about the Savant, I would quickly be identified and caught. The long hall was so dark I could not see my hand in front of my face. At night Mr. Pettyward closed the wooden shutters, to keep in the heat, but even so the marble floor chilled my stockinged feet. Suddenly, a foot in front of my feet, a wedge of sallow light sliced across the floor at the door to the music room. I stopped short. It flickered. I peeked. Clayton had the Savant's case open and was scrutinizing my cello with a flashlight. A chill came over my forearms, and then a sneeze gathered. I couldn't stop it. He threw the beam my way.

I walked back to my room and put on my shoes so that I'd be ready when the carabinieri came for me. I had no money, now, and no place to go; within minutes they would be downstairs. Here at the Pettywards' there was no trap door, no spool table, no false ceiling, no hidden space. And no way to get my cello out. The people interned in Theresienstadt had smuggled jewels, to use as money, buried in tins of shoe polish. Probably the only thing you could smuggle a cello in was a coffin.

Sitting on the bed, waiting, I had an idea. Four feet below my windowsill, on the building's facade, was a three-foot-wide ledge, the top of the building's elaborate cornice. I gathered the blanket, my bag and shoes, and gingerly climbed out. And lowered the window. Wrapped in the blanket, I slid my back down against the granite wall until I was sitting. I stared at the dark slate roof of the church across the street, the five stories to the sidewalk. The ocean of space, inviting me to plunge. The street below was deserted. There was no one walking past, no one on the block, no one whose life I would ruin by falling splat in front of them. No cars were parked on the sidewalk. There was not even the absence of someone whose car I would bash in.

My body began to shake at the fight inside itself. No matter how dire our circumstances, Yuri had forbidden me to pray: If a being out there understands anything, he would say, has the power to do anything at all, then he is a supremely evil being who watches slaughter and does nothing. But now I had no one, not even Yuri to berate me. I was the last one left.

Although I had no notion of who or what I was praying to, I sent a prayer out into the cold night sky. Quickly, quietly, so as not to wake Yuri or his evil God, I asked that I might once more touch the body of the Savant. For the rest of the night I stayed quiet, my mind gripping on nothing, exhaustion unloosing its hold.

I stirred to the sounds of traffic collecting below me. The ledge was icy with sleet. Carefully I pulled myself up to kneeling and peered inside my window. The room was empty, the door still shut. There were no flashing lights below. Either Clayton was taking his time telling his father, or the carabinieri were taking their time, the way they had with Signor Perso. I pried open the window, climbed in, and called Marie-Antoinette, who snapped up the receiver.

—When are you coming back to Milan? I asked as casually as I could.

—*Attends.*

The receiver clicked dead. Then there was another click.

—You wake up so early? she asked, as if I had a venereal disease.

—Just today.

—Sweetheart, it's only Paris. It's not as if I'm off to *les Maldives.* How are the lessons coming?

—The son's not talking, and the father—

—Says all the wrong things, she said. The usual. Introduce them to our maestro.

—Do you have Giulio's number?

—Ah, so he charmed you. My favorite part is when he says he became a doctor to save Daphne. Or maybe it was his mother.

—I left my purse in his car.

—Let me find my book. You're lucky you caught me. I turned off the phone. You know how maddening it is when people call and they need things when you're trying to leave. What was it Freud said about purses?

—Sorry.

—No no, you're my pet project. Just so you know, you're not his type. You know, I wish I were going to the Maldives! It's the only place I really feel like myself. Paris can be *so* tired. Here! No, that's not it. In London you can go into a dressing room and put on as many layers as you like, and if you've got the right bone structure, the Brits are so lovely, they just let you walk straight out of the store, and then they ring up Lloyds'. Do you know what is the greatest invention of Western civilization? Insurance. I couldn't sleep if I thought we all weren't covered. Perhaps my book will be with the ticket in my zipper bag.

—I'll hold on.

—No no no. Let me call you back.

I hung up the receiver and lay down on the bed, cursing myself again for having taken the snow boots. I had branded myself as needy, someone to be managed and set aside. I could see Mr. Pettyward reading the chatty postcard apology Marie-Antoinette would send me, pushing his reading glasses off the slope of his long, thin nose onto his high red oily forehead. See him placing it in a plastic bag for the police. After two minutes and ten seconds I realized that Marie-Antoinette had not even taken my number. I tried calling again, for thirty-six rings. Either her ringer was off, or the old maid had died.

I decided to make a run for it. No one was in the hall. In the empty courtyard, sleet pelted down, carving wet whips through the glaze of sidewalk ice. As I stepped through the wooden portone, a police car was cruising towards the building. I crossed the Corso Magenta and ducked into the Santa Maria delle Grazie. Signor Perso had taken me there on our first day in Milan, to see *The Last Supper,* which was being restored. Now, inside the dim church, a priest was saying an early morning mass in a side chapel lit by dim electric candelabras. I slipped into a back pew and lay down on the floor beneath it. Here it seemed safe to pray. I prayed for a plan for how to replace my passport without money; for how to rent a room without a passport; for how to get money without Signor Perso's papers. Every cell in my body felt like it was dying.

When I opened my eyes again the church was steeped in darkness. Behind its grid of scaffolding, *The Last Supper* was cloaked in shadow. All that was visible was a gleaming spotlit patch above Judas's head where, behind a huge magnifying glass, a conservator in a lighted miner's hat scraped at the fresco. By the altar a schoolteacher was explaining to her class that the Last Supper had been a Jewish Passover Seder—which I thought could not possibly be right. Behind me, in the back of the church, a circle of criminally handsome schoolboys were quietly discussing the prospects of Milan's soccer team next spring. Their voices wound in and around one another like a spoken transcription of the slow movement of the Trout quintet. The church's overwrought acoustics blurred their dialect beyond my grasp; without the distraction of meaning I was left with the sheer seduction of rhythm and pitch working on me and cutting me open. They spoke in the elegant, understated style of playing Signor Perso had taught me to love.

It was too much, this surfeit of spoken music wherever you went. I hurried down the aisle to get out of earshot, and stepped outside, and for a while the rain drowned them out. But then they followed me out with a priest to smoke. As I slumped against the wall, trapped by the sheet of falling water, one of them turned and offered me a cigarette. I took it. Since Signor Perso had died, I'd started accepting the cigarettes Italians seemed always to be offering. The quiet, unconditional generosity, the unspoken compact, the being taken in, in frailty and defeat—these tiny moments, now, were the best part of my day. The burning smoke numbed my lungs. I stared at the rain. I had not been this hungry since my trips with Yuri. If Clayton hadn't told, and I didn't show up for dinner on my first night, Mr. Pettyward would know something was wrong. On the other hand I could be walking into an arrest. If on the other hand nothing was wrong, then I had failed to get rosin. The boys' voices lulled me into remembering our first evening in Milan, when Signor Perso had taken me to a little restaurant near the Brera, where the owner had greeted him with the convivial reserve upper-crust Italians have perfected to an art form. *Maestro Perso,* he remarked, bowing slightly, as if he'd seated him every night for the past forty years. As he seated us, he launched a gentle tirade about how, in Signor Perso's absence, all the old trattorias had been replaced by glossy bar-restaurants, parodies of Italian taste with their metal chairs and laminated menus. Signor Perso cut him off. He saw that I'd shut my eyes and was listening to the music. The cadence of voices, the perfect falling closure of their rhythms wove in and around each other like instruments in a chamber ensemble conducted by Kleiber *fils*. I want to die here, I'd said. Signor Perso had smiled: Italian was his music, so he knew, without my saying, what I meant. For a while we ate in silence, listening to the concert of speech. Then he whispered, *Cadence means a falling*. Because he knew I was in love.

What had I been thinking, agreeing to move to Italy, a country whose spoken language was music? Why had I not heeded the shift in my gut when the passport agent at the Milan airport pulled Signor Perso aside and disoriented him? Instead of putting the Mendelssohn on my Walkman on his ears, to bring him back from confusion, why had I not just run? Because Yuri had drilled it into me never to panic, never to run with my back to anyone. As a result, I was now surrounded by a sumptuous speech-transcription of the mother-tongue I had lost.

I tossed out my cigarette and walked back to the Pettywards' in rain so hard there was no need to cry. The huge portone leading into the courtyard was open. Under the archway, the concierge gestured to me from his little booth. For a moment I had a fantasy that he was some overzealous cello fanatic who would help me find another place to stay. He bit into an enormous chocolate eclair; as he smacked through the custard, he asked if I knew who Isabel Masurovsky was. A man had come by that morning, asking questions. I nodded. The chocolate worm on his mustache wiggled. He handed me a postcard of a stone sculpture of a short, obese naked female. I stepped back, thinking he was trying to proposition me.

—Don't be nunnish, he said, smacking his lips, it's just a naked Venus. I thought you might be her. La Masurovsky, I mean.

I shook my head, casually flipping over the postcard, which would be from Marie-Antoinette.

—You're American?

I nodded. That part of my identity was useless to try and hide.

He crammed the rest of the eclair into his mouth. —My brother went to America. He said there's nothing there.

Signor Perso had sold his house in Milwaukee. There was a family living there.

—There's not, I said.

The card had no stamp, no postmark, no return address. Gradually I pieced together the Italian. Once I had asked the concierge a word I understood the meaning. Giulio was thanking me for entrusting to him my situation. He looked forward to returning my generosity. The note was discreet enough for any contingency. I almost laughed at the irony, that I had made Giulio think I was attached to someone.

As I headed away, I stuffed my hands in my pockets, where my fingers came upon a small, folded paper. It was a sheet from Giulio's prescription pad. There was a phone number on it, in scrawly, European handwriting. Beside it he had written the Latin abbreviation for twice a day, b.i.d., as a weak attempt at wit. I ran across the courtyard, slipping on the slick round cobblestones, and up to the apartment. Not until I had the phone clamped under my neck did I see the evil little lock on the zero hole. It prevented dialing out. While I'd been out, Mr. Pettyward had made good on his promise to have them installed. Because the *scatti* in Italy were billed in one lump sum and not, as he put it, parsed out in accordance with individual responsibility.

—*Fuck*, I said, into the phone.

Then I heard the lack of a dial tone, the low sound of a clearing throat.

—That we could arrange, Giulio's voice answered in Italian. Can you speak?

I could not quite catch my breath. I had not given Giulio the Pettywards' number. It did not seem likely that he would have gotten it from Marie-Antoinette.

—You have the cello?

—Oh, that, he said. You wanted it back?

He wanted witty repartee. I couldn't improvise. In the background, a hospital intercom snarled out what sounded like his name. —Tomorrow night, eleven-thirty? he asked.

—What about tonight?

—I tried this morning, he said, but now I'm on duty for the next twenty-four hours.

—I'll be downstairs, I said. Did my cello spend the night in your car?

—Don't you want to know where I spent the night?

Outside my door, I heard someone humming. I replaced the phone in its cradle.

In the dining room, Mr. Pettyward was standing behind his chair, reading, his thin rectangular glasses edging down towards the tip of his nose. There was no sign of Clayton. The long table was set with a white linen cloth and lit candles.

—Miss Masurovsky, he said, gesturing me to sit down. I stand until the women are seated. So try not to keep me waiting. I have fallen arches.

I nodded. The first dish cradled three small potatoes; the second, some withered, grayish green beans; the third, a pink gooey mash that Mr. Pettyward said was Gurney ham that a client had sent from Virginia. He served himself and passed the plate. It looked like the dog food Yuri and I had eaten once in Hungary, after he'd gotten a couple of bad addresses on someone he was looking for, and our money ran out. Still, I took a significant helping. My travels with Yuri had taught me to eat what there was.

Mr. Pettyward announced that he had had lunch at the Vatican with a cardinal. They had revisited the *Bildersturm* question. Mr. Pettyward was of the opinion that it was high time for Rome to finally demand rightful restitution from the Calvinists for the

German Catholic church art destroyed in the riots after the Reformation. He took a potato, and shook his head, muttering to the effect that people never value what comes for free. Had he been offered half of what had been wasted on Clayton, he went on, he might have developed into quite a musician. For the moment he thought he would have to settle for enlightened connoisseurship. Had I managed to give our friend a workout?

I had decided to skate lightly over the conversation, my tone a light, lively *vivace.* —Clayton's got a math test tomorrow, I said, though the two of us had not yet spoken.

—He's failing math, Mr. Pettyward said. In point of fact he has an extraordinarily high aptitude. He's eligible for MENSA, but he's too stubborn to join. I bought him a subscription to the newsletter, even had the executive director—he's a close friend—cable him directly. Clayton prefers not to take the test. I have the newsletters bound, though. Sooner or later we all come to terms with who we are.

I sneezed.

—So have you managed to give our friend a workout?

I realized he'd meant the Savant. —This morning, yes.

—Bless you. And what did you play?

—The Franck Sonata.

Mr. Pettyward passed me the green beans. —How do you spell that? Oh. Of course. Frahnk. I didn't recognize it the way you pronounced it. How many pages did you learn?

I shrugged stupidly. I knew the piece by heart, like everybody else.

—How many measures then?

I had no idea how to proceed, so I took another helping of meat.

—I'm glad you like our sad repast, he said, mashing at his with a fork. At times I wish my palate were less developed. Once you've tasted really excellent ham, as I have—not to imply you're responsible for your lack of taste, you simply lack exposure. . . . He trailed off, then seemed to gather himself again. —In many ways it's a curse to have been reared in an embassy. One was exposed to a quality of life that is virtually impossible to duplicate in the private sector.

I sneezed again. My head felt thick and swollen. I realized I had a fever.

Mr. Pettyward ate a bite of potato, chewed it forever, then lay down his fork as if the effort were too much. —The truth is that ever since my wife—since—well, I have detested food. Actually I don't hate food. I hate that I need to eat. Anyway, I won't dwell. I could meet another wife. A better wife. I could meet her tomorrow. Tell me about your life. Are you bored at the moment?

I looked down. Without a fork to occupy them, my left fingers had started in on the *Rococo Variations*. I dropped my hands on my lap and shook my head.

—Good. The cardinal and I were joined by the archbishop of Mogadishu. He discussed the life of Saint Apollonia. I had Marta dice the food in her honor. Apollonia had her teeth ripped from her mouth.

I choked, coughing into my napkin. He knew what he had in the Savant, knew I'd taken it. As I coughed, Mr. Pettyward adjusted his knife and fork along a careful parallel. When I was able to fold my napkin back onto my lap, he spoke.

—Here at the Pettywards' we are not in the habit of living like Egyptian potentates. Do not stuff yourself. You'll excuse me a moment.

I nodded, wondering if I should just get up and try to leave the apartment. Before I could decide, Mr. Pettyward strutted back in, steering Clayton by the shoulder like a vacuum cleaner. Clayton was humming the Chopin Military Polonaise. Definitely a sense of humor, I thought.

Mr. Pettyward sat him firmly in his chair and served him a scoop of ham and a potato. —Clayton, Isabel was just talking about the Franck violin sonata, which she claims to have been playing on the Amati.

—It was transcribed for the cello during Franck's lifetime.

Mr. Pettyward nodded. —We'll have to hear it, then.

I blotted my mouth. —Sorry, for before.

—Don't apologize. Few actions are mitigated by apology. I've found life to be simpler when one stops bothering with intentions. I'll give you an example. As a small child Clayton developed a taste for biscuits meant for canines. As a result he rarely clears his plate. When I ask him at any one meal whether he plans to eat dinner tomorrow, he says he'll try. But my question is, When will he succeed? The point is, a person of accomplishment doesn't *try* to pass a math exam. The report card of history remembers who won Waterloo, not who tried to win Waterloo. Well. One remembers Napoleon, but he's the exception that proves the rule. After dinner you won't *try* to play the Savant, you'll play the Savant.

Clayton stared pointedly at the opposite wall. I tried to imagine Yuri *managing* what I ate; the idea was ludicrous.

—Ah, Mr. Pettyward said, smiling tightly. I see *he's* still not talking. Isabel, would you be so kind as to serve the flan?

I cut the small, rectangular dish of pudding into three strips, lifted out the first square, and passed it to Clayton. The second square I lifted out and passed to Mr. Pettyward, then served myself the last square.

Mr. Pettyward leaned over confidentially, pointing to a piece of pudding, sticking out from my square. —Technically that was my piece of flan. You failed to cut down all the way through. The protrusion or foot on yours is in fact residual flan which belonged to my portion.

I stared down at my plate.

—That one, he said. That lump there.

I pointed with my knife. —That?

—Play that Franck sonata for me over coffee, he said, and I'll consider it a gift.

My face flooded with heat. I was finished. I nodded and excused myself. As slowly as I could, I slid back my chair. Stood. Pushed it in. Turned to walk down the hall. Instead of thinking up a plan I fell into counting my footsteps. Then, in the music room I ran out of footsteps. What there was, of course, was my old cello. I opened the case with no idea how to pull it off. I unhooked my bow and slowly tightened it. And rosined the threads. A plan was forming. Bringing an instrument back to full sound, I would explain, after such a long silence, was a gradual process. In the beginning you did not want to tax it too many hours per day. I tuned the C, the G, and the D string, but the A peg was stuck; no matter how hard I twisted, it wouldn't budge. I rested my fingers, feeling a little guilty at how suddenly and disloyally I had abandoned my cello for the Savant. That was when the A string popped. I felt a whoosh next to my ear as the metal string whipped up and yanked a clump of hair. If I had not had my chin tucked to the side to listen to the overtones, it would have whipped up and cut my eye. On the fingerboard, though I did not feel any pain, blood was streaming out of my index finger. The string had slashed it.

After so many years of ice packs and heat packs and gloves in winter, years of never opening a car door or even a can, I had a split second of old panic. But then it dawned on me that a miracle had occurred. In the bathroom I wrapped the finger in a wad of toilet paper. By the time I had packed my cello back up the bandage looked like a bright red plum. I walked back to the dining room and stood at the door.

—Now what, Mr. Pettyward said. Then he saw the blood and was aghast. He held out his linen napkin, then thought better of his generosity and snatched it back, not wanting to bloody it. But Clayton tossed me his, and I caught it involuntarily. Now Mr. Pettyward was sputtering. I rewrapped my finger and quietly apologized. I had tightened a string too fast, I said, and broken it. Mr. Pettyward asked after the damage to the Savant. I was about to reassure him when Clayton pulled out a huge generic can of NO FRILLS FRUIT PUNCH from under the table and chugged it as a decoy.

Mr. Pettyward stared at Clayton. Carbuncle spots were blooming on his cheeks. —You went to the consulate commissary? Dressed like that? Then he walked over to the sideboard, where a behavior chart was propped. —You may be excused, he said, affixing a red sticker in the box for the day. You absolutely may be excused. I think I have been unfailingly—in your mother's—and you, you—

Mr. Pettyward inhaled deeply. His face was pinched to the verge of tears. —If green is too strenuous, he said quietly, you might at least strive for yellow.

* * *

69

The cavernous living room had the eerie overspaciousness of a warehouse. Our footsteps rattled in the empty air. A triptych of serene Perugino egg-heads hung on the wall. Mr. Pettyward noticed me looking around at the odd assortment of sculpture. —My wife's collection, he said. She seemed constantly to encounter objects that were essential to her very existence. Have a seat on my Bourbon sofa. No no. That's the Biedermeyer. This one here.

Mr. Pettyward sighed in exhaustion and began massaging his forehead. I wondered if his wife had had lovers. —I have to get away, he said. I have to. To tie up, you see, some of her affairs. You'll play for me at the end of the week. I presume you'll have healed by then?

Clayton's napkin around my finger was nearly soaked in blood. I squeezed it to make more come out.

—For God's sake don't get it on the sofa, he erupted. Now. I've got to go away for a few days. You'll keep an eye on Clayton. For the time being I'd prefer that he not handle the cello. For now, you and I shall have exclusive use.

—Clayton's welcome to learn on my cello, I offered.

Mr. Pettyward arched an eyebrow.

—It's a good cello. My parents took out a second mortgage on our house to get it, I added idiotically.

—Is it old? Mr. Pettyward asked doubtfully as he poured himself another brandy.

He thought it was crappy. It meant he hadn't heard of who I used to be. —It was a row house, I said sheepishly, as if the mistake I'd made had become clear.

—So not exactly the instrument we would ideally wish him to learn on.

I shook my head.

He raised his glass in a toast to my acuity. I raised my empty glass and we clinked.

—So how shall I go about this, I said. Shall I rent a cello for Clayton?

—No no no. No no. Between us, I don't have the money for another instrument just now. You will play the Savant every day, for no less than two hours, and you may warm up Clayton on one of my other instruments. I have a more than adequate viola. That would be the thing to break him in. Clayton despises the cello anyway, so I doubt he'll jump out a window. You people all cross over, don't you?

A decade of indentured servitude, of chasing the perfect cello glissando—for a viola? On a normal day I would have replied that a viola is a cello-doll, a cello-poodle. There are more viola jokes than there is literature for viola. Holding the thing requires simian contortions. The alto clef alone—it's between the bass and the treble clef; the middle line is middle C—was a recipe for defeat. And what was he doing, then, hiring a cellist? But Signor Perso was dead; the diameter of things I was allowed to express had narrowed to a tiny spot that I had to slip through to survive. Whether or not Clayton would ever learn an instrument, indeed, whether he was suicidal, seemed beside the point.

—You need a dehumidifier, I said.

Mr. Pettyward went into his study and came back with a typed piece of paper. —This is the standard contract I use for my help. Two years, terminable and renewable by me. As you see, paragraph two stipulates the security measures. Under no circumstances will the Savant leave the premises. Nor will you reveal its existence at this location or anywhere else, to anyone. The

Italians are a race of professional thieves, you simply cannot imagine. Several people in the building have been hit in the last few years. The concierge is certainly on the take. Were anyone to get a hint of what's here, the place would be ransacked tomorrow, and you would be responsible.

He asked the spelling of my name, and filled it in. —Masurovsky. What kind of name is that?

—Russian, I said, though by now I had the sense that nationality was not quite the question he was asking.

I wondered if this was the time in the job interview when you were supposed to ask about salary. But then I thought I remembered how you never talk about money with rich people. I'd never read a contract, or asked anybody for money, had not even had the nerve, after Signor Perso was almost hit by a car, to remind him we'd been on our way to a lawyer to make a will. Yuri had done all that, had negotiated the fees, threatening and cajoling for the tiniest stupidities as if justice for the pogroms depended on whether we got sandwiches. Now, instead of focusing on the legalese, on the fact that I was agreeing to work for room and board and no money at all—I found myself playing a version of *Les Lettres et Les Chiffres,* Letters and Numbers, an old French game show for teenage geniuses that Yuri'd made me watch when I studied with Tortelier in Paris: I began to add, multiply, subtract, and divide the dates Mr. Pettyward had filled in the blanks to get them to come out to the number of minutes Signor Perso had been dead. Then Mr. Pettyward reappeared at the doorway. I gave up and signed.

—Cornelius Godfrey Pettyward is you?

—Call me God. Come. I'll show you the alarm.

The confidence I had that last summer, the blind sprawl of possibility, amazes me now. By the night of my Carnegie Hall debut, nothing surprised me. Not even Lillian Fuchs, whose recording of the Bach suites I knew by heart, hobbling into the dressing room with a bouquet from Rostropovich.

Yuri tried to warn me. He knew what it was to lose the ability to play. But at fourteen, you never imagine that your gift might really be your mother's; that her deep amber mezzo is the home your own tone seeks; that the phrases she tosses off while cooking breakfast are falling stars you catch. Your playing is as wide as the night sky, the notes as shining, the silence as black and deep. You cannot imagine that you might not know how to play a passage without her singing it over and over, the inessential dropping off like dusk becoming night. You do not know what it is to be Yuri, to feel the constant stab of a phantom limb. Because your mother doesn't see it. He never shows her that. The story she tells about him waiting backstage and following her back to New Jersey in his truck, about him showing up the next morning with a ring and a gramophone—is not about desperation. Her version is like the plot of *Così:* he shows up with Mario del Monaco, but she hates del Monaco's bad toupee and his fire-engine high notes, so she yells *Grotesque!* out the window. He sits down and waits. When she calls and has him arrested, Yuri is delighted. Renata has *taste.* He posts bail and returns with lily-sweet Giuseppe di Stefano. She slams down all the windows, but there's a heat wave; after five minutes she calls the police again. But by now Yuri has the neighborhood kids listening to di Stefano on the gramophone, so when the police come, the neighborhood mothers claim they've hired him. There's a reporter from the local paper. Finally Renata walks out on the lawn and, in the midst of Yuri's newly formed day care group, says, I'm thirty-seven and I can't have children. Yuri looks around at the neighborhood kids, shrugs, and with the hand with the bad fingers—so she too can see what she's getting—he offers her the ring.

Yuri wept. Always at the wrong moment, never at the tear-jerk scene, but at the supple sexuality she threw out in passing, at her bird-lightness, her looseness, at what she dared. At the way she could turn on a dime in performance, set aside the knowledge that her top notes were fraying, and unleash a searing cry of grief. Yuri was careful: when my mother got pregnant at forty-four, he wanted her to abort. My mother let me sleep late; if Yuri left before school started, we'd stay home and play duets. She signed an entire tablet so I could write myself a note when-ever I wanted to skip school. But when she was touring, Yuri took me there and picked me up like clockwork. With Yuri I did shows of arpeggios. With my mother there was no practice, just a life so steeped in music you could hear it in the quiet when she left.

Yuri tried to warn me. Hers was a gift, he said. Mine was a craft, like building chairs. Chairs that could loosen and come apart if I wasn't careful. People like my mother could afford to be lazy. People like us couldn't.

It goes without saying that if you know where a score is leading, you handle a passage accordingly. If Yuri had come to Russia, instead of letting me go with my mother, I would have been more careful. Before the Tchaikovsky, I had adhered to his precautions. The never wearing jewelry seemed sensible, the never doing interviews, wise. His silent shrugs after every performance, the harangues over the length of a rest, the cold rooms we stayed in on our secret side trips after concerts, the silence he tacitly enforced when we got home, even his dismissal of the kids at Juilliard who tried to make friends—after a Beethoven recital, he told my methodical accompanist that he was glad her bowel movements were so regular—it was all part of the package. The instruction was effective, and I had performed as necessary. It only takes being left behind once, because you have read a map wrong, to learn to read them right. Getting woken up with a pitcher of ice water at dawn makes breaking a string in front of the queen of England, later that same day, seem like a minor impediment. Having a performance score taken away five minutes before curtain imparts a striking ability to memorize.

(andante, going on)

My point is, Yuri tried to protect me. The first teacher he hired boxed me across the ears, but Yuri sat in the corner, watching him like a hawk. Even three years later, when Yuri discovered report cards

—I'd never shown him mine—the blast lasted less than an hour. My mother had left his favorite, chocolate-covered strawberries, which Yuri only let us eat excruciatingly slowly, at the rate of one a day. Now he flew into a rage, shoved three dozen in his mouth one after the other, bellowed that I had to know EVERY-THING. Began firing out questions about the Bill of Rights. I said I didn't need the Bill of Rights, that I was already famous. He clamped the bad hand over my face. *Too famous for thees?* I stopped struggling, to let him know that my life had nothing to do with his. Whereas he was a carpenter, I was a musician, who wasn't dumb enough to let her fingers get bashed by some stupid tool. There was one sort of bad moment, then, when he pounded his head against the wall and cut it open, but that was pretty much it. Sometime after midnight my mother came in from her closing night with champagne and piles of flowers. They had drinks. And as they left for the hospital, he gave in. *I hope you will be a veddy goot chillist,* he said. *Because you are a veddy stewpid gurl.*

The next morning he woke me up at five. It was the first time any of us had ever gotten up that early. It was clear he hadn't slept. Yuri said he understood, now, why he went to camp, why he was one of the few hundred kids out of fifteen thousand from his camp to come out. That if I was going to play a cello—which was *not* the piano and *not* the voice and thus *not* particularly useful—I would have to learn to play like my life depended on it. He had been up all night planing the ebony fingerboard of my cello, where he'd detected a groove. He leaned the cello against the bed. I opened my eyes and stared down its neck: the ebony spun out a long strand of light until it dwindled like a singer running out of breath.

Quietly, without waking my mother, we went down to the basement. What camp, I asked, while I waited for him to find the string for the light. I was waiting for him to say Auschwitz, which I knew about: it was a sort of military-school conservatory where too much marching band practice turned people into skeletons. Then the cellar went bright.

That day was Yuri's birthday. He announced we were selling our tickets to the Bolshoi ballet, that I was outgrowing my three-quarters size. From now on we were saving for a full-size cello. For three years he arranged it so that we were away on my birthday, so that he could dispense with the buying of presents. Nobody got anything new unless my mother was around. Yuri took over the shopping. He clipped coupons. Sat at the kitchen table late into the night, sending in for refunds, or paced in the cellar reading scores. Lunch was lukewarm soup he had heated by leaving the can on the stove overnight, over the pilot light. He bought huge sides of beef, carved them in the basement, made me wrap the bloody hunks in paper, and plastic, foil.

In my mother's version—the art for art's sake version—it was all simple. Yuri had a certain Russian ruthlessness in serving a cause. She'd had to marry him, she liked to say, to keep him out of jail. He made gorgeous furniture, loved us dearly, and came to every performance. Why he'd never gotten his fingers fixed, or even found a doctor who could diagnose the problem, was not worth thinking about. Yuri was smart: He bought her her figs and her salmon and her Egyptian cotton sheets and her special Brazilian coffee, the kind she'd had when she sang at Manaus. Her voice was fading, but she got work with regional companies all over Europe; it took three years for her to notice that he and I were brushing our teeth with salt.

Yuri forced me to learn the repertoire. Left to my mother, I would have played the piano transcriptions of opera scores on my cello, exquisitely, for the rest of my life. I cannot fault Yuri for not preparing me. It was not that I was not prepared. If I am not prepared now, it is because I believed my last note at the Tchaikovsky competition, the note that unraveled Yuri's safety net, when my bow pulled taut the air in the hall, when for one long infinite moment my note was the entire hall, my pulse its pulse—

(quiet, less)

The triangle is the strongest shape. I had been to school enough days to learn that. In spite of awful moments, my universe was ordered. It did not seem as if the three of us would ever be in need. If Yuri had come with me to Russia, I would have continued to trot out my gem-cut brilliance whenever, wherever he commanded; I might not know, even now, that there was another way. I was not unhappy. Yuri was my manager; the safety net he bound us in kept the world at bay. I managed the icy critiques by working out the techniques I would use to play his spitting staccato, the galloping 3/16 fury, the monotone disdain. If Yuri had been at the Tchaikovsky, enforcing in his hundred ways, that entire summer's unraveling—my Carnegie Hall debut being the last event in the sequence—might never have occurred. But his parents had emigrated out of Russia in '32, and Yuri was convinced that if he went back, he'd get shipped off to Siberia. For Yuri, time stood still.

The Tchaikovsky was the first time I'd gone anywhere without him. With my mother, it was a different world. For the first time—I was fourteen—I wore one of her low-cut gowns. She lent me jewelry and bought me a black-market mink. My mother assumed I'd use a score; right away, my shoulders stopped cramping. Yuri had made me focus when I got nervous, alone in my room; my mother told me to imagine the judges in their underwear. We went to parties. Stayed in a hotel. Ordered room service. Posed for photos. I kept waiting for something bad to happen. Nothing did. I wish now something had. If it had, I would never have imagined it possible to luxuriate in the present, to take my safety for granted. At the Tchaikovsky, I began to think like my mother. To think I was like her. When I survived and even won without Yuri's incessant management of evil, a trap door opened. I wondered if Yuri might be wrong, if we might not need to be so watchful.

When we got home my mother walked in wearing the mink; I was carrying the trophy. Yuri saw in an instant that I'd changed. When my mother went upstairs to unpack, I ran up behind her, I said, to change my clothes. When I came back down his face was crimson. Had it been hard to hoodwink the imbeciles at the Infamous Russian Puppet Circus? he asked. Then he led me back to the garage, where a bucket of soapy water and two scrub brushes sat waiting with a pair of rubber gloves. He kneeled down and handed me one. The judges had chosen their pupils, he said, and it was only because I had studied with Zara Nelsova at Juilliard that I had gotten past the first round. I nodded, though we both knew she was Canadian, that her real name was Sara Nelson, that I had only taken one master class where I hadn't learned anything.

Theresienstadt had been the *model* ghetto, he informed me, the *privileged* camp. It gathered Nobel Prize winners, decorated veterans of the Great War, and distinguished artists of every kind.

Height of civilization, I muttered, as I scraped the scrub brush over the oil stains on the concrete. I wondered if ever before I had dared to be sarcastic. Yuri stopped scrubbing. After emigrating to Berlin, he said—his voice on the verge of volcanic—my Masurovsky grandparents had taken a chance and paid their entire fortune on what the brochure guaranteed was an exclusive lake-view villa at the Czech spa town of Terezin. And even so it was *his* ability as a pianist that kept them from the transports to the East. The Tchaikovsky competition had taken three weeks, Yuri said, whereas at Theresienstadt his playing had protected him from the transports for how long? *Three years,* he hissed. Three years a *Prominenter.* Dr. Eppstein himself, Yuri went on, the head of the Elder Council, let him practice on his Steinway. To no other pianist, not even Gideon Klein, was this allowed! Of the hundreds of performers in Theresienstadt's four working orchestras, its operas, its hundreds of chamber and lieder concerts—played by the cream of the Prague musical elite!—who did I think was the only musician in the camp ever to appear on the protected list of the Jews and on that of the Nazis? To become a Prominenter A AND a Prominenter B?

Then Yuri broke off because my mother yelled out the kitchen window how sweet I was to take on such an icky job. On our hands and knees, we smiled up at her. Sounds like heaven, I muttered, because after being in Russia, where war lingered in the air like the smell of charred flesh, it was clear that his tirade had hardly scratched the surface of the massive boulder of bitterness he hauled with him, with the two of us, whenever we went on tour. I was daring him to tell her about the late-night pacing in our basement. About the flesh-rending cries, whenever we traveled, that sheared apart the dark. To tell her exactly who it was we were tracking down on our secret side trips after my concerts. To explode her benign fairy-tale version, in which the past was the past was the past.

Yuri seethed. He knew what I was doing. That Polish piece of plastic I'd won, he growled, was hers. It was *her* gift I was borrowing. I was about as capable of taking care of myself, he said, as those minks in that coat.

—Maybe I can scrub my way back to the shtetl, I proposed.

Yuri spit on the concrete.

In the months before his death, his mania deepened. Watching my fame grow, hearing the silences I mustered in larger and larger halls, Yuri got desperate. Before, we were coconspirators, detectives on a hunt. Now he was alone. More than once I woke at dawn to find him packed and setting off without me. As if he were desperate to find a tattered memory, anywhere in the world, in which his playing existed intact. One of our nice secret rituals—we never told my mother—was the one night each fall he and I camped out, on Sukkoth, under a canopy of branches we built, to remind ourselves of how lucky we were to have a roof. Now we were the people we'd been thankful we weren't. None of the postcards we sent my mother mentioned sleeping in woods or wiping ourselves with leaves. None described me washing myself with ice-cold water, in a train-station bathroom, while Yuri stood guard at the door. In September in Vienna the applause lasted a half hour. For an entire half hour the dressing room rumbled. Yuri paced back and forth as I packed up. The house manager came in. Just one, he begged softly, asking me to take a curtain call. Yuri stood still until I had left. We took a train at two that morning, as if finding this next survivor were suddenly a matter of life and death. He refused to believe the neighbors who said the man was dead. We spent days wandering from one dark village to another, deep in the crevasses between the Alps, where the sun only shone an hour a day, asking after his name and crawling over the rusted gates of Jewish graveyards. Then he decided to hitchhike. It was only luck that we made it to a tiny train station outside Brno, only luck that a train whistle screeched in the middle of the night, only luck that I woke to find Yuri standing at roll call in his sleep, only luck that he woke the next day, remembering nothing, his mania crumpled, ready to go home. Of course, with a knowledge of the future, I would have handled the passage differently. I might have wondered how it was that the world had shrugged off what had happened, as if it belonged only to those condemned to drag it along. Surely I would not have bought a whistle to take with us on trips, to blow at him in the middle of the night when things got bad. But that summer a future was hard to imagine. He was binding me to his past, limb by limb, to keep from being left alone in the camp in his mind. I was sawing away at the cords.

Yuri tried, one last time, to rein me in. In the lunch box my mother had packed for my Carnegie debut, he put in a present, he said, to remind me not to talk to reporters, a set of teeth chattering on a hinge. But I knew what Yuri meant: it was a skeleton jaw, babbling from the dead, reminding me of what happened to people who opened their big mouths. As I opened the box to eat my sandwich, the teeth clattered to the floor and snagged my stockings, and I knew everything was ruined. Then I peeked from behind the curtain at my parents' empty seats, and someone spotted me, and the applause ignited, and I had to go out. As I walked onstage I felt Yuri's tight protective barbed-wire precision—until then, my style of playing—fall away like an unfastened cape. The naked freedom, beyond his clutch, was dizzying. As I bowed I made myself a little bargain to forget Yuri, to let go just this once, to leave him behind, alone.

Musicians are so often called *masters,* as if what they do is command, but what I remember was the erotic draw of sight-reading, the tug in my gut as I opened a score, its difficult passages pulling my flesh towards desires I had not known I had, pulling me not towards mastery but submission. The giving myself over. I knew I had a piece when I could imagine destroying the score, could shut my eyes and imagine the composer sitting hidden in the audience, could imagine myself onstage, playing his desires as they came to his mind. It was not a fantasy I had ever allowed myself onstage—not with Yuri sitting there. But now, with their seats empty, I did. From the first note, my body joined with the music in a way I could not have imagined. The contours of the Bach suite I'd been tracing since I was six became the curves of a flesh luminous from years of caressing. Then Debussy poured himself out through me like molten glass. During the Carter, I felt time slow to a standstill, each note still in an infinite silence. At intermission an irresistible sleepiness rolled over me, and I did something else I'd never done. I lay down on the green room couch and slept. Then Sharon and two of my teachers from Juilliard came on and we did Messiaen's *Quartet for the End of Time.* By the time my solo came round, the Seventh Day of Rest Stretching Out into the Infinitude of Grace, I had ceased to work my limbs, ceased trying, ceased anticipating, ceased deciding, and let the music take possession. There was no wood between my legs, no scroll aside my neck, no two bodies. Just one voice, pulling towards release.

Yuri had taught me to regard applause as a crude and almost violent excess of the masses. The routine he had worked out for me was that I would smile, bow, walk off. Now I sat there, spent. Gradually I noticed the bow in my hand, the body between my legs, the white-hot silence. As the seconds swelled to hours, I searched my memory for how I'd played. My mind went white. Then I looked down and saw their empty seats and knew that I had done the unspeakable. Then the house exploded. For a moment I saw Carnegie's white-and-gold gingerbread moldings crumbling like the Dresden Oper under the Allied bombs. I hurried off. But then a simple thought came to my body: it wanted that feeling, again. So for the first time ever, I walked back out onstage. A blistering cold-heat washed over me. Though I now know about the infrasound waves that roll in under thunder—according to Giulio, they tickle the human temporal lobes into a pseudo-religious torpor while unnerving the animals in the vicinity—at the time, it was like nothing I'd ever felt.

Giulio wriggled a huge key into the colossal door of his dilapidated palazzo. Its cast-bronze panels were tarnished to verdigris and streaked with random graffiti. When he threw his weight against it, the hinges shrieked as if woken from a dream of medieval torture. Then the lower two panels, a twelve-foot-high door, gave way. The moon cast a cool blue-white glare over the deserted courtyard. The building seemed war-torn, its ravaged walls pockmarked from shrapnel, its chewed-up ornament riddled with bullet holes. Not one light was on; the windows, I noticed, were boarded up with gray, weathered boards. I wondered if the place was condemned. We walked diagonally across a cobblestone courtyard, climbed three stories up a set of worn stone stairs, then wound our way around several turns on a balcony with a rusted iron railing. I made a note to remember the way, but my mind was jangled with fever and fuzzy from lack of sleep, and I knew I'd never find my way out.

The narrow, icy passageway Giulio led me through gave onto a smaller courtyard. After another corner the passageway led to a cast-iron door held shut by a huge padlock. Giulio unlocked it, then lifted a rusted finial off the railing and shook it. Another large key clattered out that he put into the door's ancient lock. The door opened onto a long vaulted room covered in old, cracked, cream-colored tile that ended in a wall of windows. A thicket of stone columns jutted up at random heights like a charred forest. Their cornices stuck out at odd and not completely reassuring angles. There was no path. The space felt so creepy that Giulio needed to guide me inside with a pressure on the small of my back.

The thick metal door slammed shut behind us. Giulio did not turn on a light. While he went to the bathroom, I hopscotched over the shadows that striped back from the columns with frightening parallel precision. My eyes adjusted to the glinty dark. Other than the thicket of columns, the loft was almost empty. There was no order, but no clutter either. To the right a huge open armoire overflowed with clothes. An old iron bed faced the windows, ridiculously, like a magic carpet ready to sail off into the night. By the left wall a small table and three unmatched chairs sat together awkwardly. What in darkness had flickered like movement turned out to be an ornate oval mirror on a gilt floor stand, standing by the foot of the bed.

I had told myself that once I was able to see Giulio's apartment, and how he lived, I would get a sense of who he was. But this was a warehouse of objects that looked as if each belonged to a different person. The place seemed intended to drip with sexuality, but the spontaneity seemed constructed, the theme undermined by its orchestration. At least here there seemed little chance of me breaking down.

To avoid the full-length-mirror-by-the-bed routine, I walked over and stood by the chairs. I thought I should sit down, to look relaxed. But the choice was like the test with the inkblots where you say you see nothing because anything you say will be used against you. I knew not to pick the dark, carved, Indian-looking stool: there were too many little heads carved into its legs, all gods of something, whom I did not want peering up my skirt. The sleek, black-leather chair did not seem right either: it looked cold, high-tech, and its chrome fittings probably concealed straps, or some evil gynecological equipment. I settled on the stuffed Empire throne-chair, though it was covered in a malarial chartreuse and its feet, carved like claws grasping orbs, did not bode well.

—That's *Louis Dix-neuf,* Giulio said as I was easing myself down, his voice so close I reached up behind me to touch him. But then I heard him clattering around in the kitchen. It was like the time when my mother and I had stood at one center of the ellipse in Independence Hall in Philadelphia, where Benjamin Franklin positioned his table so he could eavesdrop, and Yuri stood at the other center, about fifty feet away, his back to us and his head to the ground, and suddenly we heard him whisper *I em Raspewtin,* which of course my mother thought was funny. I jumped up and hurried over to the other wall, where a group of nude sketches hung in a cluster, then glanced over the volume of the room, trying to decipher its spooky acoustics.

(leggero) —Which one? I called out casually, as if I'd been by the pictures all along. The bounce of my voice died dead against the walls. I looked closer. They were covered in silk, the whole place padded like a cell in an asylum.

—Well, Isabel, which do you think? his voice said.

I was looking at a vertical series of black-and-white Japanese porn photographs. In front of a forest backdrop, a man and a woman, in kimonos that had fallen half open, were posed having sex against a tree. Or with the tree. I couldn't quite tell. The light in the photograph was so bright and still that they seemed posed in some ritual mime of sex. A funny shape, like a piece of a jigsaw puzzle, blacked out their genitals.

Where are the genitals? was not a question I thought I could ask, so I moved down the wall. The next piece in the exhibit was a stylized, amber-paper sketch of an anorexic woman wearing stockings and nothing else. She was touching herself. I was alone in the apartment of a man who actually had a picture of a woman touching herself, hanging on his wall. In passing I wondered whether I could get past the kitchen and out of the apartment with my coat. I heard him open the refrigerator: that would be the moment to sprint by him, his head amicably buried in the cheese drawer searching for hors d'oeuvres. But the Savant was nowhere to be seen. Then Giulio emerged gallantly with a tray with glasses and champagne and a bottle of cassis.

—Just tell me which you prefer, he said.

—Just because I prefer it, doesn't make it Louis the Nineteenth.

He aimed the champagne above my head and popped the cork. I kept myself from ducking. —Because there was no Louis the Nineteenth, he said, smiling. He added a dose of cassis to the glasses and handed me a drink.

—I knew that, I said, holding up my glass to watch the heavy, swirling purple writhe against the bottom of the flute.

—Just testing, he said, clinking against me. So?

—They all seem rather similar to me.

He downed his champagne in one large gulp. —But the content's a given, no? The question is surely not what to do but how to do it.

I didn't understand exactly what he was asking. I worried he might think I thought the pictures were exciting me. But there was no neutral ground. I couldn't go back to the chairs, and the bed, of course, was out; the only other thing to go to was a series of Renaissance woodcuts of a man and a woman in contorted sexual positions. In the mirror I stared at him, wondering whether Marie-Antoinette and Fabio knew he was a porn fetishist.

Giulio glanced up and caught me and smiled. —You are offended by the woodcuts of Giulio.

How perfect to frame it like I was some kind of puritanical American zealot.

—Actually, they're Raimondi, he added. From the drawings of Giulio. As you probably know.

I smiled overfreshly. —Actually, I didn't.

—Calm down, he said in English. Giulio Romano the assistant to Raffaello. Who did all the trompe l'oeil. After Raffaello died, Giulio had to finish his projects. One of these was the Constantine Room in the Vaticano. Popa Clemente Seventh refused to pay Giulio because he had paid Raffaello already. So Giulio drew these on the walls. Then Marcantonio copied them and made the woodcuts. They became the most famous erotica in the Renaissance. Of course, they were banned. And burned. But a few series survive. This is the only set in private hands. They're in poor condition. Fabio couldn't sell them for what he wanted, so he gave them to me for helping with a reconstruction we did on the breasts of, of—

—Enter the fiancée?

—Not Daphne. Her breasts are lovely. I couldn't marry anyone I felt I had to work on.

I waited.

—Of a mistress of his I happen to know.

It dawned on me that the place was not just a set, that probably every object in the apartment was probably worth an enormous amount of money. I wondered how Marie-Antoinette would go about it. To me there seemed too few things in the apartment to steal any one of them.

—I can hardly help my patrimony, he said, and put his arm around me.

Patrimony. I thought of Signor Perso's years of useless lessons, of Vrashkansova, of inheriting the Savant without being able to play it. I wandered towards the picture window and leaned both palms on the glass. A platter of fog-breath blurred the view to globules of white. Though I was standing in a layer of icy air, I did not step backward, into the room. On either side of a dark, narrow alley, a pair of buildings loomed over the room. A series of speckled facades rhymed back between them until the diminuendo converged to a black strip of void, a long, empty concert-hall aisle that drew me towards it as if it were a light. The quiet intensified, as an audience settles to silence when they sense you behind the curtain. I scanned the rows of tiny windows of the buildings, looking for someone looking out at me. An utter aloneness settled over me. There was not one other person, it occurred to me, who knew where I was. If anything happened to me here, I would disappear without a trace. I wrote out the letters of my name on the glass, like Giulio had on the windshield of his car, so that there would be some small record of me.

I didn't hear Giulio come up behind me. A hard cold curve singed my nerves as it slid up the back of my neck. He dipped my earlobe in champagne and kissed my other ear so that I could not move without spilling the glass on my dress. I thought his kiss would be wet, messy, mixing us together, but it wasn't. It was dry. Then he sipped champagne and parted his lips. The snapping bubbles roared back into my ear like the ocean in a conch. Again I could not hear. He hooked the base of the glass on my shoulder and tilted it forward. The liquid bled down over the tip of my breast and bloomed there, a dark, indecent aureole. A hand slid up and took the weight of my breast. With the other, Giulio poured champagne into my lips. Berry-sweet cold slid down my throat. I knew I should stop—I did not like the man—but my nipples hardened and betrayed me. It came to me that my body had known all along that this would have to happen.

—Sorry, he said, not sorry at all.

—I shouldn't have come here.

—There are no shoulds to pleasure, he said, unzipping me.

—The dress is ruined.

—I have a special wool soap given to me by the wife of the sultan of Brunei. It's made from mother's milk.

My head got light, trying not to think about what it meant to make a soap from a woman's milk. I did not have the courage to ask if he was joking. Giulio stood there, smiling. Apparently, to him this was a normal situation. As a child I had never been sick and had never been taken to the doctor. Yuri had not allowed it. And so it was that I had never been naked before a stranger. But I could not let Giulio discover how much more he knew; that would be the end of any possibility. And so, as if for the hundredth time, I took off my dress and handed it to him to wash.

The woodcut in front of me came into focus. The man was holding up the woman like a piggyback ride in front. He crouched down to support her bottom on his thighs; his spine curled towards where she was clinging to his neck. Her head was thrown back, her long hair scrawled out behind her like the medusa. Her mouth was open and her eyes rolled back in abandon. I stared, trying to place the image: it was the picture of me, in the *Times,* that I found on our steps when I finally got back to our house the morning after my Carnegie Hall debut. The picture was hideously sexual.

What better moment for Giulio to come out and lie down, yawning loudly?

—I'm exhausted, he said. I work too much.

—Don't surgeons usually? I asked, without turning around.

—Your surgeons work many hours. Here we are too many, so mostly we don't work so hard. When I began, anyone who had graduated from *lyceo scientifico* could go to medical school. So at the public hospital where I work, we're all underpaid, all kissing up to the professors, who operate in fancy private clinics, like Fabio—all trying to get scheduled for enough operating time, to pass the exams to eventually get hired somewhere else.

I stared at the woodcut for a while longer. A piece of music I hate—that emetic *Barcarole* from the *Tales of Hoffman*—sat down on my brain. What I really wanted was to blend in with the columns, to face the wall like a dunce, until my dress was dry. I went to the bathroom, to stall, but when I came out Giulio was humming softly, patiently. There seemed nothing left to do but go to him.

—Hello, he said in English when I sat down. He was lying on his back with his hands behind his head. He didn't move to touch me. He was not in any sort of rush. Clearly he had slept with hundreds of women. His every word and gesture said so. He smiled, amused at my stiffness. I think that he thought that I thought he wasn't attracted to me. After a moment he reached over and put his hand on my thigh.

—These are pretty, he said. In a slow jazz run his fingers wandered up my leg along the pattern of my stockings. My skin raised up with goose bumps. His hands knew my body as well as if he'd been me in a former life.

—You know, I'm not—I mean, we can try if you want to —

Like notes off popping strings, my words seemed to twang off in silly, uncontrollable meanings. —I'm not that into men. I mean sex.

—You mean me. Or—

He lifted his hand an inch above my leg and held his fingers like a pianist, poised to come in. —You're a lesbian?

—Yes, I said, instantly regretting it. Well, no. Not exactly.

Again his fingers grazed my skin. His hands were thick and large, and I felt myself wanting them to hold me.

—It's not important.

Once I read in a horoscope that the one thing my sign had was perfectly shaped forearms. Mine are muscular, round, and solid from playing, the only part of my body I really like. I got up and turned off the lamp by the bed. Then we lay parallel, his face so close I could smell his almondy skin. A wave of claustrophobia curdled in my gut. Giulio looked at me, questioningly. I was afraid he might ask me what I wanted, so I shut my eyes and kissed him before he had the chance. One of the few things I had learned with Signor Perso was to avoid talking about sex, in bed. It's like an order form, like notation on a passage; if he played it that way and I didn't come, he'd feel cheated. That's what I love about music: you can speak without talking, without being held to what you've said. Music is expression; notes resonate only as long as they are meant to in time, and then vanish like bubbles in air. Words are like darts. Their meanings are recorded and totaled up, the totals used against you when you are inconsistent.

—Sit up.

He let me unbutton his shirt. I was not expecting what was beneath it. Signor Perso's waist was narrow, his chest hollowed out, the capillaries on his skin collapsing into fragile, transparent tissue, nestling the present of his heart. Giulio's torso was thick with cables, his shoulders capped with muscle. I had never seen arms with so many parts. They hung out from his torso awkwardly as if waiting to grasp a woman's waist. Signor Perso's body had been a blanket. Giulio's was a creature caged in clothes.

He started to touch me. I pushed him away. But his hands were steady, they held me to him. I unbuttoned his pants and put him in my mouth, which seemed to work. He lost his concentration. His was uncircumcised—fine if you're trying to avoid getting sent to a camp, but I had only ever seen Signor Perso, so I didn't know if you were supposed to do something differently. Also his was crooked. Halfway up, it angled to the left. I wondered whether it would feel good inside, or if it would hook you and hurt. I glanced back into the room: lit from the window, the columns looked like a standing-room audience. It occurred to me that Giulio had not even mentioned the Savant.

—Where's the cello?

—In a closet.

It didn't make sense. —I thought you were at the hospital the whole time.

—A closet at the hospital. I locked it in the safest place I could think of, the narcotics safe room. It's guarded. It only gets opened twice a day. We can get it in the morning.

I stared up at him, wondering if he was even planning to give it back.

Giulio pulled me up gently. —What's wrong? Did you want to play for me?

I looked down, wishing it had all already happened. In the dark my forearm looked pale and ugly against the crimson sheets.

—*Brasile,* he said. It's Portuguese for red. I studied for two years in Rio with Pitanguy—he's the best plastic surgeon in the world—and brasile is the only word I remember. When the Portuguese landed in Brazil on their way to India, the natives were making a bloodred dye, from the sap of a certain tree, whose name is—well, I wasn't lying when I said I only knew one word. More champagne?

He held the glass out to me. —I love them. They're so red, nothing stains them.

I stared at the drop that had spilled onto the bed. His sheets could not be stained by cassis; so this ritual happened often. Or did he mean the stains of women? *AS A LIVE TREE I WAS SILENT. DEAD, I SING.* Instead of a champagne glass I saw Giulio offering me a bouquet of branches, their stubs dripping the blood of other women. I had to get out.

—The wood is pernambuco, I said, fighting to keep the tone *adagio.* I eased myself out of bed. —It's what bows are made of. It's strong. But also light.

I had walked over to the table. Now Giulio came after me. I turned to face him.

—Isabel? He reached both arms around behind my back, and found my hands, and took the fresco fragment I was clutching. —Isabel, he chided gently, and then there I was.

He led me back to the bed. I lay back down and began to kiss him. But then he pulled away and looked at me. His voice wandered up like a curl of smoke through the floorboards.

—Tell me what you'd like.

—Nothing special, I said, desperate to get on with it before he noticed I was broken.

—And on what part of your body would you like your special nothing?

I shut my eyes and turned on my stomach and buried my face in the pillow. Slowly and deliberately, Giulio began. Certainly he would have made a more-than-competent musician. Everything was fluidly orchestrated, with one motif transitioning smoothly into the next. At the same time, each section had its own distinct character. The *adagios* were *adagio*. To keep Giulio from thinking that I had only ever been with a seventy-seven-year-old man, I went along with whatever he came up with, almost as if I'd thought of it too, just at that same moment. I was used to moving with and against Signor Perso, to resisting his hands just enough to make him think his strength could still guide my body—and we wound up almost falling off the bed. But luckily Giulio laughed and said, *Che comodo!* How comfortable! And we began again.

(as if lancing a boil)

What you do is you close your eyes. And smile lightly. And breathe. You smoothe the facial features. Eliminate the witness. If a heat begins to build, you lance it. Waiting for Signor Perso, I had learned to play music in my mind. Signor Perso's soft flesh was enough like mine, his love undemanding, he was a creature of habit, and once he settled in, it was only a matter of time. Beethoven's Fifth, with its perpetual foreshortening, works well to ferry you across. The Toscanini version. Of course like anyone in their right mind I could do without Toscanini's metronomic severity, the Napoleonic precision of attack, but in certain cases his insistence on pure forward motion is what is needed, to get across the time. With Giulio I am not exactly sure what went wrong. Instead of the Fifth, the funeral march from the *Eroica* wended its way into my ear. Ultimately Beethoven is always marching, I told myself, so the *Eroica* will pass the time as well. But Giulio was not Signor Perso; instead of settling in, he slowed down. I moved into the jagged Rite-of-Spring breathing, which always worked on Signor Perso. Still Giulio waited. I went through *morendo,* the *dying,* and moved into the sequence of rests. Giulio began again. I was at a loss: surely he could not have heard the funereal march bleed softly, sorrowfully into Strauss's *Metamorphosen*—the tremendous polyphonic complexity of the later, greater Strauss, which was what it was to make love with someone who had been making love for half a century: even with the age difference souring the air, with how I failed him, it had a grace not even music could match. There was no way Giulio could have seen Signor Perso behind him, floating up in the corner by the ceiling, naked in his armchair, his dry eyes full and present in the way that only music granted—as if he too heard Strauss's grief-song for his bombed Dresden Oper, as if he was watching me go, watching me betray him, the love in his eyes silently repeating that he did not expect me to love him for even one more day. I wanted to shut his eyes, to deny the fact of Giulio riding me, but when I shut my eyes I heard his cracked voice echo what he had always said. *When you come to love a younger man, I will bow to nature.* He said *bow* like cello bow. Then Giulio's torso coiled against me, closer, his flesh interrogating mine in a way Signor Perso's never had. From far off I felt a terrible heat collecting, my flesh wanting to know what it was to bow to nature, to bow to Giulio, to be a long note of *yes* stretched taut against *no*—

I had to do something. What I did was to improvise a five-minute fit of coughing. I coughed until tears came to my eyes. And then coughed more. I wanted to get Giulio into another room, at least for a moment: by the time he got back from getting me something to drink, I thought, I could pretend to be asleep. But Giulio reached down over the edge of the bed and poured out what was left of the champagne, and there we were.

I pretended to stifle a yawn. Said I was getting sore. Giulio blinked several times, and swallowed, to mask his defeat. Then he set the alarm.

While Giulio went to the bathroom, I turned down the

volume on his radio alarm so we'd be late and wouldn't have time to talk. By accident, I think I untuned the station, because during our nap I heard a sound that gradually got louder and louder—a low, continuous, crackling static. A police radio. The carabinieri were downstairs, waiting to arrest me. I had a huge map of Italy on my lap and was tracing the tiny capillaries of roads, looking for someplace to go. But each town was a place I'd performed badly, where they'd throw fruit at me, hard pomegranate breasts, if I went back. Then I noticed that the southern boot of Italy looked exactly like a cello scroll, that what I'd thought were roads was the network of hairline cracks spreading over the paintings in the varnish of the Savant as we sat freezing in the back of Giulio's car.

Then Giulio thrashed his limbs, looked at his watch, and jumped up. —*Porco Giuda.* Pig Judas. We threw on clothes. My dress was still clammy, my stomach nauseated, so I was grateful for the asylum of silence. Outside in the bitter cold, the day was clear, and the building's jagged, ravaged facade scratched against a hard blue enamel. At the polyclinico Giulio ran in and got the Savant as if he would have given it to me anyway, without any question. We drove to the Pettywards' in silence. When we stopped I jumped out. But as I opened the backseat door, Giulio did too. We had a little tug-of-war over the Savant. He looked at me sadly. I let go. With exaggerated gentleness he pulled out the instrument, brought it over, and stood it on his foot so that our bodies were hidden between it and the car. Behind its cover, he lay his hand on my belly.

—Don't forget your cello, he said quietly.

I pulled away. I prefer things just to end, without elaboration.

—*Ahme,* Isabella, he said sadly, his voice unwinding.

He kissed me. Not on the lips, but up, and a little to the side. A deliberate awkwardness. Not sexual at all. Just quiet, like affection.

And as the kiss slowly sank down and plumbed bottom, he said, —You didn't have to do all that for me.

My face burned. —I'm freezing, I said, wanting to run so badly that I almost left the Savant a second time. I jammed my key in the cutout door in the huge wooden portone and quietly closed it behind me, hoping never to see him again.

II

(as a fist unfurls)

An eardrum need only vibrate a billionth of a centimeter—less than the diameter of a hydrogen atom—for a sound to cross the threshold of hearing. In the average ear this leaves plenty of room for inrush and overlay of sounds. For the lucky wunderkind picking up minuscule amplitudes and dog-range frequencies, the air itself invades. Picture getting off a flight, pretending to wait in the luggage area, then dragging a trunk up onto a grimy, deserted bus with a cello strapped to your back. Picture a neon-dark slum cluttered with drunks. The street whose streetlights are broken. The crooked porch with its spongy, rotting carpet and the steps, ready to give way. Picture a sweltering night in a tar-paper house, on the living room couch of some aunt you met once—a graveyard, really, with its broken TV, broken La-Z-Boy, broken hi-fi (bought broken, to give the place a little class). Picture lying on a ratty sofa, sticking to its upholstery, listening for a seam in your cello to pop the way instruments do in the tropics. Your aunt is snoring; the growls and barks spewing from the corner bar wilt into crooning that finally gives way to night. Your mind slows to a doze. Then you are standing over Yuri, blowing the whistle you blew at him in his sleep to jar him from his nightmares. You start. Lie still. Tune in closer. It's the teapot of some insomniac. A roar of heavy metal from the highway washes it away. Closer by a car battery turns over and over, straining futilely towards release. There is the drone of a call-in radio listener needing to explain. Over a frantic back-forth of vacuuming—some desperate wife is vacuuming—comes the screech of a cat in heat. And sorry domestic sobs. The vacuum, the teapot, the screeches and sobs bob on a four-channel ocean of canned TV laughter that pitches and swells for miles. You're seasick. The aunt snores on. She and the rest of the world live in a muffled deafness that used to seem a mass stupidity from which you were exempt. Here in Milwaukee, you understand that the disturbance is yours.

The glistening silence that once blessed the concerts, goes. In its place there is coughing. Throat-clearing. The crackling of candy wrappers. A lisp deforming that first note. Now the famously light *ponticello* hacks at the strings like a hacksaw. A month before my parents' death, a pianist accompanying my *Magic Flute* variations had slammed down the piano lid: Either one *expels* one's emotions, he cried, or one *traps* these emotions in the body! The fourteen-year-old winner of the Tchaikovsky had dismissed his outburst as a touchy-feely wax of Viennese nostalgia, a silly attempt to remeringue Beethoven's somber variations with peaks of Mozartean giddiness. Now, with the silence gone, it becomes clear that emotions *are* trapped, not just in the body but everywhere, waiting to burst out. From twelve rows back there is the clasp of a clutch purse—the exact ca-clack of your mother's. Then the A you are playing wobbles like a mosquito's drunken buzz.

Yuri had hated my aunt Carmela, his stepbrother's second

wife. Lev had survived twenty-one months at Bergen-Belsen only to die one day when a small plane flew into the office building where he was a janitor—all because, Yuri said, Carmela made him work Sundays. They hadn't spoken since the scene at my parents' wedding, when, just as my parents were feeding each other the cake, she wailed. Though she herself loved opera, she thought her brother-in-law should know that opera singers were a loose, bohemian bunch who stayed in fleabag hotels. Plus, Renata was a northerner. Southern Italians used a word, *ruspante*, which meant you foraged the earth for chestnuts. It meant you were resourceful, a rustic survivor. Renata wasn't that. When Carmela finished her aria, Yuri turned to my mother with cake and said, *Open up*. It was a stock joke between my parents: at dinner, if Yuri sank into one of his perpetual, monumental dissatisfactions with the world, my mother would hold out a roll and say, *Open up*. Or if my mother thought she'd sung badly, Yuri would point at the backyard to send her out to forage.

We hardly knew the neighbors I was staying with; when Carmela showed up with luggage, everyone was relieved that someone, anyone, was willing to take me in. Turned out that Carmela had wanted to sing, and thought she had talent, that she felt excluded from some fancy glamour-life she imagined my mother was leading. Now she thought she had her chance. I had the flu, an infection blocking both ears; as I lay in bed she found my mother's address book, called people we hardly knew to invite them, bought huge bags of groceries with my parents' checkbook to cook in the huge pots she'd brought from Milwaukee—*For the occasion,* she kept saying. Carmela turned a reception for a Russian-Jewish atheist and an Italian Callas worshiper into a staged Catholic wake starring herself as the martyr-saint. When there was someone she thought might be famous, she clutched me to her chest. Yuri had two retired Greek helpers he called for contracting jobs, both over sixty, who were supers at the Met: Carmela perked up her posture and thrust out her bust and asked their advice on how to get onstage. After a half hour she walked up the three stairs onto the living room landing and burst into a frightening a cappella rendition of *Vincerò* that cleared the place in fifteen minutes flat. Then she charged around eating the leftover food and gulping down the undrunk drinks and cursing out my parents. Then she collapsed in an armchair and sobbed, *My one chance,* over and over. Once that was done, she got on the phone. Yuri never let me miss a concert. He had already bought the tickets to Oslo and Amsterdam, where I was booked with the Concertgebouw Orchestra later that month. But Carmela wouldn't believe that I was the one making the money; she convinced herself that the *I* on the ticket meant my mother, that my mother had another first name, before Renata, that began with *I.* She got on the phone with the airlines to cash in the tickets. Two days later, as I came home from the grocery store, I saw her getting in a taxi, wearing the mink coat. The note dared me to go on being so famous alone.

Yuri had informed me of our itinerary—and even of my programs—on a need-to-know basis. It was only after the first phone call asking where I was, in Milwaukee, that I realized I hadn't asked them to search the wreckage for the accordion file where he kept my agreements. Word spread. Most of the letters that got forwarded, now, were cancellations. I took the bus downtown to department stores and pretended I was lost, to make the long-distance phone calls. In the few performances I got to, I fell apart. Just before I'd go on, I'd decide that the notations on a piece were stifling, a death sentence, and try to play their opposite. I'd get through the first round of a competition, and then for each subsequent round I'd practice less and less, first with the TV—*Zet BUX,* I still heard Yuri bellow—then not at all. I was daring them to notice. When I improvised my own cadenza to a Bach suite and still won the prize, I understood that the listening had disappeared, that my playing was no longer hearable. Because what these beauty-pageant judges heard, these musicological *taxidermists* had in their ears was my name. At the time they were still shrieking for *Isabel Masurovsky,* no matter how she played. Because I'd won the Tchaikovsky so young, *not since Yehudi Menuhin,* Yehudi whose playing had been LOST for so many years, whose intonation was all over the place, who was running around getting his picture taken doing *yoga* with Ravi Shankar. What left people breathless, it turned out, was not the beauty of the playing but the freakishness of my age.

(still, shimmering, as if a butterfly pinned) I smiled under the blitz of camera-flash, feeling my face flatten into a snapshot. The chairlady of the competition in Champaign-Urbana handed over the check, so happy *The Isabella Masurovsky* had taken the time to compete. She insisted on complimenting that Isabel—romanticized into some sort of Princess Isabella—on her *gown.* Isabella did not correct her. She told her she'd played with Wanda Landowska in that very gown, then watched her smile sag as she realized that Landowska had been dead a good twenty-five years.

If that were not enough, I gave away the money. To some deluded charity in Bloomington whose director was at the reception for a photo-op. His scheme involved sending symphony musicians to a handicapped school to teach kids with degenerative diseases how to play stringed instruments. So that the minute these kids developed their technique even remotely, their motor deterioration conveniently leveled the performance back to zero. Probably I was daring some blood relative of my mother's, some long-lost cousin, to show up and set me straight. I remember feeling gleeful at having found such a perfectly bungled cause on which to unload the prize. My aunt glowered. Caruso got paid with a wheelbarrow of money, during intermission; I pulled stunts like this. Carmela was already rotting from cancer, and was preparing for her death as if for an opening night: with the money she found in my parents' passbook she'd bought herself a white ball gown, white ballet slippers, a white lacquered coffin with a white satin interior, all to go with the body she'd had lifted and nipped and tucked. That morning she had an appointment with a cosmetic dentist for caps because she wanted to die, she said, with *decent teeth*. Now she ransacked my trunk, found my one recording, called the record company; it turned out Yuri had signed away the royalties to allow my mother and me to travel to the Tchaikovsky in the manner to which she was accustomed. Then a letter arrived announcing the foreclosure of our New Jersey house. For the rest of the day I hid in a confession booth at the Cathedral of St. Jehosephat, and sneaked back home only after Carmela was asleep.

I'd dream my mother, onstage in her silk kimono, singing some brilliant cello piece she'd discovered hidden in an attic at Terezin. I'd try to call out, to get her to tell me how to play it. Would hear the air hiss out instead of words. There were endless rides on trains, endlessly escaping *in* to the camp, crawling under fences, to look for Yuri to tell him I would take his place. Waking in blackness, in a tangle of sweaty sheets on Carmela's sofa bed, I'd know I had died too far from the ramp of the highway where my parents crashed to find them. I would dial our New Jersey number on Carmela's old black dial phone, counting between the numbers, counting before I let the rotary scrape back to zero, counting before I hung up and started over—all for a half-second fermata as the call wound its way back east, when my parents could have been alive.

My three weeks in the high school, Bayview, were a disaster. I knew enough not to reveal my past, or what I'd done, but I hadn't been to school in years, and without the prodigy-cellist part there was a huge gap. I couldn't decipher my schedule, or do experiments with chemicals; couldn't take group showers after gym; couldn't listen to lectures on the Importance of Doing Your Homework and the Necessity of Raising Your Hand. I couldn't stop my fingers from practicing, in their stupid panic, under the desk. I couldn't master the detached pseudo-concentration the other kids were professionals at. Whenever I got called on I was lost. The bells at the end of classes made me jump through my skin.

For parents' night the art teacher made us do woodcuts of our families. I did a travel theme: my cello as Noah's Ark in the flood, with me on it. Carefully I carved little yellow flames on the belly so people would know it was maple. The high school, Bayview, was huge, so there'd be lots of parents; when I performed, people always invited me home; what I thought was that if I did a really good job on the artwork, some of them would invite me to come live with them. I thought the parents bunching around my picture, their kids pointing me out, meant it was going great. Then the kid who sat behind me, who secretly I thought I might like, asked where my parents were. I didn't answer. He asked what I was always spacing out on. I said, Chamber music. It was the only thing I let out about myself, but somehow he saw through me. Like torture chamber? he asked with a smile. Like gas chamber, I said, because there was no longer any use in pretending. Then he flashed me a picture of a rock band on the back of his notebook, men in leopard body suits with long psychedelic tongues. Some part of me got his heavy metal, got how worshiping ugliness might be a way to make a life this ugly, bearable. Got that Yuri's idea that you could always carve out a passage to safety, if what you carved was beautiful enough, was never going to work. I went to my desk, forged a letter from my aunt saying I'd moved, stuffed it in a welfare envelope I was using as a bookmark, and dropped it in the principal's mailbox. On the way home I ripped up the woodcut into tiny pieces, and scattered them from the overpass over the highway, through the holes in the chain-link fence.

By September my third and fourth fingers were never not numb. After the Tchaikovsky, Sir George Solti had taken me to dinner in New York to ask me to open Chicago's fall season with the Shostakovich. Of course, by then they'd heard about me, so when I arrived for rehearsal they had a replacement. Solti was nowhere around. They had some flutist in the orchestra show me to the last chair in the cello section. She set up my music stand awkwardly, and got me a soda, as if I were something fragile, something broken, which I suppose wasn't surprising since she and half the orchestra had played behind me in Madison, as eager-beaver graduate students, when I did the Elgar there at ten. I didn't argue. I'd been getting cramps for days; the day before, I had started to bleed. The blood confirmed that my childhood had been a mistake, that my future was leaking out. As we began rehearsing I wished I could leak away with it, wished that my mind could invent a solvent to dissolve my body, imagined my insides coursing out the tip of my finger, down a string and down the end pin and pooling on the floor, until I was flat and hard and unseen as a varnish. Then we started in, and I heard myself again. Most musicians who go bad hear only their intention. But though my limbs had betrayed me, my ears stayed true. From my hearing there has never been, will never be, repose. So in the middle of the performance, enduring *note* after *note* after *note*, I made the obvious decision.

Clayton was impenetrable. He had hummed during my interview, at dinner, and every time I saw him in between. In the morning it came out dreamy, a soft throaty blanket dragged from sleep; in the afternoon the sound was a dazed, hypnotic cloud devoid of melody. At dinner with his father, his throat was tight, the humming a dense wall of notes; in the evenings during lessons, a bath of pentatonic melancholy. Sometimes he would sit on a note forever, pausing only to breathe. I knew that to find Signor Perso's body, I would need to think clearly. I also knew that my mind would not clear until I found him. But the humming festered in my ear like an infection. Wherever I looked for Signor Perso, I heard it. I started sneaking in the back door of the Scala during rehearsals and lying down between the aisles to drown it out. Gradually I was making friends with a priest at the basilica, in the hope of getting him to tell me where they'd sent the body after the service, by pretending I was a Jewish person who was thinking of converting, even though I was no more than half Jewish, on Yuri's side, and besides, Jewishness passed through the mother, so I was doubly not. I had tracked down the station house where the detectives came from. I stared into the window glass of the stationery store across the street, where the station entrance was reflected, rehearsing a story I had prepared, in case the one who wasn't the mortician's cousin came out. I loitered in the luthier shops, preparing to filch a piece of rosin, half hoping to hear a snatch of conversation about him, telling myself that he was, after all, Milanese. Signor Perso had been prepared for burial, so common sense would have had him sent straight to the potter's field. But when I trudged out to the municipal cemetery, the caretaker told me he only managed the gravediggers, that the morgue kept the registry of the plots. At the morgue no one answered.

Yuri had always said, when I wanted to spend some of my earnings to get us out of some godforsaken place where we'd gotten stuck, that there were ways out of anything, that I needed to learn them. He'd found a passage through the chambers in the walls of Theresienstadt, by which he might have escaped if it hadn't meant leaving his parents behind. But a passage is an option only when you have some sense of where it is leading. Probably I had not found Signor Perso's body for the same reason I had lost it, because I could not imagine what I would do once I had it. To bury Signor Perso I would have to find his money. But without his passport, none of the banks would reveal whether he had an account. When I sneaked back to our old pension to get it, the Yugoslavian girl was gone from the basement, the janitor's closet locked. I did not know if Mr. Pettyward had actually worked at the American consulate, but he seemed to have a lot of contacts; whoever I dealt with there might know him. I called and gave a phony name. To get a replacement passport, said the clerk, you needed money. Plus, for me to get the copy without him, the Italians would require a marriage certificate. Persuading the *Anagrafe* that we'd had a common-law marriage, he said, was a transaction outside American jurisdiction. That I understood to mean a bribe.

I set out in the morning, determined. But as I waited for Clayton in the dwindling evening light, my wanderings seemed the absurd circles of a mind foggy from grief. I made mistakes. I interrupted Clayton's humming, to try and coax him to speak. When he lost his mother, Clayton was about the age I was on the night of my debut, so riding down the elevator one morning, I got the idea to tell him what we had in common, that my parents had died in a crash. Without quiet in your mind, you make mistakes. Though I told him about the crash as if it had nothing to do with me, with how I played at Carnegie Hall, his humming wound up tighter, like a gagged scream. Usually he let me walk him to school without talking. Now he stepped out of the elevator and hurried across the courtyard alone.

It sunk in then that this was the deal he'd cut with me, that first night, by not turning me in. Clayton would never ask where I was from, why my eyes were always puffy, or why I played the cello without sound. In return, I was not to intervene. He could show up for our lessons whenever he wanted, could conduct out the window for hours, could hum instead of talking, could simply refuse to speak. That must have been how he managed in school, and with his father: he found a weakness somewhere in the system, and wedged himself in the crack. Mr. Pettyward's noise machines—they were a fortress, built to protect against his son.

Night after night in the music room, I labored over the viola. Clayton neither played nor was silent, neither accepted instruction nor refused it. When he showed up, his ritual was always the same: he lumbered in, in his puffy parka, walked straight past me, and rattled up the wide window. With a broom he leaned out and swept the ledge. He had a little leather case he opened, that seemed to be full of trinkets and tools that he tinkered with for a while. Once he was satisfied, he would pick up his baton, fiddle with it, thrust it out the window, and conduct himself, singing a series of interminable notes. It was as if he was beaming back all the wrong notes I had played silently over the years, was taunting me by humming them in slow motion.

It was like reading a newspaper next to a burning bush: there he was, surrounded by priceless musical instruments, and yet he felt no draw, no need to learn to play—not even a curiosity. It seemed beyond comprehension. Then again, limping around on the viola, I suppose the inspiration I provided was somewhat just less than none. My job was to be the master, but what I knew how to do was to listen, and between the interminable notes he hummed, there was no way in. Steeped in his eerie off-pitches, I wished for a set of notations to follow, for an outburst from Yuri, berating us into shape. I had no idea how he could turn his back so easily, how he could feel so little interest in a skill that might be useful, if all else failed. Clayton seemed not to imagine a life where all else might fail.

One day I spent the afternoon walking in circles, in heavy sleet, looking for the basilica where the memorial was held. It was only a ten-minute drive from the Pettywards' apartment; if I walked in widening circles from the apartment, I thought, I was bound to find it. At the end of the day I got back to the apartment coated in sleet, frozen, just in time for dinner. Mr. Pettyward was away; Clayton was already seated, and was reading a comic book. We ate the casserole Marta had made in silence. And after that silence—I do not know how long it was—the knowledge had settled inside me that I would not find another trace of Signor Perso. And that evening in the music room I could no longer keep my measures ordered against his. As he raised his elbows, I put the viola under my chin, counted until I found an opening, and did what I knew how to do.

But it was like stuttering: I went from one piece to another, jerking towards his movements, speeding up, slowing down, with the inscrutable bobs of his hand. But the bumpy, erratic score in his mind looked to be something like Schoenberg with epilepsy. Then Clayton reached his baton out to his right, I supposed to signal the woodwinds, and I thought I knew what he meant. And I came in on the second movement of the Haydn. He leaned out to look into the night, closed his hands together again. Thinking he meant a cutoff, I held my bow, midstroke. The rosin I had—I had finally stolen a piece—was far too sticky. The slight twitch of his head I took as another cue. His baton bobbed, I eased in again on the downbeat. His back muscles stiffened, motionless. My bow froze again. Clayton slammed down the window on his baton, turned, marched across the room, and sat down facing me. He stared with the disgusted look he often turned towards his father. I felt myself flush. Knowing I was blushing made me blush more. He understood that I had nothing to teach him on the viola, that the game I had agreed to play with his father was an utter, complete sham. I reached under my chair and shifted in my seat. Clayton reached under his chair, as I had, and shifted in his. I crossed my legs. He crossed his. I did not dare move again. He was threatening to become my audience, if I watched. There seemed no choice but to conduct the lesson without him, to make a show of leaving him alone.

I picked up the viola, stared at the floor, and hacked out a passage.

—Like this? I whispered softly, like a student.

—It's *adagio,* not *andante,* I said, in my strong teacher voice.

I repeated the passage, again as a beginner, this time closer to the right tempo. —Okay?

—Better, I pronounced.

I acted out the lesson, back and forth, my heart pounding. Finally Clayton turned his back and returned to the window. But after that, I kept my head down. A while later, Clayton's phone rang, and he went out. Suddenly a huge jealousy overtook me: absurdly, I wanted to know who he was talking to. To control my urge to eavesdrop, I went over to the window and opened his little box. And didn't hear him coming. When Clayton cleared his throat, I was staring at the swirling snow in his paperweight of the Bastille, thinking about how Yuri had survived though he wasn't supposed to, how I'd been born, though my mother could not have children—how I had soared up when I heard my mother singing, then descended into the cellar to learn to play, how I had been lofted up next to the chandelier of the theater when I heard my name at the Tchaikovsky, then tumbled down into Aunt Carmela's slum. Like the snow in Clayton's paper-weight, my life seemed trapped in someone else's universe, disturbed by a larger hand. In that one moment I understood that it would be a mistake to think I had landed, that my fall was as low as I could go. It was at that moment that Clayton cleared his throat behind my head. The sound was simple, like someone cocking a gun, and the paperweight fell from my hand. I should have acted like a teacher, like a *master,* and stood my ground. Instead I crouched down and retrieved it like an inmate.

The decision to change the bridge was in no way a preparation to play the Savant aloud. Fitting a new bridge is a meditation on tension, an exercise in balance, not a preparation for release. It is a job for a luthier, a job a musician does out of impatience or arrogance, botches, and then finds a luthier to redo. The idea was simply to buff our stasis with a patina of progress, to gain a little time.

I'd bandaged the sliced finger as long as I could—it was infected, I told Mr. Pettyward, and not a sight you'd want to see—until one morning we ran into each other in the kitchen. Mr. Pettyward said he had made me a doctor's appointment to get my finger looked at. That was the day the infection seemed once and for all to turn a corner. The next evening it had miraculously healed; at dinner I told Mr. Pettyward I would be replacing the A string. The following night he caught me playing mute. He walked straight in, and crouched down next to the Savant's belly and asked if I wasn't jeopardizing the veneer. I said they made these silk sashes especially for the purpose. He nodded, and let me go. The next night he was back. I explained that I was fleshing out some of the subtler points of the piece, that it was a way of training your muscles, like a skater tracing figures, before you play full volume. At that Mr. Pettyward reached down and pulled the sash from the *f* holes.

I cued up the one accompaniment tape I had in my purse to the slow movement of the third Bach viola da gamba sonata, a piece I hoped was arcane enough, in spite of the Rose-Gould recording, for him not to know well. My plan was to ease into the dark opening phrase, pause at the caesura, and casually chat about tone. I thought the tape was of me on the piano. But it was Signor Perso playing, and just as I began I saw him, naked and withered, curled over the keyboard. At the same moment a freakish sound issued from my bow. I had forgotten to tune the instrument.

An apoplectic grid of wrinkles gathered on Mr. Pettyward's forehead. I attempted a joke about Leonardo being a brilliant military strategist, that building canals in as damp a city as Milan had been his way of securing the truth of his essay, "Defense of Painting against Music"—or at least, against the stringed instruments. Needless to say, it didn't go over. I bent down to tune. Mr. Pettyward tried to help by thwanging out a C on his risibly flat Bösendorfer. To get him to stop, I had to mention the perfect pitch.

Mr. Pettyward asked if I had brought the Savant to any sound at all. My response was to let out the C-string peg and blast the opening of the Kodaly Sonata. He frowned. I'd said I had perfect pitch—couldn't I hear how terrifically out of tune I was? I explained the *scordatura,* that in Kodaly's score the C string got tuned down to B. Yes of course, he said solemnly. *Scordatura.* I repeated the opening bars as loudly as I could. He asked if it just went on like that. I hadn't been able to get much beyond that point, I said, because the high bridge made the string length too short. Plus the action was low.

Mr. Pettyward walked over to the window and opened it suddenly, leaned out his head, looked both ways down the ledge, then leaned back in and shut it. He'd just come from a recital, he said, at the Ambrosian Library. The pianist was the son of his friend Nelson, who had *placed* at the Busoni. He'd been impressed, among other things, with the boy's *precision*. Just the kind of kid who wins competitions, I thought—a loud, fast, perfect banger. Mr. Pettyward said it had given him an idea. Between his birthday and the holidays coming up, he understood that I might find myself in an awkward position, gift-wise. To ease the strain on me he'd thought, Why not kill two birds.

He crouched down next to my chair and lay his hand on my forearm. What we wanted, he said softly, was for Clayton to give a little recital. Something that seemed impromptu. He'd leave the program to me, though since guests would be involved, and since it would occur after dinner, well, the Kodaly would be fine if I could play it in tune, but—his Adam's apple bobbed up and down—in the interests of good digestion, he wondered if I could come up with something a bit more *charming*.

I smiled, considering the possibilities. In Theresienstadt the prisoners had often swapped their sorry rations of broth for standing room tickets to the concerts, but some had refused Mozart because Mozart spoke German, while others boycotted only *Die Fledermaus*, because it had seemed too charming to contain the appropriate amount of suffering. Yuri never bothered with the sad, fetishized distinctions other prisoners invented to feel less helpless: in our basement he had listened to Strauss, weeping—Strauss, who, when asked why he had made no protest as the Jewish members of his orchestra were banned and deported, answered that it would have interfered with his income. But Yuri had listened because Strauss was Strauss, because the music was irreplaceable. I had to suppress a laugh, imagining Yuri's lips curling in disdain at the prospect of choosing music for Mr. Pettyward, when there was no question of anything decent being heard. At the range Mr. Pettyward dreamed of, Clayton's failure would be clear long before the salon, so clear that the salon would never take place. A normal program Clayton would botch, which would humiliate Mr. Pettyward, which would probably get me thrown out on the street. All that was left was a program of farcically easy melodies that Clayton would refuse to play.

—Why not the Verdi *Requiem*? I said. The piece took a chorus of a hundred, plus an orchestra; it was the piece the Theresienstadt musicians chose when the prisoners were forced, late in the war, to prepare a sham concert for the Red Cross inspectors who came to look at the camp. But like the Theresienstadters' choice of music—intended as a requiem for the Reich—my little irony went unnoticed. That was when I announced the need for a bridge.

Over dinner the next night, Mr. Pettyward debated himself. Of course the instrument needed to be maintained, which meant playing. Of course I was the one to do that. Still, he did not intend to invest any more capital. Carefully I led the horse to water. A luthier would see the priceless cello and charge through the roof, whereas a bridge and a few tools were a relatively cheap experiment. We agreed that I would try the economy route. Which of course meant complications. Luthiers choose their stock, and season their bridges themselves, and hang them in fresh, dry air for at least a decade. Finding a shop with a bridge on hand that was worthy of the Savant was unlikely; charming a luthier into selling his oldest piece was improbable at best. Then there was the fact that the Savant needed to be left at home during the investigation. All this meant more time.

Every major music city has one luthier whose reputation hovers over him like a halo. Milan's had been the family Leopardo since the time of the Austro-Hungarian empire, when Emil Leopardo, the archduke's luthier, set up shop in Milan after being banished from the Hapsburg court for his uncontrollable habit of stealing women's shoes. At the Scala, the cellist I asked gave me an address. Here you find the maestro, he said, the word ringing the death again like a funeral bell. I hurried through the cold gray fog towards the shop.

There is hardly any place more soothing than a luthier's. A balm of perfect humidity balances the mind and dampens sorrow. The ancient objects form a temple of worship of the durable. The hands hold centuries of quiet labor; they are healers' hands. The words spoken are helpful and tactful. The locks on the door are secure. On the second floor, the shop windows were dark. Still I ran the one flight up and rang the buzzer. Finally, I heard a bolt turn slowly. After a pause, two more gave way. The door eased open a crack, its chain still hooked and stretched taut. Behind it, a white-haired woman appeared wrapped in a black shawl. Her eyes were glassy.

—Three days ago he died, she said.

I nodded. We stood facing each other.

—The stock will go to Luhrman in Vienna.

I nodded, and tucked a wisp of hair that had fallen in front of my face back into my bun.

—*Non si può*, she said, shaking her head.

I nodded again. Her raw grief was like a hot balm on the ache of mine, and I stood before her, thinking of Signor Perso, absorbing its heat. She undid the chain and opened the door again, then turned away, shuffling back through a maze of crates. The shop was on the verge of disappearing. All that was left of the furniture was an empty glass counter, a tiny padded chair, and a stool. Wooden crates stuffed with tissue and shredded wood stood piled on the floor and stacked against the walls. The rack stood without a single instrument hanging from it. She walked over to the sink, filled a cup with water, poured it into a battered metal pot heating on an ancient hot plate, and collapsed into the padded chair, picking at the stuffing that poked out of one of its arms where faded flower upholstery had worn away. Outside it began to rain.

—Sixty years of marriage, she said, and you're left packing boxes.

The water came to a rolling boil. Surely, her husband had known Signor Perso. I turned it off, secured a wooden lid on the crate between our chairs, took a cup from the sink, and washed out the coffee ring on the bottom. She lit a candle. The room's dark gray gave way to a warm glow. She had lit a single candle. As she poured the tea, steam fogged the storefront window. A weary smile came over her face.

—So what did he promise you?

I glanced at the wall between the two back windows, where a bridge, a nut-brown Belgian beauty, hung in the middle of a neat row of tools. Its long, elegant legs would be perfect for pulling out the Savant's choked sound. I had never seen one so dark except once, on the 'King' cello, Amati's other surviving masterpiece, that Signor Perso had once driven me all the way to South Dakota to see. I burned to show the bridge to Signor Perso.

We sipped our tea in silence. Her den of misery seemed to offer the perfect solace, and I began to feel better. After a while she noticed me glancing back up the wall.

—Those I should have buried with him. Nobody wants them. You know the saying, Tools hate new hands. But I can't throw them away.

—I would hang them in just such a row, I said.

—Funny, she said, from the way you hold your hands I would have guessed you a musician.

She lifted herself out of her chair again and began wrapping the tools in newspaper. I took a plastic bag from a pile in the corner and packed. When we were finished she unhooked it from the wall, put it in a plastic bag, and tossed it in. —This was hanging here when he took over the shop from his father. Probably it's too old to sell.

My heart began pounding. That much luck did not go with my life. I wanted to tell her to wrap it up but of course I could not. She watched me walk down the stairs and waved, glad for the load I had taken from her. On the street I stepped sideways and leaned against the building to shield it as I slipped it in my pocket. Then I forced myself to walk steadily back to the Pettywards', told myself it must have a crack. But in the maid's room room I examined it. The maple's grain was as fine as the wood Stradivarius had imported from Yugoslavia. There was no crack. The date penciled on a foot was 1914. What I was holding was Leopardo's crown jewel, the one he could never bring himself to sell. It was impossible luck.

There are only two kinds of bridges, French and Belgian. That night at dinner I explained to Mr. Pettyward how I had narrowed it down to a choice between the two. As I detailed the advantages of each his eyes glazed over wonderfully, until finally he rose and stretched and shut himself in his study. In the music room, I unwrapped my treasure from its tissue. Fingering it again, I felt almost nauseated. There was no room for error. Either I would carve the Savant's perfect bridge, or I would destroy it.

I waited until dawn to begin preparing, for the last thing Mr. Pettyward needed was to catch me plunging a needle into the belly of the Savant like a voodoo practitioner. As the light came up I set about measuring, to mark where the vertical midpoint of the new bridge would go. I was just on the verge of poking a tiny marking hole with a needle when I noticed a tiny white dot slightly lower down, exactly like the mark I was about to make by filling the hole with chalk dust. The old, weathered bridge, I noticed now, stood just above the level of the notches in the f holes. My heart skipped. What I was removing, of course, was Vrashkansova's last bridge. Her luthier had set it higher on the cello, and shortened the length of the strings, to accommodate her tiny hands.

I studied the belly. The friction from the feet of a bridge grinds the rectangles of varnish beneath it to powder. Beneath Vrashkansova's bridge, two thin naked strips of wood confirmed the outline of where a lower, older bridge had stood. Placing the new bridge back down lower, in the location of the original, would relengthen the strings to fit my larger hands. At the same time it entailed a huge risk, for lowering the bridge would mean exposing two naked strips above the bridge, where Mr. Pettyward could see them, and decide I had done something wrong. I shut the Savant away and went to bed. It was absurd. The sight of a place forever held for a bridge, two squares that remained naked and waiting, moved me almost to tears. Somehow the prospect of restoring that small bridge to its rightful place seemed a mission that I had to accomplish, no matter what the cost.

The next day I began to loiter at the luthier shops. And fell in with them like family. Within a few days, though Signor Perso was more with me than ever, the need to find him had faded. The luthiers came to expect me. I gave them my middle name, Maria, and told them I was called Masha. I offered cookies and chocolates pilfered from the cabinets at the Pettywards'. They learned how I took my tea. Masha was a mediocre musician who was thinking of apprenticing as a luthier. It was pathetic; none of them had ever met a woman who wanted to be a luthier.

Women are the instruments, one proclaimed. But he taught me anyway. In the quiet calm of dark winter, in exchange for the daughterly flirtation I offered, I learned to shave and to shape, to carve and plane. At dinners with Mr. Pettyward, a slower narrative progressed. I mocked the messy shops I visited, the inadequate specimens they offered. I told him about a lead I had on a man named Leopardo, who people said was the luthier's luthier.

How the cellist at the Scala had wept when he told me the maestro was dead. Though in private I was working through my project like a score, breaking it into small, solveable components, with Mr. Pettyward I continued stalling. We looked together at the little white dot on the belly of the Savant. I let him watch as I shaded the naked rectangles on the belly of the Savant dark with graphite, aligned the feet of the bridge against the dot, and pressed down. He watched me shave off the blackened spots of high contact, and press down again. Mr. Pettyward seemed almost hypnotized by the process, seeing the high spots, watching them get cut away.

One evening as I was close to finishing, out of the blue, Mr. Pettyward asked how my Italian was coming. The question was a normal question, asked over a normal plate of pasta primavera. The blood rushed to my head. Then he asked, would I care to hear a joke in Italian that Réné at Jacques Français had told him. I said, Why not. He smiled and thoroughly blotted his mouth. When the Savant arrived from Italy, he said, the French court cellist for whom it was made insisted he and his wife have separate beds. Year after year he slept with it. Finally someone asked why he didn't sleep in the bed with his wife. And he said, Find me a woman this beautiful, with two *f* holes, and I'll change my ways.

At this Mr. Pettyward laughed so hard his eyes began to water. I chuckled along, my stomach tightening for the blow.

He looked at me dead on. —Réné says a bridge change takes a day.

—If you're a luthier.

—How long if you're you?

—One more day, I said.

What happened the next evening did not happen because I was planning to play. Like anyone whose work is in their hands, I simply fell into my body working. The next evening, for the first time since I had lost Signor Perso, my twin gargoyles, memory and anticipation, released their clutch and flew away. My swirl of schemes fell quiet. I shaved and planed and sanded and was blessed. Even when I realized that I had no template to cut the curve on the top of the bridge, I traced the curve of Vrashkansova's, and went on. Only when I had tightened the A string and was adjusting the fine-tuning screw did I remember where I was, and look up and see Clayton. His body was balanced horizontally on the sill. It was as if he had been frozen halfway out as he dove out into his orchestra. Probably he had decided to jump, then reconsidered, and now he was deciding which way to fall.

Of course the viola would have been the responsible choice of venue. Had I had the little dwarf handy, I might have used it. On the other hand, who listens to a viola? Played by a joke of a teacher who manages only to squeak? Shall I say here that I knew by now why Mr. Pettyward had hired me? That I was the last person on earth who could keep his son safe? The upshot was that I panicked, picked up the Savant, and unleashed a huge, bloodcurdling shriek. Clayton lost his balance. Suddenly he was tipping forward out the window. I ran over and tried to grab his legs, but he was bigger, denser than I'd thought, his body heavier than my idea of it. Out of nowhere, he had a man's body. He let loose a piercing yelp. All at once I knew where I was hurting him. I let go. Clayton doubled up into the fetal position and balanced on his side—absurdly, it occurred to me to wonder whether Giulio's penis had gotten bent in an accident with one of the governesses—and then his legs slid through my clutch until, in defiance of gravity, he stopped. Clayton was fixed in a handstand on the ledge.

I leaned over into his crotch, and guided his legs around my chest.

—Lock your ankles, I said. I'm going to lean inside and pull you up.

His hands shifted. Coins from his pocket dropped, converged, vanished.

—Fuck you.

—Baby's first words.

He clamped his legs around me. I could barely breathe. I leaned back away from the window, pulling with all my strength, but it was like trying to drag a building. His legs began to lift me off the floor. For a second we balanced. In the distance, I heard my telephone ring. Then his legs' grip broke open, and he fell, and I hit the floor deadweight.

From the floor, I caught my breath. The window framed an orderly grid of city-sky. I leaned out to look. All I could see was a tow truck dragging a car to a side street for street-cleaning. Somewhere below, Clayton was crumpled on the sidewalk; the night had gulped him down. If Mr. Pettyward's apartment lay in the same precinct as the pension where Signor Perso and I had been staying, I thought, there would be no way I could keep the detectives from putting the two deaths together, from seeing that I was the element they had in common.

Then, over the street symphony, I heard a quiet trace of humming. It seemed that Clayton had imprinted it on my brain, that the humming would be there, forever, *inside*. I hoisted myself up, straddled the sill, and climbed out the window. Even the fresh air smelled like Clayton. When my feet hit the ledge I felt for the second time the bracing absolute of the space before me. I stared out over the dark choppy sea of roofs, the horizontal halo of light at the horizon, the stripe of street below. What had been possible to avoid for years with Signor Perso was no longer possible to avoid. I was the last of my family, the sole surviving Masurovsky, living in place of children of those who died in the camps, with their specters watching. But even if Clayton were dead, and his *humming* stuck my ear for life, Yuri would say that suicide was not an option. But would jumping really be carrying on what Hitler started? Wouldn't jumping allow that monster to control my fate from beyond the grave? Could anyone really have an obligation to live for others who were lost? And what, in the case of my broken-down life, could that possibly mean?

As I pondered, the urgency faded. Then—a scratch, a flame, an orange ember glowing. To my right, Clayton was sitting against the wall, his arms resting on his knees. I slid my back down the wall and hid my face in my hand. Then I smelled the smoke, closer. I held out two fingers in a V. He inserted the cigarette between them. The smoke hit my blood, riled it up. He picked up his baton and laid its tip in my lap. It had a string and a hook attached.

—I was *fishing,* he said softly.

—For what?

He lifted the pole and dangled it in front of my face. I closed my hand around some staccato clusters. It was a woman's brooch, in the shape of a starburst. I glanced at him. He was fishing for his mother's jewelry. He shrugged. It was a child's game, and he knew it.

We finished the cigarette in silence. It occurred to me that the new bridge I'd cut could not have been a complete failure if the cry I'd played came out that loud. Then an unsettling shadow of terror, that I was even contemplating playing again, given what just one note had brought on. I threw the cigarette out into the night and watched its ember vanish. Clayton crawled to his feet, then took my elbow and carefully guided me up. He interlocked his hands. I stepped up and climbed inside. He followed me in.

—If I decide to jump, he said, pausing at the doorway, I won't need your help.

—I'll keep that in mind.

After Clayton was gone I shut myself in the bathroom. The cry I'd let loose on the Savant was echoing in my ear. I turned on all the faucets to try to drown it out. But there was no way to hide it: from the minute Mr. Pettyward had first opened the Savant's case, I'd felt a flutter of wanting. This time I'd been lucky. But only a fool could fail to see what I could bring on, letting go for even just one note.

As the December streets thickened with shoppers, I stopped looking for Signor Perso. Their steady heartbeat of need and get, their smartly wrapped packages, the hope they contained —it was all too much. My favorite luthier now seemed always to need the little footstool where I had been perching for a quarter of an hour now and then. Mr. Pettyward had a rule, that Clayton was supposed to call my room, as he himself made a practice of doing. But when Clayton knocked and said, *Open up,* two days before Christmas, I was so grateful for the rattle of a human being that I could have thrown open the door and hugged him. Instead I told him I'd meet him in the kitchen. I was wearing some pajamas I had taken from his drawer.

—He'th home, he whispered urgently. The lisp Mr. Pettyward had mentioned, it seemed, happened when Mr. Pettyward was around. I threw the blanket around myself and opened the door. Clayton's eyes were pressed shut. On his shoulder he held a tray covered in a cloth.

—I'm wearing purple socks today, he whispered. For the first time.

He came over, stood next to the bed, and pointed his shoe out in front of him.

—Cute.

—They're not cute. They're handsome. You didn't get the full effect. He put down the tray, took off his shoe, and wiggled his foot under my face again. —So what are we doing?

His face made my throat well up: first day of his Christmas vacation, and here he was with breakfast, seven in the morning, trying not to look lost. —Ta-da! he said, as he flicked out the cloth and draped it over my lap. He had brought coffee and chocolate croissants and strawberries. There was even a tiny radio oozing Christmas cheer.

—What happens when your dad—

—As of this month I'm bigger. Clayton handed me coffee. My pajama sleeve poked out from beneath the blanket, and I watched him take note of the strangely immature pattern of flying airplanes on the flannel.

—I have some just like those, he said.

—My brother's, I said.

Clayton nodded, stood up, and pulled two rubber balls out of his pocket and began throwing and catching them, one in each hand, at different speeds. It was an exercise I'd demonstrated for him, one evening when he still wasn't talking, to unsynchronize his hands.

—Do you have a brother? he said.

I shoved the rest of the croissant in my mouth. A snow of pastry flakes blanketed my lap. I brushed them away, then flipped the radio. I like carols only in July, when you're not expecting anything. Further down the dial I found some Villa-Lobos, a lush, tropical piece I'd played at Juilliard as a kid.

One of Clayton's balls fell to the ground. He pointed to the radio.

—*Bachianas Brazilieras,* I said, swallowing. Hector Villa-Lobos. Brazilian cellist, this century. He rewrote Bach, Brazilian style. It's for eight cellos.

—*Trés schwa,* he said. *Schwa* was his word for cool.

—It's okay that you hate the cello.

—God told you that?

I nodded.

—He's a liar, he said.

—He's diplomatic.

—Diplomacy is the art of misrepresenting your interests as their interests. Kissinger. I wanted to play the cello, three years ago. He wouldn't let me. Now he clues in that he needs to keep the precious cello sounding nice.

All of a sudden, without knocking, Mr. Pettyward swung open the door. His eyes strayed over the blanket I had wrapped around me, then down to a strawberry that had fallen onto the floor.

—I bought them with my own money, Clayton said defensively, picking it up.

—Which as far as I am aware is a subset of my own money. So it would appear that I have bought at least some of the nice stuff. A subset, by the way, is a mathematical concept.

—We were thinking you might take us ice skating, Clayton said, his voice so tiny I could barely hear him.

—*Ice* skating. Mr. Pettyward fingered his sling nervously.

Clayton's shoulders drooped.

Mr. Pettyward smiled his plastic smile and ruffled Clayton's hair. —I suggest you use your time more wisely. Anyway, I'll be leaving in about a half hour. Just for today and tomorrow. And perhaps the weekend. I'll be back middle of next week, latest. Don't feel bad for me. Christmas was Jesus' birthday. I care about *God's* birthday. Isabel knows what I want.

Mr. Pettyward's voice was breaking up. It seemed as if he could not bear Christmas with Clayton, as if he could not bear the holidays without his wife. But to Clayton the reason hardly mattered. His shoulders sank, defeated, and his face crumpled. I watched him force himself to stand up straight against the pain. Still he stared at the doorway where his father had stood. Finally we heard Mr. Pettyward shut himself in his bedroom suite.

—How much weight do you think that doorway would hold? Clayton asked quietly.

—Why?

—You know what a portcullis is?

I shook my head.

—It's the spiky gate you drop in the wall of a castle, he said. If you time it right, you can gore the guy in the chest.

My phone rang. It had been ringing consistently during my weeks at Mr. Pettyward's, though when I picked up, no one was ever there. Clayton glanced at me.

—I have no idea, I said, and answered the phone.

—*Joyeux Noel!* chirped Marie-Antoinette. It's Anna-Maria. I've been to Brazil.

—You're back?

—I'm in Lech. In Austria. That's the town. Fabio and I are at this silly ski lodge *à l'Americaine* with horns on the walls. And these lemmings, always plowing into you while craning zair necks looking for His Royal Anus. Fabio and I were at an auction where an inlaid pistol came up: I bid it up until he promised to get me something really excessif. But tell me about you. *Le chargé* is well?

—He's right here, I said. First day of vacation. We're about to start practicing for a recital.

Clayton stared at me in shock. Of course, Mr. Pettyward had left it to me to tell him.

—And the father? Marie-Antoinette asked.

—Leaving on a business trip.

—Gone, for his son's holiday. *Bon,* she sputtered. I hate men. They irritate me. Who said that?

—So how was Giulio? I said, after a moment.

—He was with one of his usual *type,* she said. One of those bored, rich women who've got nothing else left to buy.

—Well, sure, I said. Outside, the church bells were clanging a loud bright A, the pitch of my phone. Suddenly it was clear that Giulio had been the one calling again and again. But why, I didn't know. Surely he couldn't think I had money.

—By the way, she said. I hope you didn't spend the night with him.

—With your friend Giulio? I finally said, as if the idea were absurd.

—*Bon.* Because when this woman went off to the ladies' room, Giulio interrogated me about you. You told him you were married?

—He came up with that himself.

—Good, she said. Anyway I did you a favor and painted you as very boring.

Clayton leaned towards me and dangled a strawberry in front of my lips. I swatted it away.

—Meaning what?

—Giulio is the kind of man—well. For example. Fabio once had a *petite histoire* with Daphne. She has a little Corot he wanted. Every time they were out together, Giulio was spying on Daphne and calling her the next morning to tell her where they went, what she was wearing, even how many minutes they were sitting in the car.

—I thought his fiancée was in Geneva.

—Daphne *works*, she sighed. Don't ask me why. But her mother is in Milan.

—Giulio followed them?

—When he found out they had opera tickets at the Fenice during *Carnavale,* he drove to Venice and ran around at inter-mezzo lifting the masks off people's faces. Fabio gave up. He said he couldn't afford to take a suite at the Bonaparte every time he wanted a little privacy.

—Don't misunderstand, she went on. I love him dearly, the man's done wonders for my cheekbones, he's thirty-two, and already he does things Fabio can't, and Fabio knows it. But jealousy is his bête noire. She giggled. —Ironic, since you never know where he's been.

—When are you coming back? I asked, swatting Clayton away.

—Due to some very boring legal complications, she said, I will be remaining at large.

At that moment the line clicked. An operator interrupted to say there was an emergency call from Giulio Salvagente.

—He does this all the time, Marie-Antoinette said. If someone died, I'd never know it.

The operator asked if the *signora* would take the call.

Marie-Antoinette said, —I suppose so.

The operator said that the call was for the Italian number, not the Austrian.

A pause followed.

—Tell him I need to speak to him immediately, Marie-Antoinette said. Tell him it's a medical emergency.

—You're having more surgery?

—Soon I'll be brand-new, she said, and hung up.

Clayton stared at me now. —He wants us to play a recital?

—I already taught you *The Wind and the Rain,* I said defeatedly. He had hummed so aggressively during that lesson that I could tell he hated it.

—Can't we do that Villa-Lobos thing?

I looked at him. He leaned in. If I had turned my face slightly, we would have brushed lips. I held myself still. Clayton picked up another strawberry and rolled it over my lips. Biting was the price of his cooperation.

—I'll be one cello, he said, and you be the other seven.

I swallowed hastily. —I can't play seven cellos.

—No? he said softly.

I flushed. Clearly he had figured out that there was more to my playing than what he heard on the poodle. I wished I had known him when I was fourteen, that I could go back and be that age with him, wished I could erase the time between us. If I could have relived the last decade in the shine of his faith in me, everything would be simpler now. I told Clayton to shut his eyes again, so that I could put on my dress. While it was over my head, the phone rang again. Clayton picked it up; this time it was one of his friends. He launched off in a racing Italian I couldn't follow; it almost seemed as if he actually had a friend. The minute he hung up it rang again.

—Your line was busy, Giulio said. It's never busy. I thought something might have happened. Do you know what day it is? It's the one-month anniversary of when you lay yourself at my feet and declared your uncontrollable passion for my semi-balding head. I thought we might celebrate.

—I have a date.

—What about Christmas Eve? I have an appointment at a lovely inn, a deconsecrated monastery, near Bolzano. You could come along. I know you like basilicas, but this is probably the next best thing.

Of course, if I went, then Giulio would know I had no one else. —I have a date then too.

—*Va bene.* That's my beeper. I have to go. I'm on duty for the next twenty-four hours.

—So why did you ask me out for tonight?

—For you, I would have switched.

—You can just switch?

—I've worked every night since we met.

—Keeping an eye on the fiancée?

—Who? Oh, *Daphne,* he said, after a minute. I never tried to hide her from you. I don't lie to anybody except Daphne. I'm faithful that way.

I waited out the silence.

—So Marie-Antoinette's been gossiping. We were at an auction last week in Geneva. She won't be back anytime soon. Of course you know she managed to get herself caught trying to sell a piece of stolen property to the wife of some high-up Christian Democrat. The husband got her off—he cut a deal with the prosecutor, also some cretin Christian Democrat—that she could avoid trial if she left Italy. She doesn't seem to mind terribly. Paris agrees with her. And why not? It's what Milan was before the Americans left us with this pile of rubble. Which reminds me. I have to go make the world more beautiful.

Clayton:

On a day such as today and indeed throughout the so-called 'holiday season' you may be wondering just what the word 'merry,' or indeed, 'happy,' amounts to. While pursuits such as the ritual exchange of trinkets, religious practice, the excessive ingestion of comestibles, or the acquisition of the languages of lesser peoples may each purport to offer its own species of satisfaction, it is crucial, especially at your age, not to be misled on this count. The only reliable joy is that obtained from the owning and spending of large sums of money. Money is the only decent thing in a world infected by women.

CGP

The notepaper had a treble staff and some notes—some stupid atonal fake-music—printed across its head. The gifts were similarly special. Mine was a box of chocolates shaped like lightbulbs that some Lithuanian lightbulb guy Mr. Pettyward dragged home had presented at dinner, still tied with the same gold ribbon. Clayton's was a gift subscription card to the *Wall Street Journal Europe*. Then and there I decided that I would give him a present if it killed me. Clayton was getting better, I told myself; I would take the risk and give him a lesson on the Savant. But Mr. Pettyward had not been lying about Clayton being klutzy: all morning, his fingers had romped over the strings like paws, until just before lunch, when he had scratched his cheek with his bow and nearly poked out an eye, and dropped the viola, which clattered to the floor. The neck had a hairline fracture where it had separated from the body. I tried to fasten a bandage over his cheek, a simple medical ministration, but the more I fussed with the adhesive tape, the more Clayton fidgeted. Then he pulled the bandage off and made it bleed again. Finally I gave up and sat back down, my heart like a lead plumb, knowing I simply could not bring myself to risk being parted from the Savant. I tapped the count with my foot again, it was as if Clayton had read my thoughts. He stood up and shoved his fists in his pocket and said he needed air, and left the room. I looked again at the viola. I would have to have it repaired before Mr. Pettyward returned. Before long I heard Clayton's loping shuffle coming towards the music room. He had his coat on and was holding mine in his arm.

—We're going shopping.

I stared at the floor.

—What? Clayton said. Don't worry. I'm not getting you a present.

My face burned. He knew I wasn't paid, that I had no money. He forgave me.

—You have money?

He smiled wryly. —He gives it to me. I don't get him a present, he won't get any.

I nodded. He even forgave his father for his mother's death. I stared at him, wishing I had the money to buy him a huge, room-sized present, wrapped in gold foil, and even felt a wave of sorrow for Mr. Pettyward.

—It must be a constant weight, I said. That he was driving the car.

—Huh?

—In the accident. With your mother.

He frowned. —She was already gone by then. And anyway there wasn't any accident. He hyperextended his elbow throwing change in a toll booth basket.

—Your mother's alive? I said stupidly.

He looked down. Shrugged. —One day she left, he said, in a flat husky voice that had a lake of misery beneath it.

I lay my hand between his shoulders.

—Let's go, he said, holding up my coat.

Out on the street, Clayton walked straight up to a big navy Alfa sedan idling in front of our building. Giulio was inside, prescribing something on the phone. They had arranged something, I realized, when Clayton picked up the phone that morning.

—Merry Christmas, Clayton shouted, as he opened the door in the front. On the seat was a huge box wrapped in tin foil. I had not received a present since Signor Perso had lost track of his days. I frowned, trying not to cry—I wanted badly to open it, but knew I could not end up in bed with him again.

I walked over to the driver's side. He lowered his window. —Maybe the two of you should go.

—Just skating, I promise, Giulio said. It doesn't have to be the Super Bowl. Stop pretending, he said, when I didn't move. You're happy to see me.

—Now that you've kidnapped me, I grumbled softly, getting in the car.

—This is not kidnapping. I was kidnapped, Giulio said.

—Were not.

—Was too. By the Red Brigade. When I was nine.

—Cool, Clayton said.

—Liar.

—What happened to you? Giulio asked, pointing to the Band-Aid on Clayton's cheek.

—Got in a fight, Clayton said.

Giulio nodded.

We were slowly weaving through Milan's dark, narrow cobblestone streets. We turned a corner. Outside my window lay a giant excavated honeycomb of low, uneven brick walls.

—What's that?

— *Ruine Romane.*

—Of what?

—Roman buildings. In Italy you don't build anything without first digging out two millennia of past. It gets tedious.

—Open your present, Clayton said.

I slid off the lid of the box. Nestled inside the tissue was a new pair of white leather skates and a pair of blue wool socks. —They fit, Clayton announced. I took your boot and traced it on a piece of paper.

—Bought with your own money?

—I know where the household money is to pay the cook, he said.

—Thief, I said.

—My grandfather Granco called it redistribution of property, Giulio said.

—If your father's father was named Granco, then why are you called Salvagente?

—He was an anarchist. To protect my father, he told him only that anarchists had potluck suppers where you never ate well. But at his funeral, the labor leaders who carried his coffin to the headquarters told us he'd gone to Paris when he was nineteen and met all the famous anarchists and fucked Emma Goldman. When he came back to Bologna, he refused to join the Fascists. They took him out in the woods and poured motor oil down his throat. That's what they did if you didn't join. During the war he didn't have to fight, because he had flat feet, so the Fascists put him in charge of supplies. Which was perfect for the *resistenza.* Whenever one of the partisans in the hills needed food, he'd redistribute. That's when they started calling him *Salvagente.* It means, the life ring you throw off a boat.

We plodded out north of the city, through dreary clusters of factories, through town after town, until finally we turned onto a country road. After a time, from behind a broad swath of trees, our car came out on the edge of a lake where craggy, viney bushes grew in a maze of wild arches. Then the car swung out onto a gravelly stripe of road that ran alongside it. At its end stood a gray shack where a hermit or a hunchback might have lived, a cardboard shoe box tacked on the horizon, half to the earth, half to the sky. It looked like a shack in the Jura Mountains Yuri'd made me sneak up on in the dead of winter, while he hid in a thicket, where the old man inside was keeled over on his breakfast. I wondered if it might be a place for me to stay, after Mr. Pettyward kicked me out. I would have to lead Giulio around into telling me what roads we'd taken.

Clayton tied up his skates and sprinted off, his body wiggling like hot air rising from macadam. Then there was just Giulio and me. Giulio skated over and knelt in front of me, helped me lace up my skates until they were right. I braced myself on a door handle of the car, then held on to him. Together we clomped out onto the ice.

—Pick up some speed, he said.

—I know, I said, though I'd never skated.

Giulio clasped my hands and began to pull.

—Sorry we ambushed you. But otherwise you wouldn't have come. I've been calling.

—I've been out of town.

He smiled. —Oh, me too, me too. In fact it's lucky you didn't answer. Saved me money.

He clasped my hands and skated backward in a smooth, snakelike motion, pulling me so that I fishtailed, gently, from side to side. Somehow he was able to steer without looking. Faster now, we curved between and around the green arches of the huge dark bushes growing out through the ice. Whenever we approached a low branch I thought he was going to hit his head, but always, at the last minute, he ducked.

—How do you know when something's there?

Giulio pulled me in close and breathed a warm fog over my nose and face. —I steer away from the panic in your eyes, he said quietly.

The silence was immense. I glanced around for Clayton. I didn't see him anywhere.

—What if we get lost?

We were curving around the side of a hedge. Giulio slowed us to a halt.

—We won't.

Suddenly, Clayton zipped under our outstretched arms. He was sitting on his heels.

—Hey, losers, he yelled out.

—I love my skates, I yelled after him.

Giulio laughed and pushed us off again. —He has tumbled on his backside with joy.

I tried to squirm out of his hands. —He's hurt?

Giulio held fast to my wrists. —He's jealous. Remind me, how exactly are the two of you related?

—Hey, Clayton yelled, as he skated by again.

—I'm certain he's jealous, Giulio said.

—Maybe you're jealous. When we met you said that people only suspect things in others that are traits they find in themselves.

—*I!* he laughed. I'm jealous never. Of all emotions, jealousy has got to be the stupidest. Because, the thing is for your lover not to want someone else. If they want someone else, they might as well have them. This is the only point I'll ever give to the church, that the line between thinking and doing is irrelevant. But anyway, I trust myself. Usually, the more lovers a woman has, the more she appreciates what I have to offer.

—I'll keep my stable, then.

He felt for my two wedding rings, under the glove. —Shall I assume that anyone with two marriages has only one lover?

—Don't fish.

Suddenly Clayton zoomed in front of us again, heading straight for the bush. —Watch, I yelled, as he tumbled into a somersault that left him flat on his back.

—Is he clumsy, or does he just act clumsy?

—*I'm* clumsy, I said.

—People who love through a lack are always closer than those who share a strength.

Clayton plowed into me from behind, knocked me down.

—Watch where you're going, he said, and skated off.

For a long, stretched-out rest, I lay on the ice, idly wondering whether I ought to sneak away to check out the shack. Then I heard the steady sliding cuts of skates. Giulio's head and parka floated into view.

—*Buon giorno,* I said.

Giulio corrected my pronunciation. We repeated it back and forth.

—*Perfetto,* he said, skating in close to my head. —Except that it is *Buona sera.* It's just after four. No matter who else you're seeing, I think I'll have to call you once a week to check up on your Italian.

—Who says I'll be speaking Italian?

—Well, whoever he is, ask him to cure you of that American *accento.* Even if he's American.

—Top of my list, I said.

Giulio stopped over my head, upside down. —*Contessa comatosa,* he said, do you have any plans to get up? I don't know how to tell you this, he said, but as a doctor it's my duty to inform you that eventually the pond will melt.

The cold was beginning to chill the back of my head. —*Sono fredda,* I said. But I knew I hadn't gotten it right.

Giulio crouched down over my head, straddling it with his skates.

—You mean *ho freddo,* he said. We say not, *I am* cold, but *I have* cold. It's like *ho fame,* I have hunger. In Italia we have the desires instead of becoming them. Of course, in Europe in general, we're more detached from our wants.

—You believe your ridiculous theories?

He shrugged. —Everyone else's are just as absurd. No, really —Europeans, we don't lose ourselves in grandiose wanting the way Americans do. Our empires are over. Everything matters slightly less.

I nodded. —And who has called whom every day for the past month?

Giulio shrugged. —*Ho fame,* he whispered.

—You think Americans become their desires?

—It's part of speaking American. Your thoughts come out in American *cookie-cutters.* Aren't you proud of *cookie-cutters?* In New York I had a wonderful lawyer-girlfriend who baked. It always made me laugh in America when people said, I'm hungry. Like it was their name. It reminded me of the seven midgets of Snow White. Anyway, *sono fredda* means something very different.

—*Freddo* for you, no?

—No, he said. As if he'd read my mind, he knelt down on his knees, lay down on top of me, and looked me in the eye. —There is no *sono freddo.* Only *sei fredda.* The expression is used only for women.

—You didn't have to say that.

—I didn't say it, he said, and he blew a fog of warm breath over my face. You did.

He had me pinned. A vision came to mind of this story Signor Perso had told me, of Houdini beneath the ice, self-birthed from his chains and locked trunk, searching with his palms for the hole cut to the surface. I wondered whether the ice was thick enough to hold us, one on top of the other.

—We're too much weight in one place, I said. The ice might crack.

—You know what the poet Horace said?

—What, I said.

—Plunge it in deep water, it comes up more beautiful.

I shut my eyes and saw the cold swollen alabaster flesh of Houdini's dredged-up body. In some way, of course, it would have been more beautiful than the man. For all its horror, there was a poetic logic to Houdini's drowning during an escape. Like a perfect coda, that sort of ending brought meaning and closure. But like Yuri, I had the messier problem of how to live with a loss that dragged on. If I had died with my parents, all that would have been left of me was the brilliant prodigy, a shooting star combusted at its zenith. As it was, I was a broken-down has-been with no idea how to get from one measure to the next.

I stopped pushing Giulio off. Whether we fell in no longer seemed to matter.

—How did you know?

—I didn't, he said. For sure. Until just now.

I stared at him.

—That night, I wasn't sure, he said. I kept thinking you might come. Besides, I didn't know you well enough to embarrass you.

—And now you do?

Giulio rolled off me, crouched on his heels, and offered me a hand. —I shouldn't have said anything.

He braced the fronts of my skates with his and began to pull me up. —One more thing, he said. This maestro you came to Italy with. You perform that way for him?

—He taught me *music.*

—But that's the food of love, he said. So says Shakespeare.

—I'm his assistant.

Giulio nodded.

Clayton was shouting something, waving us towards the car.

—So why then do you hoard? he asked.

I fixed my eyes on his. —Why do you squander?

Giulio appealed to the sky for help. Snorted. —I'm going to see the hermit who lives in that shack. And give him some money. Then we'll go eat oysters. My grandfather used to say that oysters were the closest he'd come to a spiritual experience.

—You know the guy who lives there? Clayton asked, skating up.

—He's an ancient partisan, Giulio said, a friend of my grandfather, who's still hiding.

It seemed so easy to him, saving people; being the life ring for others was almost imprinted in his genes. Imprinted in mine was not having saved a soul.

—So you'll come for oysters?

—We should get home, I said, somehow imagining I could hide from what he now knew of me.

Giulio nodded. —What about New Year's Eve, then?

Clayton glanced at me. —I have a date.

—Mardi Gras? Giulio joked.

I shook my head.

—So then too. Tell me. What exactly do I have to do to get you to have dinner with me?

I wished I could play the heat collecting against the walls of my heart. But words would mean explaining how, onstage at Carnegie Hall, I'd taken my father's life ring and tossed it back to sea; and how little idea I had of how to save myself. I wanted him lying on top of me again. But at the same time I felt I could not let him come any closer.

—Fine, he said. I give up.

—You're not the type, I said, silently begging him not to.

But Giulio lowered his eyes, his smile a thin glaze over bitterness. —Anyway holidays should be canceled. No matter who you are, they gouge out a piece of your normal life. The wound takes days to stitch.

Giulio skated off towards the shack. I unlaced my skates, then got in the car and watched his body slide side to side, smaller and smaller. In the back seat, Clayton had dropped off into snoring. So the shack was occupied. As Giulio skated around my head I had fantasized about making my way back here, about figuring how to eat bark and ice fish—it had all, I saw now, been pretty lame. I stared at the shack in the distance. That was the trade-off: if being a prodigy means you can read a thirty-six-part orchestral score, being an ex-prodigy means you haven't got a clue as to how to sight-read life.

—*Oysters are veddy reech een tseenk,* Giulio said. Did you know Casanova ate fifty a day?

Without warning, Giulio had pulled over to a rustic roadside restaurant attached to a freshwater oyster farm. We had shaken Clayton, then left him sleeping in the car. From the oversized bowl, Giulio gracefully served up two plates of linguine. Then he stabbed an oyster from the platter, tipped back his head, and dropped in the treasure. His eyes shut in a moment of private, incommunicable pleasure.

—Was that what killed him?

—He lived to be quite old. Actually I think the oysters were the key to his success. Zinc, you see, is a big component of what I offer when we—

I set down my fork.

—*Dio. Mi scusa.* I've been eating with doctors too long. Although it's interesting. Usually women aren't squeamish. In medical school it was always the men who fainted at the sight of blood.

Giulio blotted his mouth, then held up his little pinkie. —It's true, though. A deficiency of zinc does very bad things to men.

—So you're stocking up.

—I need a steady supply.

My fingers, on the tablecloth, were plowing through the Brahms double concerto. I held them still. —For the near future?

With his napkin, he reached over to blot some red sauce on my collarbone, and grazed my neck with his fingers. —Perhaps.

—You said this didn't have to be the Super Bowl.

Giulio smiled, took my hand, and drew it to his lips. —I did. To get you to come out. But you wouldn't want me to abandon every hope? My enormous, swollen, oversized hope?

He stabbed another oyster, and dangled the long gray muscle close to my face. It looked like part of a dissected heart that he had preserved in formaldehyde. I shook my head. —Not even one? Giulio shrugged and gobbled it down. —There's really no evidence to suggest that eating extra zinc does anything. But I like to pretend there is.

—Because you need so much of it.

He swallowed another oyster. —Tell me something. You and your maestro. How long have the two of you . . .

He trailed off. While we skated I had forgotten Signor Perso, forgotten him for four hours straight, while Giulio had coaxed me into coming, coaxed me into skating, coaxed me into coming out for oysters. For him it was like twirling pasta, I thought, pulling out a strand of the past, turning me round and round until I was all caught up in him. There seemed no use pretending. I held up two fingers.

—And this, shall we say, *seasoned* lover, is how old?

—Seventy-seven.

Giulio gave out a low whistle. —Hard to imagine.

—Nobody asked you to work up a sweat.

—So does he still manage—

I shut my eyes, and reached out to grip the edge of the table, and knocked my knife and spoon to the ground.

—So he still can be pleasing, he said, hopping off his stool after me. We met groping in the shadow beneath the table.

—Not everything is reducible to orgasm, I said quietly.

—I don't know, he said softly. One of my mother's ancestors —they converted in the thirties—was this famous eighteenth-century Jewish mystic, a nutty Paduan rabbi named Luzzatto. He comments on a passage in the Zohar on the Song of Songs. 'What is he?' it reads. What is man, upon whom the whole work of creation is incumbent? And the answer is, 'How he was created.' The Padua rabbi thinks you can only read this as one thing: fucking. Then the *Zohar* asks, 'What is he thereafter?' And answers: 'How the body is perfect.' For the rabbi the body is the vector of divine knowledge, perfect in the moment of bliss. It's history as a continual chain of orgasms.

Just then he held up the spoon. We stood up and brushed ourselves off and sat down again. —So how is it with him?

—He has a mild aphasia, I said.

—Aphasiacs always remind me of puppies, the way they understand everything and nothing?

He reached for his wallet and tossed a credit card onto the check. I stared out over the parking lot. —But, can I just ask— where was your family? I mean, wasn't there anybody to object to your moving to Europe with a seventy-seven-year-old aphasiac?

—I had an aunt.

—A blood aunt?

—The second wife of my father's brother. We didn't get along. I didn't earn money in wheelbarrows, at intermission, like Caruso.

Giulio laughed.

—She died years ago, I said.

—And the others?

I stared out over the parking lot. Clayton was heading towards the front door of the restaurant. I stood up to wave, glad to escape Giulio's gaze.

—So you're the last one left, Giulio said quietly, raising his arm to signal the waiter for another plate.

—Diarrhea, Clayton said.

It was late February, the first warm fog of spring was wandering in through the window. We had managed to practice through the holidays, and even all through January, waiting for Mr. Pettyward to come back and demand his recital. At dinner I had entertained Clayton by making up a nightly story about where his father was, a thousand-and-one nights of Mr. Pettyward roaming the world to find the perfect Christmas gift for his beloved son, wandering the markets in Hong Kong, tracking down a rare books dealer in Buenos Aires, hiking up some Himalayan mountain to ask advice from the Dalai Lama. Clayton, too, developed a routine doing imitations of his father, his favorite being his father slipping a glass sliver into his mouth to cut his lip on, that Clayton said he kept in a pillbox, so that he could get meals in expensive restaurants for free. But with each day that Mr. Pettyward failed to appear, I watched Clayton's energy dissolve into a fog of bitterness and anxiety. Now he twitched at every stray noise, his head cocked in anticipation that, after a silence, leached back into his curved, defeated shoulders.

Our lessons were a tug-of-war between two impossibilities. Clayton's body ran into itself almost on a molecular level: watching his fingers trip on the same phrase, over and over, I wanted to stop pushing, to hand him the viola to smash. But allowing myself to love would surely mean my end. I knew the claustrophobic rage of jumping like a dog at a stick held just out of reach, but a catastrophe was lurking just around the bend: I had been given one task, and if I failed Mr. Pettyward would throw me out without a second thought. Clayton knew, without my saying, what I thought of his father's wish for a recital. But admitting that would mean my downfall. And so, to get Clayton to work during lessons, I played Yuri's game of withholding indifference, made him practice until he was close to crying with frustration. When I broke down, and forgave his failures, Clayton joked around and slacked off, and I hated him for not understanding the problem. When I succeeded, and we made progress, I hated myself. Then I was Yuri at his worst.

—Di-ah-RHEE-ah, Clayton drawled again. In the eighteenth century, they thought diarrhea was the most beautiful word in the English language.

It was the first night of Carnavale, the Friday before Lent. For three straight evenings we'd worked on *Hail to the Chief,* which I thought might placate Mr. Pettyward; but like everything else, Clayton simply couldn't get it. To ease the tension, I suggested a walk, but after a few minutes the revelers on the sidewalk had marooned us on our island of misery. Then from down the street one of the luthiers who had tried to flirt with me, short, stocky Cristoforo, yelled out *Masha!* I had to steer Clayton away. Luckily he was short and stocky—he was dressed as the Hunchback of Notre Dame—and could not catch us through the crowd. We hurried on in silence. Clayton picked that moment to start whistling. Why any human being would think it appropriate to inflict his off-key labial farting on another is beyond my comprehension. By then we were already both on edge; I suppose I was unnecessarily sharp with him. When we got home, to make amends, I gave him a transcription I'd done for fun of *A Little Night Music* that gave the viola the melody while I covered the rest on piano. But three times in a row, where the melody becomes the accompaniment, he reversed the parts and skipped to the end.

Clayton sighed loudly. —I'm not a musician.

—Pretend.

I'd been patient and determined for weeks; why I was irritated now, I didn't know. I tapped the count and we started in. But again he rushed through like a train, plowing through all the life in the piece, just to cross it, to reach the end. He looked up even before he'd played the last phrase, his face expectant, and snorted mucus back up his nose, to avoid blowing. I couldn't contain myself.

—Must you flap your elbow every time you play two strings?

—YES.

—Why?

—Because I *feel* like it.

I took hold of his elbow. He jerked it out of my hand.

—Why can't I play left-handed?

—You'd bump into everybody else in the orchestra.

—So everybody has to be right-handed. That's totally Fascist.

My head felt sodden. I could just see Clayton's scene in Hitler's propaganda film, the unfinished classic documenting the happy Jews in Theresienstadt, *Der Führer Schenkt den Juden eine Stadt.* Hitler Gives the Jews a City. Could just see Clayton playing left-handed in the prisoners' orchestra, bumping elbows with the heap of skin-and-bones who shares his stand, getting dragged off by a guard to be deported, with all the other screen stars. He'd have been cut from the film.

I noticed a tingling in the Vs between my thumbs and fingers. Independent of my mind, a will to strangle was collecting in my hands. Clayton could not see the miles between where I was and his protected little life. The glib way he could call orchestra seating *Fascist*—his innocence itself—seemed a kind of brutality. I knew I should back away; in my mind I saw Yuri doing his one-finger push-ups on my scores, to keep himself from hitting me. But the piece we were working on was the simplest thing we had; if I couldn't get Clayton through this, he'd never learn anything.

—We're doing it again.

Clayton stood up. —I've had enough.

—Just like that.

He nodded. I raced him to the door, trying to slam it. As we jostled for position, there was Mr. Pettyward, trying to tiptoe by unnoticed. He was wearing a tuxedo and holding a bloody tissue to his lip.

—Enough of what? he asked, blotting his mouth.

—You're back.

He nodded. —And I've cut my lip, he said resentfully, as if that were the price he had to pay to get home. But tell me, how's everything? The viola's an amusing instrument, no?

—It's just grand, said Clayton, who was frozen in place.

Mr. Pettyward stepped by him into the room and pulled out a volume of Grove's. —The fact is I've been thinking about you both nearly continuously, he said, paging through the encyclopedia. You, and your repertoire. I heard a terrific piece by Berlioz the other night called *Harold in Italy.* How about that?

—That was written for Paganini, I said. Who was a virtuoso.

—How about Satan in Siberia, Clayton muttered.

—If that won't work, I have other ideas. You could do Telemann. It says here Telemann broke down the barriers between secular and sacred music, secular meaning the opera coming out of Italy at the time, sacred meaning church music, i.e., Bahgh, who was his contemporary. Bahgh used fugal, complex lines, whereas Telemann used simple, melodic lines.

Clayton raised his eyebrows.

—He avoided the hard stuff it takes to play Bach, I said.

—Our fearless teacher, Mr. Pettyward said, and hiccuped.

—He also popularized the periodic phrase structure, I said quietly, which eventually became synonymous with Mozart and Haydn.

Mr. Pettyward nodded. —So even if she doesn't actually play, she does know something. The point is, Clayton, Telemann was more famous in his time than Bach.

Clayton collapsed in a chair. —*Sic transit gloria mundi,* he said. Worldly glory is fleeting.

—Don't be obtuse, said Mr. Pettyward.

—It's genetic, Clayton said.

I motioned to Clayton to come and help me with the music stand. As we wrestled it apart I stepped on his foot, hard, to get him to stop antagonizing.

—You see, Clayton, Mr. Pettyward said, for worldly glory to fleet, one actually has to earn it. I heard your rendition of "Hail to the Chief," one of the simplest melodies ever written. If that's the caliber, I mean, what on earth have the two of you been doing?

—Working up our Christmas carols, Clayton said, hard as nails.

Mr. Pettyward sobered. —Have you been enjoying your present? I saw the papers piled in the hall.

Clayton rolled his eyes. He had simply taken the *Wall Street Journals* in the hall on his way to school, unrolled them, and tossed them on the pile. Mr. Pettyward turned from the room. I tapped the count with metronomic steadiness. Was the note Mr. Pettyward had left still in my coat pocket? Would Mr. Pettyward look there? Couldn't Clayton have learned even one piece? Why had I not insisted?

Clayton plucked at the strings of the Savant. —We're in a nodus, he said. That's Latin for knot. But could I ask you something? I mean, one cello piece?

—Sit down and play.

—And if I don't? You going to shoot me?

I could not find words. Perhaps the feeling of safety was simply a failure of imagination: because no one he knew had ever come close to being shot for playing badly, he could joke as if it were not a possibility. Part of me wanted to throw him on a sidewalk, alone in a foreign city, with nothing but an instrument. He'd learn to play then.

—I see why your mother left, I said, the echo of Yuri's disdain burning in the silence.

I do not think I will ever erase the image of Clayton's face crumbling. All I had wanted was for him to conceive of my life, for my situation to sink in. But probably experience was always the limit of feeling and thought. However sad his life, Clayton had a father, a place to live, the freedom to fumble. He could afford to fail where I could not.

A rowdy noisemaker wailed up from the street. Mr. Pettyward

reappeared at the door in a huff. —Jesus. I have to be in Modena tomorrow at six in the morning. This recital was the one thing I asked you for this year. The one thing. And if you two can't give me that—well, I'm sure Isabel can find herself another job.

I stood up and walked across the room and shut myself in the bathroom. The tiled cubicle was an echo chamber, absorbing nothing, every sound bouncing back into the air. I sat down on the edge of the bathtub and thought of my father, trapped in his isolation chamber, of how I must have sealed it that last summer by taunting him with my safety. That his past would remain hidden from my mother was a premise she never questioned. What must it have felt like, I wondered, for him to live wrapped in love's promise of company, while trapped in a past that condemned him to solitary confinement? If Clayton's innocence was a brutality to me now, how much more had mine been to Yuri?

I splashed water on my face. Trying to get Clayton to understand my life would have meant forcing him to live it. Clayton would not save me from his father. To hate his failure to bear witness was to torture him for the erasure of time, for innocence itself.

As I opened the door a horrendous screech, like fingernails scraping down a chalkboard, sliced the quiet. Outside, Clayton was sawing the bow over the Savant like a mental patient.

—What the devil? Mr. Pettyward yelled from across the apartment, as I opened the door.

—We're practicing for your party, Clayton yelled, his body a frenzy of motion. Ripped bow hairs flung out wildly.

—This is my house, Mr. Pettyward yelled.

—It's Thravinsky's chef d'oeuvre!

—Isabel! Mr. Pettyward yelled. The instrument!

—She lives with me! Clayton screamed. He slammed the door so hard it bounced back open. And then, at the top of his lungs, —PHILITHTINE!

As I left I took one of the three small hand towels, whose texture I had grown attached to. After a night of sleeping in a station, your life can be saved by a linen towel. When I came out an ominous blur was coming from the hall. The white-noise machines were on full force. Here in the music room Clayton was retrieving an urn on the bookcase. The way he gingerly pulled it down, so careful and unclumsy, made me guess that it contained his mother's ashes. But then he took off the lid and extracted a biscuit in the shape of a bone, and held it out to me. For him this was clearly the perfect time for a dog biscuit. I shook my head. He put the urn back on the shelf and shrugged. —More for me, he said.

In the distance I heard my phone ringing. That would be Mr. Pettyward, calling to fire me. I stood up to go and walked over to where Clayton was sitting. Clayton refused to look up, to let me say good-bye. I took the top of his head into my hands and kissed it. Clayton took the bow, began tapping a count, and picked up the viola. I sank back onto the piano bench. But before we could begin, the force of another metronome, the metal taps on Mr. Pettyward's loafers clicking over the marble, overtook his count. I told myself to keep going, to not turn around or look back, to not freeze into a pillar of salt. The tapping ceased. A rip of paper, again and again. The flutter of the pieces of my contract, falling to the floor. Then the taps again, until the apartment door slammed like thunder.

The revelers' noisemakers, howling through the window, underscored the silence.

A few beats later Clayton came in.

I had seen these moments over and over at Juilliard, the broken kids who concentrated their will and spent all they had in a brilliant last stab. The notes Clayton played were clear, and plain, and mournful. It was as if his months of fumbling had been an act. When he was done he laid down his bow, stood up quietly, and left. He would not, I knew, play again. A little while later I found him in his room, in front of the open window, staring out into the courtyard. What I had said about his mother leaving him, the cruelty of it, sank in and in and in.

His sweet, milky smell mixed with the fresh spring air drifting in. The awkwardness of his body, the way it tripped always against itself, moved me. Clayton, the poverty of his life, his trying so hard to love, moved me almost to the point of tears. He kept failing, as I had with Yuri. He was as unable to conceive of my terror as I was my father's, as unable to imagine being sprawled on a sidewalk in winter with nowhere to go as I was to imagine playing for my life in a camp, on a three-legged piano, amid filth and misery and starvation. A past was not something anyone could love you out of. There seemed no point, in a way, in letting anyone else near it. Watching Clayton stare at his fish tank, I understood my father better than I ever had.

Clayton stood at his fish tank, his face glowing in its wobbly light. His room smelled different, denser, not like a boy's. I stood watching, a wad of pain balled up in my chest. I admired his resistance, his outburst, his failure to comply. It was what I'd wanted to do nearly every time I went onstage.

—Just go, Clayton said. Have a nice date.

—Date?

—You told Giulio you had a date for Mardi Gras.

—People say things that aren't true, I said, to make the other person understand the truth. It's like, if you play *lontano* on the French horn, and you put your hand in the bell to make it sound far away, then you have to play B to hear C.

Clayton tipped his head towards his father's study. —You don't like him?

It dawned on me that Clayton thought that his father and I were a couple, that his father had come back for me, for our Mardi Gras date. That he was jealous.

—Actually my date is here, I said quietly, and I put my hand between his shoulder blades, to let him know the date was with him. But he shrugged it off.

One of Clayton's fish was suctioning the glass with its lips, over and over and over, searching for invisible bits of algae. —What's its name? I asked.

Clayton wiped his eyes on his shirt.

—Hey, I said. Tell me what your fish're called.

—Changes.

—What are their names now?

He reached in his pocket and took out the other half of the dog biscuit, and began to crunch it. His desolate, mechanical chewing made me want to hug him.

—They're Tartar Control, he said. Whoever makes these isn't a fraud. You'd think they'd lie about the new ones being better tasting, but they really are.

After a while I pointed to a blue fish with a hump and asked if it had a name. There was no answer.

—Your father said one of them was Beethoven, I said.

—He named it that, he said sullenly.

—So what did you name it?

—First it was Boris. For Boris Karloff. Then it was Boris for Boris Pasternak. Because I read *Doctor Zhivago*. Then it was Horace, for Horace. I was reading the *Odes*.

—What's its name now?

He picked up a tiny squeegee and listlessly scraped it against the inside of the glass.

—Spell, he muttered.

—Doesn't rhyme with Horace and Boris.

—That wasn't on purpose, he grumbled.

—What's that one?

—Isabel.

—Hmm?

—That's its name.

—Not the blue one. The orange with the frills.

—Isabel, he said again.

—Fine, I said. I won't ask anymore.

—Okay, he erupted. They're all named Isabel. Okay? It was my Christmas present.

—I don't know what to say.

—Not to you, he said. To them.

I cleared my throat. —They're all named Isabel?

—Could change, he said.

—That doesn't bother them?

—They like all being family, he said quietly.

We stood in the spell of the watery light, the steady gurgle of bubbles, the dart and glide of the fishes' silent ballet. Our breaths clouded and cleared on the glass. What I wanted was simply to lie on his bed beside him, my eyes shut, and say nothing more. But the unspoken was too close, the air too dense, our wants gliding past each other, but then darting back, as if trapped together in a tank. Sound travels four times as fast through water. In the middle of telling myself that I could both love and not love, that I could open up and love him, while keeping from him who I was, it came to me that he was hearing my thoughts through the silence. I tried to back away, but I had lost track of my body, and I knocked into him. Then in stretched-out time I fell backward, and hit the floor, and watched Clayton grab a leg of the aquarium's stand. And let go too late. He thudded onto my chest and knocked the wind out of me. Then I felt the splash of water, heard the aquarium's shattering crack.

I lay on my back, my head in a pool of wetness, with Clayton's body motionless over me, his weight rising and falling with my breath. Under the frantic fish-flutter slapping the floor an immense and horrible stillness settled over the room. Flooding through me was a terrible relief, that I had done the damage I would do, that the worst had already happened, that nothing worse could occur.

Then at its center, Clayton's body noticed mine. For a moment his weight vanished, and there was only the place where his erection pressed against me. A jolt seized both of us. Clayton rolled over and sat up. The skin around his right eye was studded with shards of glass. A tiny jet of blood pulsed out on a tiny shard of glass sticking out horizontally from his temple. Then the slaps of fluttering flesh distracted his attention. I do not know why, instead of helping Clayton, I crawled around grabbing handfuls of fish and rushing them to the toilet. Probably the Isabels seemed easier to save. Then I looked again and Clayton was standing, the blood dripping from the side of his temple. *Don't move,* I said. I sprinted out and got our coats. I checked his pocket—he had gone over the border to

Switzerland on a school art history trip, and his passport was still in his pocket, along with some Swiss francs. I gathered up what little we had.

After what Mr. Pettyward had said about the wait at the public polyclinico, I knew that the right way was to take him to the expensive private clinic where they knew Clayton and had his records. But Niguarda was outside the Milan city limits. Even if we could get in without his father, the little money I had would never get us there, and Clayton had hardly any cash. The polyclinico where Giulio worked was half a mile away. I took the Savant in case I needed to bribe someone to treat him fast: I did not know how long Clayton could last, bleeding that way. In the taxi, I put on lipstick. In searching for Signor Perso, I had found that everything in Italy took less time if you wore it.

The taxi driver couldn't find the emergency entrance to the polyclinico. As we circled the maze of buildings it occurred to me that they might not let me stay with Clayton because I wasn't family. Clayton saw my face and gripped my hand in his. Finally the driver found the emergency room. It was where we'd come in. I gave him the money I had. He cursed softly, but didn't argue. By now Clayton was dizzy. I gripped him under his shoulder and guided him through the sliding doors and towards the reception desk.

The emergency room was a chaotic circus of Mardi Gras revelers. A Sophia Loren transvestite in a tattered suede dress and heels held an ice pack on the side of his purple, swollen nose. Two parachuters, in gear, kept jumping up and down. Seven drunken popes with tall, white, pointy hats sat cross-legged on the floor, singing a drinking song and swilling from a wine bottle they were passing between them. A Charlie Chaplin listlessly poked at an elf in a wheelchair with his cane. Shrill voices mingled with weeping in a disembodied cacophony.

I made my way to a nun with a badge standing in front of the reception desk. She looked at Clayton, then accusingly at me, asked how this had happened as if I were some sort of child abuser. I asked her to find Giulio. She frowned. We were friends, I said. She laughed. Clearly Giulio had lots of friends; clearly, she wasn't one of them. My Italian was falling apart. I told Clayton to show her his head again, to ask her to page him. Clayton turned to display the tiny glass shelf protruding from his temple, and they had a chat. Then she walked down the dank green corridor.

—She says the Lord won't let me die.

Halfway down the hall, a man with dark sores on his face sat on a rickety bench. We weaved towards it and collapsed next to him. Clayton's head slumped down. I eased it onto my lap. My sleeves were soaked in ink-dark blood. A sickly sweet odor, like rotting leaves, infused the air. I imagined Yuri's lips curling at the notion of her "Lord" as someone to rely on. Then my breath flattened, and time seemed to tunnel down; all at once I got a sense not of the far future but of the depth of the present, of what was about to happen. There was no notation, now, no way to manage the passage, no passage through, no passage back. Then I remembered the story Yuri had told me about Rabbi Zusha, who wept on his deathbed because he feared being asked on the day of judgment not, Were you like Abraham or Moses? but, Were you like Zusha? Did you do all that Zusha was capable of doing? And what I knew was that I had not done all I was capable of doing to take care of Clayton, that I had no idea even how to begin. Outside my will, an inhuman howl erupted from my belly. I watched myself shove a metal cart against the wall. Two orderlies in green—how aesthetic and Italian it was that here, the men in white coats wore green to match the walls—came running down the hall and grabbed me by the upper arms. Clayton came to and jumped one of them, piggyback. They reeled around together, the blood spurting from Clayton's temple like a tiny lawn sprinkler, and went down. The hall went silent. Then, at the far end of the corridor, Giulio burst in wearing a tuxedo. He looked around, saw us, and came running.

—*Ecco mi,* he cried, almost in a panic. The orderlies released their grip. —A Fiat was in my space. His eyes focused as he touched my bloody cheek. —What has happened?

I pointed to the glass in Clayton's forehead. Giulio looked at me, his face softening as he absorbed that it wasn't me who was hurt. Clayton cocked his head sideways and showed him his temple. It looked as if he'd sprouted a stubble of glass. I handed Clayton's chart to Giulio. As he read it emotion dropped off his face, replaced by a cool veneer of expertise.

—Pettyward, he said. So that's your last name? You're the son of that American diplomat? Fussy, mannered, crying out for leather?

—You know him?

Giulio shrugged. —Somebody introduced us at a party.

—They beeped you on your pager?

Giulio hesitated a moment, then nodded, though that did not make sense. Clearly he had known we were here in the hospital, but how? If he'd been out parking his car, there was no way he could have heard the hospital intercom paging him; if he'd been somewhere else, at some fancy black-tie party, there was no way he could have arrived at the hospital so fast.

—So can I just ask—he's the big date for Carnavale you mentioned?

Giulio had been sitting in his car outside Mr. Pettyward's apartment, I realized, waiting for me to go on my big date. He had followed our taxi here.

—I can't *see,* Clayton said, his voice on the edge of crying.

A half hour later, in the operating room, a nurse was squirting fluid over Clayton's temple, then suctioning it clean. I shut my eyes, concentrating on the machine's hollow gurgle, wishing it could suck the cyclone from my chest. After a time the room grew quiet, the scurrying graceful, the voices hushed and subdued. A reverential silence descended. I opened my eyes. Giulio sat masked and draped above Clayton, his gloved hands poised to begin. Above us, in a dimly lit gallery, a half dozen people had gathered to watch him operate. Signor Perso had tried to teach me to approach music the way smart musicians approach music, as a problem of thinking; the truth I never had the heart to say, what I had known at eight, was that, if you were thinking about what to do, it was already too late. At my best, my limbs had known better than my mind and before, had found the notes like fruit on a tree, in a paradise-time in which desire and knowing were one, when there was no gap between wanting and having a sound. Giulio's hands, now, were in that time. Everyone in the room felt it. Physical genius is domineering and absolute, and in its incandescence, all you can do is watch.

—So how did this occur? Giulio asked.

—I tripped on my fish tank, Clayton said, when I didn't answer. It fell from five feet up.

—Out of the blue? Giulio picked up a syringe casing and unwrapped a long needle. My breath caught in my throat. —*Calma*, he ordered, squirting an arc of fluid above my head. He muttered something to a nurse's aide. The huge, wheezing woman lumbered out.

—You're kidding, right? Clayton asked, as Giulio aimed the needle.

—It's called twilight anesthesia, Giulio said. I need you conscious. As he sank the needle into Clayton's temple, Clayton flinched. I thought of his fish, flailing on the floor, and took his hand. But Giulio said I was blocking his light, so I had to back away.

—Play for me? Clayton asked.

—She can't, here, Giulio said like a general. He began plucking out shards of glass with a tweezers, his curved fingers prancing as exuberantly as a harpist's, the shards clanging like tiny bells in the metal pan the nurse held out.

—Remind me how the two of you are related, Giulio said.

—We play Bach together, Clayton said, when I didn't answer.

Giulio stared at me, and held out his thumb and forefinger. I pointed to Clayton's eye. —Could you please just—

The nurse wordlessly placed a tiny set of tweezers in his hand. —It's just sewing, he said. I'm a good tailor. During my military service my unit already had a doctor, so I became their tailor. That's actually how I met Fabio. I was called up to fit his wife's gown one night when all twelve of the Scala's costumers came down with the Asiatic flu.

—Caballé was a freak, Clayton said.

—Don't talk like that, Giulio said. Irrigate. In fact don't talk at all. Caballé is a beautiful singer. Did I ever tell you the story of how I was kidnapped?

Giulio pulled a microscope in and returned to plucking out shards. His hands moved with a quick, unconscious grace. I realized mine were shaking: Giulio's hands, their bravura, had once been mine. Luckily, the nurse's aide lumbered back in and handed me a paper cup with two cheery red pills, followed by one with water. I threw them down my throat.

—In the 1973 recession the strikes were horrendous, Giulio began. There were laws against firing a person, even if they did nothing. My father had a clothes factory, which kept open even though he wasn't making money and he would have made more as a tailor—because of his workers. He was loyal to the party.

—The communist party? Clayton wanted to know.

—Don't talk. When you're poor, you want the opposite of what you have. We have a long history of political bandits among the peasants. He held the tiny triangle of glass up to the light, dropped it on a tray, and asked for a clamp. All the colors in the operating room, I noticed, were getting fuzzy. The relief at placing Clayton in Giulio's hands was melting into the discomfort of standing in the glare of their genius. It seemed to me that his hands were too confident, too sure, for him to have endured anything.

At the skepticism on my face, Giulio threw up his hands. —Look it up in *La Repubblica*. I love the way Americans always think politics are things that happen to other people.

Giulio said his father had gone to lyceo with a couple of the early *brigatisti*. That Americans knew the Red Brigade from the violent kidnapping of that American general, Dozier, but when they started, they weren't like that. They did capricious things, kidnapped a Mafia pornography king and sent pictures to the newspapers of him naked and tied to a tree. People had sympathy, because when Pinochet took Chile they worried that a right-wing coup might also happen in Italy. He said something about two Christian Democrat parties, both full of ex-fascists. Somewhere far away, I noticed the scraping sound of his scalpel. The pills, I supposed, were taking effect.

—You see? Giulio said, holding up another piece of glass.

—Where was your mother? Clayton asked.

—Don't talk. On a cruise ship with a rich industrialist named BoBo.

Giulio tied off a vein in Clayton's temple. He said his parents' marriage had been a typical high-low thing, that his mother's family had hated his father, but forced him to marry her once she got pregnant. That because she'd been so snobby, his father had stuck with the communists way too long. That when the brigatisti started shooting people in the knees, his father stood up at a party meeting and made a plea that the communists have no more to do with them. When he walked out, many people left with him. Giulio's hands poised for a beat; the nurse reached in to clamp something. Then he said that the brigatisti hadn't wanted to provoke the masses, so they kidnapped him to change his father's mind.

The story was so well-paced and -orchestrated that I wondered if it might be true. Giulio said he was on holiday with his father and his father's girlfriend and bookkeeper, Laura. On their way back from seeing some cloth makers in Como, they stopped for lunch in the hills between Florence and Grosseto. When Giulio's father went to the bathroom, some friends of Laura's drove up in a sports car. One got out, and then they shoved him in the car.

—And since that time, Giulio sighed, my father has never trusted women. Whenever I have a girlfriend, he follows her around.

I nodded. He lies like a performer, I thought, tells his stories over and over until they're true.

—So did they kill you? I asked.

Giulio held up his pinkie, the one chopped off at the joint, and then I didn't know what to think.

Wordlessly, the nurse took her eyes off Clayton and looked up at his face.

—I see it, Giulio said quietly. Open?

Clayton opened his eye. Giulio covered the good one and passed his hand back and forth in front of his face. —What exactly do you see?

—Like a shadow, Clayton said.

Giulio eased back his stool and muttered something to his nurse, who spoke sharply at another nurse, who hurried out. —So the brigatisti took me to a cave in the hills, he said, as the other nurse burst back in with a package of slides. With a tiny spatula, Giulio scraped up a bit of muck onto one. —A culture for fungi, he said. The shepherds know those caves like the inside of their mouth. They watched me all the time. I was only allowed outside after dark. I learned to go to the bathroom twice a day, morning and night. It was good training for surgery.

—They fed you? Clayton asked thickly.

—Once a day. Also good practice for surgery. A shepherd came every evening with rustic food. I've never had better pecorino.

The nurse returned to say that the person Giulio wanted was in Corfu.

Giulio turned to me. —There's a piece of glass lodged in the bone. It broke off while I was extracting it. I can't go in that deep—I did a rotation in eyes, but I'm out of practice. Everybody who could is either operating on somebody else, or out of reach. The one guy who's here just started on a his-and-hers motorcycle catastrophe. He won't get in here soon enough without my having to close and open again. So we may as well close and see what happens. Glass is inert. Unless it's contaminated it could theoretically stay there forever. How clean do you keep your fish tank?

—Clean, Clayton said.

Giulio seemed to look to me for permission. But the pills I'd taken seemed to pack his words in layers of cotton, and I had no idea what to say in response.

—Okay then, he said. I'm going to close, and we'll hope for the best.

Before I could understand what happened, Giulio's hands began again at virtuoso speed, and soon he was finished. As he wrapped Clayton's eyes in bandage, he concluded with a short discourse on the aging of cheese.

—Half an inch lower, he said to Clayton, and you would have bled to death.

—Really?

Giulio peeled off his gloves, threw them in a basket, and punched him lightly on the biceps. —It's a good thing to tell your friends.

Clayton reached for me, and our hands gripped; in that moment, we agreed not to speak of what had gone between us.

Once the nurses had wheeled him out, Giulio turned to me. There was bleeding in an anterior chamber, he said, which could be putting pressure on the optic nerve. Until the swelling went down, there was no way to tell. I could feel his words come at my head, feel them bounce off like particles deflected. I opened my mouth, to ask him to say it all again, but could not speak. Part of me was relieved, almost to tears, that Clayton was in Giulio's safe hands. Part of me loved Giulio for saving him. But another part of me knew now how Yuri must have seethed, what it must have felt like to swim in the jealous underground river of the broken and dead, watching the survivors above ground who made it, get on with their lives. I stared at Giulio. All I could see were his hands working, their maddening timing, their quality of mind.

It was like an IV of silence, slowly seeping into my veins. Clayton's patience, his blindness and stillness woke me on the cot where I was sleeping, pulled me to his ward, and kept me there late into the night. Amid the wheezing coughs of patients and the beeps of their machines, I began to play as I had not played in years. Clayton wanted nothing more than the low tones escaping from my muted cello; suspended in his blind attention, I took my bow and began to play. It was as if he were a cracked treasure, now protected and wrapped in tissue. As if, in the hospital's care, nothing worse could occur.

The fever rose at dusk when Giulio left. As Clayton healed and hemorrhaged and healed again, I worked my way through Shostakovich and Schubert and Brahms. Under the cover of the ward-mandated silence, the blanket of Clayton's blindness, the anonymity of resting, now, in a place where no one knew me, I began to play. Pieces I had learned in secret, pieces even I had forgotten that I knew, flooded into my ear and through my hands.

My cocoon was broken one night around midnight with a soft, slow applause.

—Lovely. Giulio's dark voice cut through the shadows.

My face was burning in the darkness. I yanked the sash from the *f* holes and began wiping my sweat from the belly of the Savant. Giulio stepped out from behind the curtain. He was wearing a disheveled tuxedo, the neck open, his bow tie stuffed into his jacket pocket.

—That ending was just— He gathered his fingertips together and kissed them open. —No words to describe.

—I suppose your performance this evening was wildly successful.

Giulio shrugged. —Just explain me something. What is it with you women who hope for silent sex? If we were anatomical inverses, if women had vaginal orgasms, as Freud thought they should, we would never have needed to talk. We would be, how do you say? the *segs machines,* fucking mute as dogs.

—Women don't need talk to get pregnant.

—True, he said. But in all species the norm is that the female chooses the male. Even if the history of male-female sexuality were a story of male rape and domination, would we have needed to talk? No. And so clearly this is why language developed. To bridge that little inch between what pleases men and what pleases women. You see? We owe the birth of language to the clitoris.

—Hey. I brought you something. He reached into the breast pocket of his jacket and extracted a pair of earrings. Their teardrop emeralds caught a shaft of moonlight. —Lovely, no? They're Russian Baroque. You can tell by the filigree.

—You stole them?

—I'd say I *acquired* them. During the course of my work.

He dangled them before my face. They seemed too beautiful to touch.

—What's the matter? You prefer pierced? I prefer clips, but that's just me.

I stared up at him, wondering what I'd owe if I took them.

—Just take them, he said.

—What if I lose them.

He smiled. —Somehow I'm certain they're insured.

—Having nice things doesn't save you.

The corners of his mouth curled upwards. —I wasn't offering redemption.

He reached out and clipped first one, then the other, on my ears. I shut my eyes, liking the feeling of their weight, holding my head down. I stood up and looked at my reflection in the metal of the paper towel dispenser. Of course, his instincts were dead on. He'd had a vision of my face, framed by her earrings, so he'd taken them from her to give to me, shifted their ownership like features on a face. The way he felt free to remake the world to his perfect utopian vision of it frightened me.

—So what did you do to get these?

Clayton thrashed in his sleep, muttered something, and slipped back into dreaming. Giulio tapped out a cigarette from his package. —Let's go to the office so I can smoke.

—I mean I've always been attracted to the feminine, he said in the hall. Even as a boy. Not sexually, but aesthetically. I love the female proportions. That someone as tall as you can have such small feet, such curved, round heels and toes, I think is magical. The elegance of the design! And of course I love surrendering myself to flesh. We Italians, flesh pleasures us. Without it we feel deprived, jealous of our ancestors, which we do anyway, we're *la razza stanca,* the tired race, defeated already for two millennia, but you have to dispose of the day somehow.

—Hardly an answer, I said, as we entered the ward office.

Giulio locked the door behind us. He crossed around behind the wide metal desk and switched on a fluorescent light over the small porcelain sink. Then he changed his mind and switched it off, letting the moonlight coat the room again. He washed his hands thoroughly. —It's my way of worship. Luzzatto's idea was that in each act of making love we re-create God's original act of creation. So you see, it's in the genes.

From the metal dispenser on the wall Giulio pulled two tiny paper cups. He plopped down on the swivel chair behind the desk, took a bottle of Amaro from a drawer, and poured us a drink. Then he lit up a cigarette. The Russian filigree earrings caught a swath of moonlight, casting wobbly bubbles onto the wall.

—Do you even enjoy all this seduction?

From the metal tray behind his desk he picked up an instrument, a small rubber triangular hammer with a metal handle. —I love the moment of invitation, he said, banging on my knee. Involuntarily, my foot swung out towards him. —It's wondering what a person's like, and then they invite you in.

The heating pipes began to clang and hiss. Giulio guided my legs to cross the other way, then started banging again. —I like the buildup. The unfolding. I mean it doesn't even need to be a nice body, he said, banging. It's the moment they drop everything.

I covered my knee with my hand. —So it feels like falling in love.

Giulio shuddered briefly. —It's twelve hours, maximum. Then you're done with it.

—I meant for them.

—Oh, he said. Well. For them. For them, the love thing can be a problem. Afterwards you have to find a way to let them know they enjoyed it more.

He leaned in and kissed my cheek. —Hey, he said, pressing his cheek to my forehead. You're feverish.

Giulio rocked back in the chair, reached back behind him to a small drawer in the metal tray, and took a thick black handle with a sideways cone at the top. He clicked it on and a bright beam of light came out the point. —Open?

On its own, my jaw went slack in the face of his quiet authority. He pressed a wooden stick down on my tongue. When he clicked the instrument, its tip shot a beam of light down my throat.

—Good. Giulio nestled the cone-light in my ear, clicked again, and lowered his eye to peer inside. He stared a while.

—Find anything?

—Symphonies.

—So do you use toys? I asked, after he had done the other ear.

He loosened the belt of his trousers, pulled out his waistband, and shot the beam down into his pants. —Would you like to see my secret Carpathian underwear?

It took a pause, for me to understand that he was joking.

—You're looking for a—a something, he cried. But women don't fetishize that way. I mean each has certain, well, tricks, that, once you know them, you can make her come. But what I do is more, to reach in and get at what they can't bear about themselves, and then, for a couple of hours, love it. I'm like a good priest. I take away shame. As soon as they understand I don't judge, it coaxes them right open.

Giulio tossed the cone-light back in the drawer. He eased it shut with his hip as he washed his hands in the tiny porcelain sink. No wonder I had gotten no sense of him in his apartment: it was in rooms like these that he was at home.

Giulio poured me more Amaro.

—So you pry them open, and then you leave.

He gently pressed his fingers on either side of my throat, and shook his head. —Then I find the grain of sand, the thing they can't stand about themselves, and pull it out and show them it's a pearl.

I held up my paper cup to toast him. —One, two, three, I said, and drank.

—No, no, he said, mapping my throat as I swallowed. *Festina lente.* Hasten slowly. That was Virgil's motto.

He placed a palm on my shoulder blade. For a moment, I thought he was finished. Then I felt a tug on my zipper.

—It comes off, doesn't it? I mean even though you wear it every day, it's not bolted to you? No. Here's the hook.

I glanced at him.

—Just to the waist, he said.

I nodded, and turned my back. Giulio dragged down the zipper and helped ease my dress down off my shoulders. Then he led me over to the cot where I slept. I clutched at the dress to cover my breasts.

—You've never had a physical?

—Not for a while, I mumbled.

Giulio crouched down in front of me and held my hips, and pressed his cheek against my belly. He inhaled deeply. —Already I would know that smell a mile away, he said. With his cheek still close he eased my dress and tights down over my hips. I stepped out of the pile. He folded my dress neatly over a small metal chair next to the cot. —If you lie on your stomach, he said quietly, I'll examine your spine.

He laid the sheet and blanket over my legs, folding them with care. Starting at my neck, his thumbs began working their way down the sides of my spine with tiny circular jabs.

When he arrived at it, Giulio unhooked my brassiere. I inhaled, then exhaled slowly as his thumbs jumped to a new vertebra.

—So what were you playing? I heard you moaning all the way down the hall.

What the mind can know, and also not know, at one and the same time. For hours I had enveloped myself in a fog of phrasings, without allowing myself to hear the piece. Now it came flooding in: the smelly parlor, the battered phonograph, the recording the old Ukrainian woman had played for me, while Yuri snored on her sofa after she bludgeoned him with an hour of screaming for deserting her in Czernowitz. When he woke and heard it he swiped the needle off the record. But already I had picked it up.

—The *Kol Nidrei,* I said. By Bruch. It's—

—The Hebrew prayer, he said, plunging into my lower back. I thought you were one of us.

—You don't believe in God.

He shrugged. —The God I don't believe in is Jewish.

In the hospital, playing for Clayton, thoughts of my life had evaporated. Now each plunge of Giulio's thumbs released a new pocket of sadness: how Signor Perso had always understood everything and nothing, how I had wanted to run away from him in the airport, how, by taking care of everything, Signor Perso had taken care of nothing when he died. How I needed Giulio to take me to the morgue. How scared I was for Clayton. Luckily, just then Giulio reached the bottom of my spine. He lay a palm on the middle of my back, pounded on his flattened hand, repeated on the other side.

—Tender? No. Good. Your kidneys are good. On your back. I'll examine your breasts.

Giulio covered me with a blanket, then rubbed his hands together briskly as I pulled it up to my neck. He slid his warm palms underneath and raised my arm, his fingertips pattering over my armpit. Then he danced his fingers down in circles around my breast. For a little while I pretended it was all right. But then he was rolling and pinching the nipple, making it tingle. My hand flew up to cover it, and then his hands flew up, as if to show me he was unarmed.

—Okay, he said. Okay. How about I listen to your lungs?

I sat up, clutching the blanket in front. Lungs somehow seemed safer. Giulio's fingertips grazed my back lightly, as if going over a set of Braille instructions. From behind I heard him inhale deep, then exhale slowly, to guide the pace of my breath. I fell in with his steady rhythm, drawing in my air with his, releasing it with his. On an inhale a warm metal disk pressed the bottom of my rib cage.

I had seen stethoscopes on TV, but never felt one. As it made its way around the terrain of my back, to pick up what it could, the thought of him having a special ear, of being able to listen in deep inside, stirred and frightened me. Giulio inhaled loudly to slow down my breath. Then I held my breath, knowing that too was wrong. Finally my tempo settled.

After a moment he cupped a hand under my left breast and suspended it with a grunt, as if from the strain of the lift. Tucking the stethoscope beneath the fold, he began listening to my heart.

Having my flesh plumbed so deeply, while I was not making even the slightest sound, moved me beyond speech. I focused on silencing my insides, so that he might not hear my streams of sorrow, of wanting him, how close they were to the surface. But as his listening deepened its force grew, and instead of my insides quieting, a silent voice rose up in the silence. With crystal clarity, it spoke. The *Kol Nidrei* was the Hebrew prayer of atonement, the prayer that acknowledged, at the start of each year, that our best intentions go astray. Veiling it from myself, I had been praying, compulsively, to prepare in advance in case Clayton died. My eyes brimmed. I blinked. A stream rolled down my breast and onto Giulio's hand. He unhooked his stethoscope from his ears and glanced at my face.

—What is it you're looking for?

Giulio stared at me as he undid the tuxedo buttons from his shirt. He hung his clothes piece by piece over the back of the chair. I slid over on the narrow cot to make room, and opened the covers. He lay down beside me, wrapping his limbs around me, gently as tissue, cradling my head.

—I was trying to find what you think is wrong with you.

I pressed my head to his chest, wishing I could make myself tiny, could open a tiny trap door into his chest, crawl through, and pull it shut behind me, could hurl myself against his beating heart.

One thing I liked about Giulio was that he liked me right away, savored the distance between us, enjoyed the ways I kept him away. I liked that he'd bribed Clayton with a skating outing, that he would sit in his car outside Mr. Pettyward's apartment, do whatever he needed to do to see me. But that was the frightening thing about him, that nothing gave him pause. In the days in the hospital I came to see the greed in his vision, the way it sucked up everything in its path. I had watched him glide through the operating room, flirting sequentially with both the men and women, until they were so attuned to his movements that they drifted through the space like tentacles attached to his brain. It was Giulio's habit to turn his gaze away from people he'd just met, to glance at them shyly from the side: when I mentioned it, he said he couldn't stand to look at a face straight on until he'd rearranged the features in his mind to the way they ought to be. Giulio remade the world to his wanting.

I am still not sure that the big bang he told me about was not just another in his long line of fabrications, a story about the breakdown of the universe he made up to break me down. We were eating lunch in the doctor's lounge off the cafeteria. Though

Clayton still could not see—his eye had hemorrhaged twice in the past few days—Giulio mentioned, as if it were nothing, that he had to go to the mountains near Bolzano later that day. He'd postponed an appointment there, he said, the night Clayton got hurt. Then he looked at me, questioningly, asking if I would come. I said I wanted to wait until things settled down. Without missing a beat Giulio changed the subject to the beautiful fifteen-year-old girl he'd stitched up that morning, whose dirt-poor parents had paid him some pathetic sum they'd collected in church to close the incision. Before the operation, when they'd thought it was a cyst, he'd decided to take her to bed. Then the pathology came back ovarian cancer. Now she had a hysterectomy, and they hadn't even gotten it all.

Giulio was picking his way through his meal; as usual, I was finished. On the table beside his tray lay an envelope. Most beautiful back you've ever seen, he sighed, and pulled an X ray out. The film was of Clayton's brain. Giulio held it up against the light box on the wall and pointed to a white dot. He said it was the sliver of glass—like a needle—lodged in his eye socket. I must have been looking right at it, he said, from above, because otherwise I'd have seen it. I mean it's not a cancerous ovary, he joked. Nowhere near big enough to cause the hemorrhaging. But just to make sure, he said, they'd take it out as soon as the swelling went down. He had the best eye surgeon in Milan lined up to do it after the holiday weekend.

I was sleeping at the hospital, and Giulio had quietly arranged for extra portions of food to be sent up with Clayton's meals for me: my whole life, now, had casually come to depend on him. I tried to listen for the undertones beneath his words. He'd gone out each evening, and slept at home; was he trying to protect me by reminding me of the other women he was sleeping with? Trying to incite me to jealousy I could not afford? Was he trying to introduce the possibility that Clayton, too, was mortal? Or simply to reassure me about Clayton, so that I could leave for a night?

There were too many possibilities.

—I wish Clayton's mother were here.

Giulio rolled his eyes and lit a cigarette. —Better that she stays away.

I tipped my head sideways, silently asking why. Giulio told a story about the last time he saw his mother, she came to visit in this silver dress with metal threads, with her hair supershort. Giulio started screaming that she wasn't his mother, because his evil governess, Fräulein Edwige, had said she was never coming back. So Giulio thought this was a robot his mother had sent to take her place. She was wearing a pin with jewels that looked like a real heart. She took it off and jabbed it in his finger. Then she pricked hers, pressed their two fingers together, and said, Now we're related. Giulio kept screaming. After that she never came back.

Giulio smiled bitterly. There was a sizzle as he stubbed out his cigarette on his salad plate. —I don't know why I told you that. I'd rather you cut into me than make me talk about my mother. My point is, Fabio's totally transformed her.

—Marie-Antoinette?

Giulio shrugged, as if the whole thing were obvious. —Seeing her now, for the first time, would really upset him.

I nodded. In the distance, I heard a quiet cloud of cooing from the birds nesting in the trellis. Behind the surface of the world I now knew was another order. Marie-Antoinette had sent me to the Pettywards' because Mr. Pettyward was her husband and Clayton was her son. What little I had clung on to, since Signor Perso died, was simply an illusion. I sunk down inside, wondering what I could hang on to, what I could know was true.

—She's having plastic surgery to try to come back to Italy as someone else?

—At first I thought, the plan's insane. But Fabio's done extra–ordinary work, especially the cheekbones. If you ever want a new face, he's the guy to go to. So, you'll come with me?

I shook my head. Then he asked what I was waiting for. I said, for things to stabilize. That was when Giulio decided to tell me about the big bang he and Fabio had joked about. Giulio said that stable was not the nature of things, that the universe had begun with a giant explosion, that as we spoke it was still flying apart. That gradually it was winding down, its heat leaking out into a cold, dead nothingness. Which meant, scientifically, the universe was dying. Even the stars, he said, even the stars had mostly collapsed upon themselves already, that starlight took thousands of years to reach us, that most of the lights we saw were ghosts of stars, already long gone.

I ran my finger over the few crumbs on my plate and licked it. Thinking there had to be some part of the Italian I hadn't understood, I asked him to say it da capo. When there was no mistaking what he meant, I asked what came before the big explosion. I wanted a beginning, a time before the furnace blast, a time to go back to, to hope for a different ending. But then Giulio said, They have evidence. And the way he said it, I knew I'd lost. Lost the anniversaries I'd invented, the minutes and hours and days I was collecting, the buffer between me and Signor Perso's death. For what is the point in counting moments of survival, if the infinity on either side is loss? If the future is just the past becoming visible?

Then Giulio smiled, as if he hadn't just explained that the universe was exploding, and went to get espresso. I stared at my empty plate, wanting something else to eat. An old man at the other end of our table was wheezing the way Yuri did when he got overtired, when as we trudged along in search of someone we both knew was dead, he would gradually have more and more trouble breathing, breathing out, until his asthma clutched him, and he had to stop, to gasp at the task of rebuilding a ruin, his ruined faith in life, brick by brick by brick. Yuri had survived by counting, by searching for and counting survivors, to prove to himself that he wasn't the only one left. I was glad he wasn't here to hear what Giulio was saying.

I remember the wave of cold, the shudder that ran through me. If the future was just the past becoming visible, then there was no dissolving my past in Clayton's innocence, in his love, no falling into his safe life, no going back in time. By the time Giulio returned with tiramisu I had decided to leave. I gulped it down. We set our trays on the conveyer belt. He casually mentioned that I couldn't sleep in the hospital anymore if he wasn't there. Then what little I had left collapsed beneath me. I stared at the line of trays sliding towards the hole in the wall, wishing I could gather up all the half-eaten food, before it disappeared, to have in case of emergency. Giulio took my elbow and guided me towards the elevators.

—So? he said again.

—I'd have to change, I said, though the truth was, I already knew I was going.

The elevator doors slid shut. We were alone. —You don't need to change. Whatever happens, as long as it's true, is fine. If it's not true, it's just a nothing.

I swallowed. —I meant my clothes.

Giulio smiled. —I got you a present. It's in the trunk of my car.

By the time the elevator doors slid open, I think I had convinced myself that Giulio would take care of everything. That was how Signor Perso had loved me, by taking care. Back upstairs, everything seemed all right. Clayton had finally been released from intensive care and was being rolled into a ward; his cot's squeaky wheels seemed practically to sing of survival. He was sedated, his breathing tempo steady. At the other end of the ward, an old man was choking; but Clayton was on an IV; there seemed little chance of his choking from something lodged in his throat. I remember gazing at the sweet freckles sprinkled on his cheeks and neck, the stab of home I felt, imagining the constellations dotting his body beneath the hospital gown. Both eyes were bound in gauze, which was unnerving, but other than that there seemed nothing else to anticipate.

The transfer of the instrument happened quickly. Probably I was so focused on the present that my mind was incapable of anticipating the consequences of accepting it. Giulio went on rounds, and I went to take a shower. When I got back Clayton was managing, blindfolded, to flirt with a young nun who hurried out of the room, flushed with embarrassment, when I came in. I explained the situation, that I could not stay without Giulio there; before I could finish, Clayton broke in and asked if I could give him a night off so that he could get some quality time with the nuns. The trick in life, he said, was finding women with less experience than you.

He asked if there'd been any sign of you-know-who. I wondered if he had forgotten the episode with his father, whether he thought we'd simply go home and patch things up. To avoid reminding him, I lied and said I'd left a note. I leaned the Savant against his bed and put his hand on it and told him Yuri's story about a cello protecting you while you slept by turning the bad guys into anthills of cinnamon sugar. I asked again if he'd be okay overnight. His mouth rumpled. He asked for a kiss good-bye. Somehow, though he couldn't see, he saw me nod. He reached out into the air. I gave him my hands. His IV pole was between us. I said I'd go around the bed. He clutched my wrist and told me to go over it. I watched myself do as he asked. I suppose it will come as no surprise that he pushed my wrists out from under me, that I fell smack onto his chest, my mouth a breath from his.

—How're my Isabels? was the question.

I have never been good at improvisation. Trudging along behind Yuri, I used to fantasize about turning and running, but what stopped me was that I could never imagine what I might do once I'd escaped and caught my breath. Now, though I had told one lie, I could not keep up with the performance, could not invent a new lie to keep the first afloat, could not find a way to admit that I hadn't been home to write the note, or care for his Isabels. In my mind I saw the fish floating dead in the toilet, and I jumped off the bed. But it was too late. Already Clayton had a blind man's senses, and he knew I'd let them die.

I started backing out of the room, but Clayton reached up and fumbled behind his head for the Savant. I went forward to guide his hand to it, to tell him I wouldn't touch it or take it. Then he did something extraordinary. Instead of clutching it to himself, he passed the neck back to me.

I could not have imagined such a gift. So at first, I didn't understand.

And then I did.

—You can't do that, I said, pushing it back towards him.

His lips pressed together, determined. Again he pushed it my way. —It's in my name. For tax purposes.

A nun clattered in with towels. —That's Natalia. Natalia, he said loudly, I'm giving her this cello. You're the witness.

—*Va bene,* she muttered on her way out.

—You want it, I said, knowing it wasn't true.

—I want to translate Latin, he said, and try the new Milk Bones with Cheese.

He was biting his bottom lip as if he'd asked me to marry him. I sat down on the bed. The weight of owning the Savant, the risk of all that could happen, sank down in my gut like a weight pulling me underwater. And yet I wanted it so much that I could not catch my breath. I searched for a way to refuse him. Clayton felt for my shoulders, pulled himself up, and brushed his cheek against the curtain of hair aside my face. The air between us ignited. With an infinite rest under the gesture, he passed the Savant my way.

There was nothing to do but take it. The fierceness of his love, from being held at bay, would admit nothing else.

Of course, reconstructions flatten and simplify, they doctor the past with present knowledge. Listen to Busoni's editions of Bach, you'd swear Bach was writing for a modern Steinway. Though my memory of those days of waiting has sharpened that shudder, the more I try and retrace my thoughts, the less sure I am that it happened. Did I leave the hospital to keep Clayton safe from my desire, the wanting I had to tell him everything, to wash away all I had known, all Yuri had taught me, in his warm, blind innocence? Had Yuri pulled me into his world to protect me? Or simply to have company, to escape the utter isolation that exposure to evil, to ugliness, had left him with? Is my memory of shuddering, of the jolt of knowing I had to protect Clayton from myself, just the shape I have cut from the stone I cannot swallow, the fact that I left? Is it even possible to reconstruct the unbearable? Or is the story that sticks as memory simply the version that allows you to bear the chaos, the bridge over the abyss that lets you walk on? Probably questions like these are useless; trying to strip off time's overlay, to retrieve what you knew then, is like playing a piece backward. If Signor Perso were here he would put me in the bathtub and read to me about the wife who turned to a pillar of salt, a frozen column of tears, because she looked back. I suppose I will press on.

III

(as if suspended over a void)

Giulio unlocked a monstrous black Alfa Romeo. When I asked about the navy one, he said he'd traded up. This new Alfa started without any trouble, so there was nothing to keep us from leaving. The car smelled foreign, manufactured, not like the bodily smells of the hospital; already when he slammed my door, we were miles away. As Giulio headed east on Milan's ring road I kept telling myself that I had taken the Savant for safekeeping, that I would find a way back to Clayton's love. A sunset sprawled out behind us across the horizon: a huge, heroic angry spread of red, a sky Beethoven would have composed towards the end. The window to Clayton's ward faced west. A pang struck, that with his eyes bound, Clayton would never see it. I had not played aloud for Clayton to protect him, to keep what happened on the night of my debut from happening again. Still, I stared back at the bloodred sprawl, wanting to turn around, to go back and play that sky for him before it was gone.

I glanced down at my lap. A handkerchief had appeared there.

—Your eyes are leaking, Giulio said quietly.

—Allergies, I said, and blew my nose like the foghorn tuba in *The Flying Dutchman*.

Giulio nodded. —Tell me something. This precious cello. The one you refuse to play. Is it old?

—Because what I am wondering, he went on, when I didn't answer, is why the old instruments give the greater sound. My theory is that the beautiful sound lies in the slow death of the wood. That the cells of the dead wood resonate more freely, like women who have loved and lost.

I smiled at him, floating his theories by me, for me to shoot at like ducks in a gallery. —When it's cut down, most of the wood is already dead. It's only the bark that's alive.

—So it's the opposite of people. The layer we touch of each other is the dead one. That's what I love about operating: inside a body, it's hot and it's wet and you know what you've got in your hands is alive.

We slowed for a red light in front of a crumbled brick portal from Milan's old city wall. Three prostitutes leaned against it, smoking. After what Marie-Antoinette had said, I wondered about the sex he had with the women he hung around with. Having to sweep away one rich, dead-bored woman after another seemed to me like having to perform the same program, over and over, to one tone-deaf music-hater at a time.

—And what about your other life?

—What other life?

At the green, Giulio slid under the arch and turned towards a sign for the highway. —Oh, that, he said finally, as if I'd found a decade-old recital program of his in a closet. Giulio reached to take the tollbooth ticket. He had not said a word for ten minutes.

—What do you love about it?

—You mean besides the money? he said, resigned.

—You think about the money during?

He glanced at me. —If things get tedious.

—So besides the money. I mean, why exactly do they pay?

Giulio heaved a sigh. —No one's ever asked me that. I mean who I've already slept with. Listen. Say it's your sixteenth birthday. You're in a bar on the grand canal with a friend from lyceo. Say a beautiful woman sits down next to you.

—So?

—So say you're a guy.

—What's the question.

—Say you talk.

—What do I talk *about?*

Giulio rolled his eyes. — *Women.* You talk about topics. Now, just say, by some miracle, that she seems to like you.

—I suppose in those days I had a lot of hair?

—You have hair. You had hair then. Now say you kiss. And things happen. You're blushing, by the way. It's attractive. Now, hypothetically, say you leave together.

—What about my friend?

—He's smart. He leaves. So when you get outside, she says she charges.

—Charges what, hypothetically?

—Hypothetical *mon*-ey, he said, rolling his eyes. You tell her you'll give her what you have. It's not anywhere near enough, but she agrees. Now. There's nowhere to go. You go somewhere in your father's Renault Cinque and park.

—I thought my father drove a truck.

—Your father drives small cars. He thinks it goes with being a communist. Now say she wants you to enter her in the ass.

I stared out at the darkening horizon. Along the road, a line of cypress trees rose up, slammed by like huge jail bars. Giulio was driving wildly fast, in the left lane, his left blinker on, to tell people to get out of the way.

—Watch the road.

—Of course, he said, and then, not taking his eyes off me, charged across all four lanes of the highway, horns honking at us, to pass a flank of busses.

—I'm a virgin?

—You're *sixteen*. You're not twelve. But that, you've never done. I suppose at sixteen you were singing in the church choir?

—I had a job.

—Doing what?

—At the basilica in my neighborhood in Milwaukee, I admitted.

—You mean a church. I don't imagine Milwaukee was crawling with basilicas.

—The Basilica of St. Josaphat was made a minor basilica in 1929.

—By which pope, he said skeptically.

—The dome was eighty feet wide and two hundred and forty feet high.

—It wasn't a real basilica.

—Look it up in *La Repubblica*. One of the requirements to be a basilica is that you have tours and pilgrimages. We had them. I led the tours, I said, even though my job had been to wipe up the chalky alabaster dust that had snowed down onto the pews every day, after the dome got renovated.

—But, Milwaukee is where you grew up? You don't seem like one of those people from the Midwest. They're all so—nice.

—As a child I traveled, I said.

—And your father? Somehow I picture him a Russian Jew.

I could feel him circling above my past, like a patient vulture.
—Go on with your story, I said.

—Okay so now you're close. You're proud of how long you've lasted, but you've been close since the moment you kissed, he went on, and now you've been at it awhile, and you know you can't hold out. So you reach down to touch her, and—

—And she's a he? I said.

Giulio burst out laughing. —Why do Americans think 'homosexual' at the slightest whiff of anything other than the missionary position? You're like those hunting dogs who see a leaf far off and think it's dinner. At some point in adolescence most Italian boys have a penis pal. It doesn't make you gay.

I looked out my window, annoyed that I hadn't seen it coming.

—She's a she, he said softly. For God's sake. That's why I like women who look like women. No unpleasant surprises. Luckily, I already have evidence of your femininity.

—That was a contraption I strapped on for the occasion.

—That would explain a few things.

A light mist had fallen on the autostrada, which rolled beneath us now like a dark stream of polished lava. Giulio flipped opened the wooden panel to the left of my feet—transplanted, somehow, from his other Alfa—and produced two glasses. The corked bottle of white wine he held up was nearly empty. He threw it on the back seat, pulled out a new bottle of red, and, steering with his knees, began uncorking it. The speedometer eased up over 150 kilometers an hour. I stared out into the thickening dark, into a sticky vision of our mangled bodies, the totaled Alfa, the Savant crushed to tinder, the rhythmic screams of ambulance light igniting the carpet of glass. And Clayton in the hospital, waiting.

I was sure I did not want to hear the climax of his story. To avoid it, I turned on the radio: there was Bernstein, coming to the radiant climax of Beethoven's Ninth, the one he did when the Berlin wall fell. The *Ode to Joy.* Somewhere, I thought, somebody had a sick sense of humor. I clicked it off. —So go on.

—Then you feel welts all over her stomach, he finally said, handing me a glass.

—We're in a dark car? I said, still trying to crawl my way out of what I knew was coming.

—You know what they feel like.

Involuntarily, stupidly, my hand reached for the door handle: if he had known violence, then of course he was capable of it. But at that moment, the locks in the car flicked down.

—So now purely hypothetically, he said. What do you do?

—I get out of the car?

—No, no. You've paid. And not even full price. That would be an insult.

—But I do stop.

—The answer is, he said, that though you haven't hit anybody since grammar school, it comes to you to beat her. And when you do, she comes.

I saw myself, under Giulio, him slapping my face hard, spitting on it just as I let go. I wished I were anywhere but in his car. One of Yuri's refrains had been that the quickest way to trap yourself was by wanting to believe you were safe.

—Let me guess, Giulio said. Our musical aesthete, who can't lower herself to perform for an audience, finds the idea of prostitution morally repugnant. I mean, it's not just that you're

American. Even if you had twice the experience you do, I'd never believe you'd been married.

—Doesn't take a genius to know that if someone goes away with you on Mardi Gras, they're not married.

Giulio held up his glass as if to toast my astute observation. We clinked.

—That doesn't mean they're about to fall in love, I added.

He crooked his finger to reel in my ear. —Nobody said anything about love.

I drained my wine and set the glass on the floor. Yuri had taught me how to punch in cases of emergency. Giulio's wine spewed everywhere.

—That's wonderful. Magnificent. Giulio reached back and grabbed a towel from the laundry pile and blotted frantically at the murder-stain on his chest. When that didn't work, he pulled out a bottle of seltzer and ripped it open. It exploded all over the windshield.

—I guess you can't open everything so quickly.

The muscles in his jaw carved dancing mounds of tension on his cheeks. —Why are you so *hard?*

He began to wriggle from his shirt. We swerved. —*Steer the car,* he barked. I took the wheel. —Why don't you tell me what that precious cello of yours is worth, he said, and then we'll know how much you sold yourself for on our first enchanted evening. Don't tell me. You're shocked. You're saying you slept with me that night because you wanted to.

He was weaving between lanes.

—I needed it back, I said.

—Well, *I* need a lot of money, he said, pulling his shirt off over his head.

He leaned forward to wipe the windshield with his shirt. We were accelerating. Tossing the shirt behind him, he leaned over and scrounged under my seat. The truck in front of us swelled across the windshield, its black rubber panels flapping like wings. Finally he sat back up with a dry-cleaned shirt in cellophane. As he ripped off its package, an orange rectangle of a rest stop sign rose up in the distance. —Pull over.

We were barreling down the left lane. —*You* pull over, I said. Giulio grabbed the wheel. We screeched across the lanes to the exit, hit a bump, flew into the air, landed skidding on the frozen brush girded by the ramp. Branches cracked against the windshield. The car shuddered sideways, its underbelly scudding onto the asphalt. The pavement shimmered. We hurtled across the parking lot towards a bus trickling nuns. Giulio pumped the brakes. We fishtailed into the moment my parents fly off the highway—the branches slap, we're skidding back, there's Clayton dead, Signor Perso alive—then our back bumper slammed against the bus, knocking time in place.

I was plastered against my door, Giulio sprawled over my lap. I took in the chain of small, daily sounds, the hum of the motor running, the muffled, frantic chatter of the nuns, the distant waves of traffic farther off along the highway. Giulio reached over and turned off the car. After a moment we were gathering ourselves. He pulled a suit bag hanging in the backseat and got out of the car. Almost as an afterthought, he glanced over at me.

—You're all right, he said, and got out and slammed the door.

I heard him flirting with the nuns, taming them, until their voices cooed like doves. When that was done he turned to leave. Then he hesitated, felt in his pockets, turned back, aimed his key ring at the trunk, and popped it open. I opened my door.

—I paid off that dwarf at your pension some time ago, he said in a low voice, and hurried up the walk towards the rest stop.

A caesura. I sat flattened in my seat. Finally I dragged myself to look. Giulio had salvaged everything: the smashed heap of clothes, the tapes of our old 78s, the smell of Signor Perso, rising up like bread. Here the familiar fabrics, their jumbled patterns the chaos of the death. Our years came streaming down my face. I pressed Signor Perso's crumpled nightshirt to my face and inhaled the old, safe smell of his skin, wishing I could hurl myself in the trunk and shut the lid behind me. Then my eye fell on his threadbare Harvard bow tie, now creased and worn. It had been hanging freshly pressed under a dry cleaner's plastic when I'd dressed the body. Giulio had tried it on, or worn it. He had been driving around with our things for months, scrounging through them, had scrounged up talk about Signor Perso, knowing he was dead. To get inside, Giulio would stop at nothing.

Washed and shaven, his new suit hanging as if pressed on his body, Giulio emerged from the rest stop like a reengineered recording of himself. Amid a landscape of perfect plastic shrubbery, he paused to check his cuff links, glanced to either side as if to reassure himself that no one he knew had seen him messy, then headed down the walk towards the car. Up close I saw that his fingernails were buffed, his black loafers were shining. He dumped his dirty clothes on the laundry pile in the backseat and walked around inspecting the car. Once he saw that there was no damage, he praised the Alfa's huge rubber bumpers. He jumped in, pulled up to a gas pump, reached across me to the glove compartment, and pulled two surgical gloves from a dispenser box. Then he saw my face, the tears, and laid a hand on my arm.

—Really, it's nothing.

It took me a minute to understand. Giulio thought he'd unleashed a waterfall of gratitude.

As he put on the gloves he asked if I knew why there were no more wooden flutes. I stared at him. His face had a cheery placidness. He was planning to pretend he hadn't just almost killed me.

—I *love* myself, he said. The one musical thing you don't know. He smiled, jumped out, and swiped his credit card with a flourish. From the rearview mirror I watched him open the trunk, take out a metal canister, and begin filling it. The gas battered the sides in a low baritone shudder that tumbled up the scale. —This way I never run out, he said smugly, screwing on the top.

—So why was it empty?

He shoved the gas nozzle into the car. —I ran out. Anyway all the wood came from a certain island in the Caribbean, owned by two flute makers who were fighting each other for control. Finally, one tricked the other out of his half. Then the other one set fire to the entire island. It'll take a hundred years before the trees grow back. Now here is my question to you. Would you rather be the flute maker who got the island or the one who burned it down?

If that was how the world was divided, Giulio was the one who would always come out with the island, with the genius hands that worked, the one who would risk the accident, but arrive at his rendezvous immaculate. Who would survive at any cost. Detonating in my chest was a wish to maim him. In the open glove compartment, next to his carton of cigarettes, were matches. I lit one, lit the pack with it, threw the burst of flame out the window at him. But Giulio deftly jumped aside, and it hit the concrete spitting sparkler-bits.

Giulio stamped it out with a belly laugh. —Exactly. Given the right circumstances, anyone's capable of anything.

He peeled off a glove, reached in through the window, and grazed my cheek with his hand. His hand smelled of almond and neroli, and the faint tang of martini: at the Agip bar, I realized, he'd had another drink.

—*Le donne violente,* he said. Probably there's something wrong with me that I find violence attractive in women.

A cool, clammy tingle crawled its way down my spine. Was that his point, to trap me in his moral relativity, where everyone was guilty? Or would be if you pinned them on the right board and prodded them in a circumstance? Where beating a woman became an anecdote you told over a glass of wine? I thought of Clayton, of the way I had crushed him, told him his mother had left because of him, just to get him to practice. Was Giulio right, that what repulsed me about him was what I could not bear in myself? Was crossing into evil as simple as deciding to survive at any cost?

I eased myself over the stick shift and crawled into the driver's seat.

—What's happening?

I buckled myself in.

—You want to drive my three-day-old Alfa?

I gripped the steering wheel and stared straight ahead.

Giulio took a deep breath and got in the car. I inserted the key in the ignition. He clicked his seat belt. I put on mine.

—What's the problem?

—No problem, I said, and turned the key.

The car lurched forward.

—I left it in gear. Don't tell me you only know how to drive an automatic?

He unlatched his seat belt. —I'm driving.

—You lost your chance.

He narrowed his eyes. I kept perfectly still, wondering if his long, slow exhale was the windup to a punch.

—So put in the clutch, he finally said.

I gripped the stick and tried to shove the car in gear.

—On the floor. Your left foot.

I managed to start the engine, revved it, got the stick into first. As I let out the clutch there was a sound like a chainsaw ripping into a redwood. With feigned nonchalance Giulio pulled a manicure kit from his black medical bag on the floor and began buffing his nails. I stalled. Restarted. We lurched forward. The lone tree in the parking lot jumped out in front of us. I slammed on the breaks. Giulio's nail buffer flew out of his hands.

Giulio retrieved it, switched on the hazard lights, and resumed his manicure. I started up. And stalled out again.

—Had enough? he asked, buffing away.

The old cramping, the muscle memory of performing without a score, clutched my shoulders. Why had Signor Perso not imagined his death, or the time after it? Why had it never occurred to him to teach me to drive? Silently I seethed at my impossible body. But I was not about to hand myself over to Giulio again. Driving a car, I told myself, could hardly be more difficult than playing the *Rococo Variations.* It occurred to me to listen for the sound I wanted, the smooth, rhythmic groans from the groin of the engine that Giulio had made, and work backward to the movements. That was the secret: in seconds, my limbs had molded their motions to the needs of the machine. I managed to circle the parking lot without chugging, and then I was coasting up the exit ramp as if I had always known how.

Against the darkening eastern sky, a low moon was rising. Beneath it, the hill towns looked stagey, like a painted backdrop for a *Trovatore* set. Or perhaps it was the scent of Giulio's martini breath permeating the car that made the journey seem unreal. I have no idea how long we were on the highway. For a long time I floated on the childish high of having mastered a physical task. Then the road forked, and I had trouble getting over to the left, and my mood fell, knowing that whatever lay ahead would not be as easy as coasting on this highway. The road began to weave through the Alps, circling around cliffs, then seeming to head straight over them as it snaked back and forth above a riverbed. Gradually I learned to lean into the curves. I liked the feel of the car righting its weight, like a bow balancing. At a certain point rough strips cut into the surface of the road that began to jackhammer the car at regular intervals. But then I gave myself over to the vibrations, let them pass through. By the time Giulio pointed to the exit for Trento, I managed the toll-booth with a smooth *rallentando*. After a short while we were heading up the side of a mountain. The air between us began to thicken with what Giulio was about to do.

—Is it much farther?

—A little ways, he said, lighting a cigarette. Downshift.

I stamped on the clutch and did as he said. The gears tight-ened like muscles in anticipation, and the car surged upward, its power firm in my hands.

—I mean, Christ, Giulio burst out. The whole thing's Daphne's fault. She had tickets to some benefit, then she wouldn't go because she got a cold sore on her lip. She made me take one of her friends, an executive for some big weapons manufacturer. It ended up, we spent the night together. She said she hadn't slept with anyone in years, that if she dated anyone she worked with she could never let herself care about them, because later on they might not get the security clearance. I tied her up and made her tell me some classified secrets. Which drove her wild. God knows, I didn't give a fuck. The next morning she panicked and made me swear that the evening would stay between us. A couple of weeks later I got a package with some antique cuff links. The note said our night had made her realize that her security clearance was a prison, that all she wanted to do was violate it. She said that after seventeen years, she'd left weapons and taken some U.N. job where security wasn't an issue. And she'd finally met someone. The cuff links were to thank me.

—So okay, he went on, stubbing out his cigarette. I thought that was the end of it. But the next Sunday, the phone rings. It's a friend of this woman, Swiss, whom I'd met at the charity thing. She's just in town for the day. She asks if I'll meet her later, at her hotel, for a drink. Daphne was still in Geneva, and I was reading at home, so I said, Why not. This woman is a mother of three, never worked, nothing like her friend. But clearly the friend had talked, because the conversation keeps dropping off a cliff. All she can talk about is how she loves her husband. She has this nervous giggle that I kind of liked, so finally I say, I think you called me for a reason. What reason is that? she asks, like a little coquette. We circle round again. I mean, after a few drinks, I'm thinking, out with it, or I'll go home and read. Then I start studying her like a patient. And something clicks. I think, this is textbook, the housewife who wants to whore herself, but can't say it. So I ask if the rooms are nice. She says, Would you like to see one? I say, Why not? Upstairs, she goes to the bathroom. I start reading the newspaper. When she comes out I turn a page and tell her to undress. She's a little heavy, awkward with her body, so I'm thinking it might take her awhile to warm up. But no, she puts on a show, takes off her clothes very slowly. I glance over the paper every so often. And keep reading. She comes over and stands in front of me. I reach in to check—she's wet. So I turn the page. She kneels between my legs. Would you like to open my pants? I say. Would you like me to open your pants? she says. And I say yes. I give her little lessons. She wants them. Like this? she says, very innocent.

—And you both lived happily ever after, I said, not wanting to hear any more.

Giulio thought a minute. —I mean what do you do in a case like that? It's like pouring water through a sieve. I say, It looks like your hips want me inside you. And she says, Would you like to be inside my hips? I kept thinking, I'm going to hit on what turns her on.

—But you never do.

—Well. It goes on like that. I mean for hours. Until I'm at the end of my wisdom. Finally she's on top, sitting with her back to me, and then I hear moaning, a guy, coming from I don't know where. Then I see the closet door's ajar. Then she lets go, and they share their special moment.

I slowed for traffic, remembering him boasting in the hospital that he always enjoyed it.

—Two days later, I come home after being on duty for thirty-six hours. Under my door is an envelope. When I open it, ten thousand Swiss francs fall out. I felt physically sick. I wanted to burn it, but I just, I just couldn't. I never had touched that much cash in all my life. So I just slipped it into my wallet, and threw away the envelope, and went on with my day.

—So you saw them again?

—No. But one thing led to another. The first one, with the cuff links, was just something lucky that happened. But after this one, it was something I did. You know what the worst part was? Watching myself slip the money in my wallet, and in that next second becoming a completely different person, a person who did that. It was the easiest thing in the world. Has that ever happened to you?

It seemed a power, the way he had of leaving one self behind and putting on another, like a pair of wings under your coat to fly away with if you needed. But as I glanced at him, his eyes seemed desperate, as if looking for food.

—I guess not, he said, with a tight edge in his voice, as if he couldn't bear the judgment he knew was coming.

We rounded a sharp curve. He signaled me up a steep gravel turnoff. I downshifted again, my new competence settled now into my muscles' memory. After some slow going, an ash-white monastery rose up in the headlights. Giulio pointed to the side to a gravel lot where a row of cars sat parked facing the drop-off on the edge. I steered us parallel and nudged us forward. The car shuddered to a halt. For the first time in hours, I took in his whole face. It looked ravaged. But it was the exhausted relief at the end of a battle: finally, he had stopped performing.

—Leave it in gear, he said quietly. It works better than the parking brake. I have to go in. Could you just wait a few minutes, then get yourself a room? I'll come find you in a couple of hours.

—Irrespective of her marital status, I said, our musical aesthete does not find prostitution repugnant.

—And how does she find it?

—The question is how you find it.

Giulio lit a cigarette, cracked his window, and exhaled smoke. —Have you ever seen anyone die?

I saw Signor Perso's quiet, dead face, his fragile, tissue-thin eyelids, and shook my head.

—So little changes, he said. Except the body's empty. The

thing about medicine, the unbearable thing is, that you cannot find what a body needs to live. The death one finds over and over, but look as hard as you want, with the MRI and the barium and the X ray, you cannot find the life.

He reached down for his medical bag, pulled it up to his lap, and smiled bitterly. —All we can tell the relatives is what organ it escaped from. I mean women pay me, and paying makes the transaction simpler, easier for them to let go, but I think I'd do it even if they didn't. Because, *figurati*. In one evening, you are handed the sacred knowledge of a body: not what it needs not to die, but what it needs to live. You can't imagine—I mean the death you see as a surgeon, *day* after *day*—

I lay my hand on his arm. He threw his cigarette out the crack in the windshield and stared out at the sky.

—I wish bodies, he said, when they were ready to go, would burn up like stars.

With Signor Perso, my gut had simply said: *not burnt.* But in running from ashes, I had erased him a different way: now he was rotting without a headstone in some slab-studded stretch of barren ground where I would never find him.

—That would make things easier, I said, staring out at the vast black beyond the mountain's edge. I had never seen a sky so tightly studded with stars, with specters unwilling to vanish.

The wooden entrance door was carved with the faces of devils. I leaned my weight against the door and eased it open. Giulio was still leaning his elbow on the reception counter at the other end of the entrance hall, flirting with an ancient, misshapen widow clearing a coffee service from a side lounge. A Marie-Antoinette doll balleted from the office behind the counter. This one had a better figure than Marie-Antoinette; her doe-eyed face—except for the weird, square chin—qualified her as a more standard beauty. But she had the same mincy walk, the same flawless skin, the same suit cradling her behind like upholstery. Did Giulio pick them that way? Or did he just habitually make them all come out the same? I wondered, again, where I might possibly fit into his scheme.

The doll wisped around the counter, wrapped her arms around his waist, and concaved her little body into his. Her sling-back shoes framed her feet like tiny thrones, making them look curvy, pliant, inviting as torsos.

—Darling, Giulio said, flicking his wrist behind her head to glance at his watch. You've taken up coming here?

—Your other darling gave me her appointment.

The tone was flattened to a staccato monotone—irritation wrapped in sugary calm—but the cadence was unmistakable. Marie-Antoinette. Probably you could char a person's flesh with a blowtorch and the voice rising out would still sound the same. How could she imagine that her voice would not give her away? Either the Christian Democrats who wanted her out of the country cared only about the appearance of getting rid of her, or the Italian police did not have voice print equipment. Because if they did, the only way for her to return to Milan would be never to utter a word.

Giulio slipped from her embrace. —She left?

—You're only three days late. Or do you imagine time stops for us all until you arrive?

Giulio inhaled. Exhaled. —I had an emergency.

He glanced around at the empty living room, then walked over to a scrawny potted evergreen left over from Christmas, with Carnavale masks hanging off it, and rang a little bell hanging from a branch.

—Severina, how do you like your new padrona?

—Don't start with me, prince, said the old, gnarled woman behind the counter.

I tried to ease the huge door back, to wait until they were gone, but it creaked, and then there was nothing to do but go in. Over Giulio's shoulder, Marie-Antoinette gawked at what must have looked like a lost, oversized orphan. By now, my dress was threadbare. Giulio turned to see who she was staring at. Then he too stared, as if I had come to the inn on my own and he was stunned to see me. I fought the urge to turn and run, and walked straight towards him.

—How *are* you? he said, cupping his hands around my face like a set of blinders.

I wriggled out of his hands and turned to face Marie-Antoinette. But she was sprinting up the stairs.

—I need the key, I said quietly.

The old woman arched a disapproving eyebrow. —We're serving till ten, she said severely, and handed me the huge latchkey she was holding. Don't lose it.

Giulio's head flushed. —No no. He uncurled my fingers, took back the key.

—Giulio? I said. You were telling me why you chose plastic surgery? The tactic was idiotic, I knew; but I couldn't stand how embarrassed by me he was.

—Because I hate sick people, he said softly, like a trapped animal. He ran a hand over his head, recovering himself, then turned to the old woman. —I'll be a little while. Could you—

The delta of wrinkles around her puckered lips deepened with amusement. She nodded. Now that she'd understood that the three of us were not going to be up in the same room, all at once, she seemed to be enjoying Giulio's predicament.

—I'll put her in nine, she said.

—Nine. Nine is nice, Giulio said, then sprinted up the stairs, two at a time.

The old woman pulled a key off the board, then glanced at the Savant.

—You don't have in mind to play that loud, do you?

Me. Play loud. I smiled and shook my head. Still, she put back the key she had and pulled another one off the board to give me. She pointed to the narrow stairway at the back of the entrance hall.

Room thirteen was halfway up the stairs off a cramped, poorly lit landing. Its small dark wood door curved to a pointed arch that was hardly taller than the Savant. Even before I could insert the key, the door swung open. The tiny space seemed some sort of closet. Three of the walls hugged a rumpled single bed. Its stained sheets gave off a musty smell. On the floor next to it sat a bucket of cleaning supplies. I heard footsteps, and hauled the Savant inside and shut the door. This was the sort of situation I knew well, in which no other asylum would be forthcoming.

The one window, a narrow slot high up on the opposite wall, shot a sliver of moonlight onto an old, yellowing wall lamp. I tried the switch. Nothing. I felt: it had no bulb. I wanted to wash my face, but there was no sink. Wandering the halls, looking for the bathroom, my ears would surely pick up random strains of desperation or desire. Less and less room in my chest to take in air, then less and less air, my breaths quicker, useless, hemidemi-semiquavers, giving no relief. Where was Giulio? I scanned my cell, hoping the walls might yield instruction, a hint or a command. If only I could fly through them like music, could fly out like a sound wave, traveling forever into the infinite night, back towards the light of the stars—

(going on)

I thought of Leopold's widow, grieving. Of how she had kept packing, even as we talked. The notation was a simple *andante*. To make the bed, to lie on top of the bedspread withought allowing myself to speculate on the stains beneath. To shut my eyes and take myself en route to somewhere else. To conjure basic forward motion. The jostlings of a train. Better yet, a plane high in the air, far from any ground.

I flicked out the sheet, smoothed the bedspread, lay down, and shut my eyes, imagining my cello strapped in the seat next to me. A lady on the aisle, knitting. The click of seat belt, the tray flipping down—the success of mental journeys elsewhere rests on banalities such as these. On the engine's monotonous plainchant. On the knitting needles' steady skris skris skris. The knitting woman twisting her overhead nozzle, and air blowing down. But the nozzle seemed to be blowing only air, only air. If something else was mixed in, I couldn't smell it. Of course, if you were going to put something in, it would cause less panic if what you put in was odorless. But wasn't gas odorless? A stewardess appeared and began her ritual semaphore. For the first time ever, I took out the card and looked for the exits. What I had to do was concentrate on learning, on learning the rules of how things worked. Because sooner or later, the plane was going down.

In the middle of the flight I opened my eyes. The ache in my head made it seem as if hours had passed. I had the new car key, but probably Giulio had a second one: I wondered if, after our scene in the lobby, his plan was simply to leave me here. I gathered up my things, sneaked out through the deserted lobby, and went out to the parking lot. Giulio's new Alfa was still there. If I waited in the car, he could not leave without me. I sat in the driver's seat and held the little bar by the door to make the seat go back flat. Then the plane had landed. I was arriving in Milwaukee, standing with my cello in the baggage claim area of the Milwaukee airport, listening to the fake-cheery Musak, waiting for my trunk. Clayton was also waiting. We were the last two people. Instead of watching the conveyor, he was staring at my body. I looked down and saw that it had grown up during the flight. Now inside my old self was a new intruder, curving out, whose shape I had no control over. I pulled my cello in front of my body, made a decision to walk around with it strapped to my front from now on, the way they had in Renaissance pageants. Then my knee knocked against something. Giulio's car phone was off the hook, beeping angrily. I woke, sat up, pushing random buttons. There was a series of tones. Then it connected and was ringing. I had pushed the automatic dial. Then I heard a click and a pop and Clayton's lonely, tinny—*Pronto.*

—Clayton? I said, not understanding.

—You're not here, Clayton said. Giulio's phone had speed-dialed my number at the Pettywards'; he was at home, I realized, in my bed. —So where are you?

—Near Bolzano. They let you out?

—They said I could come back Wednesday.

Of course I ought to have asked why the hospital had unbandaged his eyes and released him, when three hours before there'd been no talk of it. To have considered that to get home Clayton would have had to remove his bandage and use his hemmorhaging eye. But on another level his sudden improvement seemed obvious: my loving him had been the danger, and I had moved myself away.

—How are you? I said, waiting for him to tell me about the fish.

—Never better, he said. I got dog biscuits, I got drugs, and I brought my little TV in your room. I'm watching an old movie of some bleach-blond porn star who got elected to Parliament.

—You had dinner at the hospital?

—Catered by the brides of Christ.

—How did you get home?

—I have my ways, he said.

I had no idea what that meant. —I'm sorry, about—

He cut me off. —I said a few words in Latin and flushed the toilet. I only need one Isabel, anyway.

Through the windshield, a wedge of light widened as Giulio stepped outside the side door of the inn. A tangled cloud of finches exploded from the arched, leafy trellis, then clotted again and disappeared within its quivering black vines. Clayton had gone back home, I realized, to be in bed with me.

—And how's your date?

Giulio reached the car and got in. That was the moment when I ought to have told him about Clayton leaving the hospital, ought to have considered that, to get home, Clayton must have removed his eye patch, moved the injured eye, and ridden on a bumpy tram. But I was speechless with awe at his stubborn, naked, unprotected love, its tide rushing at me no matter what I did. I had bullied and betrayed him, lied to him and left him, had killed his family of fish. And still his love burned as faith. If I had burned his skin he would have found a way to love me with his flesh.

My silence was crushing him. I could hear it. Clayton was in my bed, waiting for the rest. But the gap between us was too great. There was no way to explain that I was loving him by leaving, to speak of what would happen if I stayed. I heard the line go dead. Still I held the phone against my ear. After a minute it began beeping. Giulio gently took it from my hand and pressed *End.*

—Seeing someone else? Giulio asked softly.

—Not anymore, I said.

We lay side by side, staring at the beams in the cathedral ceiling. The silence was immense. I lay listening, remembering how it had fallen on me like a layer of fresh snow, each time I performed.

—Quiet, I said.

Giulio picked an apple from the fruit basket beside the bed. —That's why I love the mountains.

His bite scissored through the silence. He offered me the apple, but I shook my head. I had never been able to stand the violence of the crunch needed to eat the fruit.

—At least the Mediterranean doesn't roar like an ocean.

He threw back his head like a sword swallower and lowered the apple core into his mouth by its stem, crunching seeds. —Oceans give me nightmares.

The small round sandstone tower was lit by dozens of votive candles burning in a slanted, heart-shaped rack. It was the kind of hideout that, at any other time, I would have dreamed of discovering. But I had never imagined myself, once inside. Outside the alcove windows, clusters of tiny lights dotted the other side of the valley. A wave of homesickness rushed through me to be in any one of those places, where one day was like the next. I thought of Clayton, sleeping in my bed.

—*Scusa,* Giulio said. I'm sorry that took so long. But what could I do? I mean the reason I know Marie-Antoinette is that she's Fabio's patient. I had to calm her down. And she wasn't thrilled to see me here with you.

—What method did you employ to calm her?

—Sometimes you speak Italian like an eighteenth-century chambermaid.

—I learned Italian from librettos.

Giulio took a sip of wine. —Who writes those librettos, anyway?

—Answer the question.

—*Porco Dio,* he sputtered. It's not that interesting. Marie-Antoinette left Pettyward because he couldn't perform. His foreskin's too tight. He needs a simple operation, which he refuses to have.

A working penis was not something anybody needed Giulio for. Silently, I pressed him. He shook his head. —Really. What I do with anyone else is of no use to you. You need what you need, and she what she needs. It must be like music. Probably Beethoven needs what Beethoven needs, and so with Brahms.

—You serve up pronouncements like you're living in Plato's Republic.

—But isn't it true?

—What you need can change.

He smiled. —Only once you get it.

My chest tightened. Being locked into what you needed, to what you lacked—it sounded like a life sentence, trapped in the prison of your own deficiencies. Like a slow-building charge, the work I had done to change the Savant's bridge detonated inside me—how much I wanted, I still wanted, to play it. I was terrified of letting go that way again.

—Before my parents died, I said, I needed to perform. Then they died, and I stopped being able—I broke. And now I'm not that person. And I don't need—

I stood up. I had let out too many words.

Giulio took hold of my wrist. —Just sit a minute, he said, his voice quiet as gauze. He downed his wine, and poured us each another glass. —All I meant was, when I started surgery, I thought that by mastering technique, I would become a master. I imagined leaving some tiny immortal mark of my art in every body I operated on. Instead each breast, each face, needs a slightly different art. And I must remake myself to them. And to each person. Some women need to be loved away from self-mutilation, while others can only love a self that isn't them, can only love themselves by altering what they are. So they have to cut to come to rest.

—What you need can change, I said again.

I stared out the window, wishing I could fly off with his set of wings. But there was Giulio, holding out his hand to lead me to the bed.

—It doesn't help to hate what you need, he said quietly.

On the bed, my eyes closed, I felt him lay his finger on my nose.

—What are you doing?

—Measuring.

—So you can fix me?

A soft kiss, on the tip of my nose. —So that when you're gone

I will have in my finger not just my finger, but also the length of your nose.

He took for granted that all this was temporary. —That's the kind of thing you said to her? I said, trying for witty repartee. Giulio winced at the edge in my tone. I wanted to swallow my words. —How do you know I'm leaving?

Giulio took my hand and began stretching my fingers back and forth in splits. —I haven't done a thing for you.

—Careful, I said, worried that he'd crack my knuckles, that he might injure them, that I might not feel the release coming.

—You know in some ways, Isabel, health is self-forgetfulness. His fingers clamped onto the fleshy muscle at the base of my thumbs. A jolt ran through my limbs. —It's all right, he said. Do you know what this little cushion on your palm is called? The mound of Venus. I love probing the curve, finding the trigger point beneath it. When you're in pain, he went on, it's like that touch: Your whole body is the hurt. Then for a while, even after your body gets better, your mind is still sick with memory. Because your life still revolves around protecting yourself from the past. It's only when you stop always protecting—that is when you are healed.

—I know.

—Of course you know. I'm just saying. It's just a gift.

—I thought you didn't believe in God.

He lowered his face to my ear. —Not God's gift to you. Your gift to me.

The almondy smell of skin, his quiet immoveable bodily persistence—it was like trying to swim against an undertow. Even my breath, I suddenly noticed, had fallen in with his tempo. I could not stop thinking about what Giulio had done with Marie-Antoinette.

It was the erotic draw of sight-reading someone else's score, the gravitational pull of giving your body over to the wants of another.

—I want to do what you did.

—You want?

—What you did to her.

Giulio shook his head. I nodded again.

—You're not kidding.

I shook my head.

—It's a *nothing*, he said. Mary Ann can only come in a chair.

—And?

—And I wear a suit and tie.

—And?

—And I look at my watch while we do it. As if on cue, Giulio's beeper went off. He pulled it out of his pocket to check the number. He smiled, looking slightly too pleased with himself, then glanced at his watch.

—I mean I don't have much time, he said, putting on his pants.

He dressed quickly and confidently. It was as if my request had lowered a needle onto a groove, and all he had to do was let the record play out.

—This isn't right, I said.

Giulio looked dismayed. —What seems not right about it?

—It is wrong from beginning to end.

He thrashed his limbs around. —So a few things got altered, he said as he got up. At the fireplace, he began stabbing at the logs. The fire flamed up. A spark popped loudly.

—Of course you're right, he went on. Probably that's what love is. Breaking in where you don't deserve to be, and being allowed. And letting someone else break in. I suppose it's violent by nature.

He set down his poker, came back to the bed, and lay back down, curled on his side as if punched in the stomach.

—Whoever you are, he pleaded softly, I'll hide you and heal you in my horizontal confessional. But that's a trust I just can't break.

I curled around him, breathing in his scent, and let myself see the obvious. He too dragged some unspeakable past. He too could not let himself be known. He kept all his women from needing him by skating them out onto the same thin ice. But even as I was busy understanding, I was drinking in his wide feet, their architectural arches, his indestructible fireplug torso. I could feel my hips expanding. It seemed as if, if there were no possibility of loving, we could do each other no harm.

After a while he turned me onto my back and looked down into my eyes, searching for a judgment. When he found none his eyes widened, then watered in disbelief. He kissed me slowly, all over my face, for longer than I could have imagined, until I reached up and pulled him to me. Then we tore at each other like two refugees who had just been released. But the moment he entered me something inside him backed away. After a moment, I felt him go soft. His torso was grinding through the motions, but something in him couldn't do it. I took his hips in my hands and stilled them, to let him know he could cease what was now a charade.

Giulio rolled away, lay his head on my stomach, and held my hips. Clutched. A wave of silent shuddering rolled through him. I felt a hotness, the wetness of tears on my belly. Then, like a storm passing, his grip unfurled.

—You see, he said quietly, I—I can't really love.

I gathered him up to me and took him in my arms. The truth in that distance, in his failure, made me feel closer than I ever had. I cradled his head. Then I shifted sideways and eased his face in between my breasts.

—I could live here, he said softly, and then he was asleep.

A while later he woke with a start.

—Is there anything you want? I asked, stroking his head.

—I'm so tired, he whispered. I want not to have to want.

Giulio got up and threw two more logs on the fire. I crawled out of bed, wrapped a blanket around me, and opened the Savant's case. The soft paintings on the belly of the instrument glimmered in the firelight. I leaned it between my thighs and tuned. Giulio went back to bed and threw his arms over his head and stretched, the ropes of his muscles shuddering. Finally I poised my bow.

—Shut your eyes, I said.

—I want to watch, he said, like a child.

—I can't play when I can see the person's face.

—It might be nice for the person.

I bent down behind the cello and pretended to adjust the end pin. Then I rosined my bow. The caesura stretched longer and longer, as for some reason I remembered again the carton of rosins from the Nazi storage depot on the floor of the luthier's janitor closet, and my stomach sickened, thinking as I had not before about each of those cubes of chalk as the square-packed dust of a person. The impossible thought that seized my mind was that I was rubbing my bow with some musician's remains. Giulio must have wondered if I would rosin until the end of time, for after some time, who knows how long, he came over and took the cube from my hand. Then he set aside the Savant and softly bit the scruff of my neck, like an animal ready to carry its young. An arm wrapped around my breasts, the other around my stomach. Slowly he pulled me up from behind. He sat down. Sat me on his lap, across him. Took the bow from my hand. His humming sank down into my gut, warm and burning. Slowly, he drew the bow across my belly. Latticed my thighs and my belly with streaks of white. Drew the grainy grit across the tips of my nipples until they stood hard at attention.

—Now you're covered.

I stood up. He stood up behind me. I turned. He pulled me to him, mixing the powder between our skin.

—If we're not careful, he said, we might get stuck.

—Fuck you.

He smiled, then stretched out on the bed, folded his hands behind his head. —That's what I'm asking.

I shut my eyes and tried to drop everything out of my mind and hear the music, for somewhere, I knew, it had to still be there. What could possibly go wrong? I told myself. I tried to focus, to let time slide out like syrup, to remember the way each note could slow to a stop for me to play it. To imagine floating out, the phrases rolling over Giulio and winding up the walls. To put myself where there was no bow, no hand, no skin, no wood. But then I opened my eyes. I glanced again at Giulio. His smile looked too pleased. It came to me, that playing was what he'd meant for me all along. And I knew I couldn't do it.

Giulio saw the distress on my face. He came to me, eased the bow from my clutching hand, and guided me to the bed. He held me until our failed performances faded, until all that was left was the smell of skin, the warm overtones of flesh, the rise and fall of our coupled breaths. After a time I felt him harden against me, but still we lay there, the silence stretched out and building. Then Giulio crawled between my legs and took me in a kiss that was slower than one of Bocherini's excruciating middle movements. And drank until I lost all measure. As my last note faded, a wash of distant sobbing came into my ear. All at once I knew what had happened, that the sobbing was Marie-Antoinette. She had called the hospital, and discovered Clayton was gone. Giulio had told her about Clayton's injury, and she had called the hospital, and when the nurses discovered he wasn't there she sent someone to find him at home. That was why he had been so confused on the phone. He was bleeding to death. Probably he had been hemorrhaging, even as he called me from my bed.

The jagged western Alps reached up and up into a fog thick with moonlight, their bald stone ridges looming like a gargantuan muscle, as the car climbed north. Through patches of low-lying clouds the moon cast a fuzzy lunar glare on the stone. Enough traffic clogged the road to force me to focus, to drive the echo of Marie-Antoinette's sobbing out of my ear, the sobbing I had run from with Giulio's wallet and keys, the minute he got in the shower. The sobbing I had run through, to get to the car. Had heard even as I started the ignition, as the pair of headlights, a police cruiser, flickered around the curve in the road and came to a halt at the inn. Had left the car in second gear, all the way down the mountain, to drown out. But at the bottom, when I reached the T in the road, I could hear it again. South would be warmer, but the weather was clear: sooner or later, the carabinieri would be looking for me. The road north to Bolzano blazed in artificial light. As soon as I turned right, I knew where I was going.

Now an alarm rang in the car: it was Giulio's car phone, ringing. I swerved and nearly hit a car in the next lane. Again it rang. I reached down and picked it up: static, then a beep. It went dead.

I put it down. It rang again. I pressed at buttons to turn it off, but an ocean of static filled the car, and then there was a voice.

—Tell me where you are. Giulio's voice slithered out through the speaker like a snake, its muscle tightening around me, pulling me back. Could he track me down because I had answered? Then glaring yellow light swept around me, brighter than midday, and I was inside a tunnel. The phone went dead. I clicked it off, grateful for the quiet inside the mountain, that there was only one road now, that it went straight. I would simply go straight until I could think of what to do. I'd been hoping against hope that Clayton was alive, but I knew why Giulio was calling. As the car flew out of the tunnel, the phone was ringing again.

I pushed the green button. Ambient fuzz filled the car, then snippets of Giulio's voice. —Clayton left the hospital.

—He went home.

—You learned this WHEN? Giulio shouted.

I gripped the steering wheel and stared forward. By running from Clayton, by trying to protect him from me, and from his own desires, I had caused his death. There was no place to go, nowhere to be; wherever I went, I would do damage, would leave someone behind. The cars were breaking for traffic. Around the curve I saw the sign for the Brenner Pass into Austria. I pushed *Off;* the phone went dead. I was approaching the border, with no passport but Clayton's in my purse. But there was no break in the rail, no exit to make a U-turn. The slopes below the highway were thickly covered with sharp, spiky evergreens that looked as if they'd impale you if you pulled over and jumped. It was just after three A.M.; I wondered if I might take advantage of a guard change. I steered towards the longest line of cars. With eight cars between me and the checkpoint I rooted in my purse for my old Milwaukee library card and pried the photo out of its old-fashioned metal corners. I wondered if I could somehow stick it onto Clayton's passport, if maybe somebody might not notice. But when I saw his freckled face, in the only picture I would ever have of him, I could not bring myself to ruin it by tearing it out. Then I glanced up ahead and saw I needn't bother. The drivers ahead were dangling their unopened passports out the window as they rolled past the snoozy border guard.

I stalled out, restarted the car, and edged by, drenched in sweat. A little while later I paid a toll, then stopped for gas. Giulio had more currencies in his wallet than I would have thought possible; to avoid using his credit cards I paid in a combination of lire and Swiss francs. In the bathroom it hurt to pee, as if my body had thought to solve the identity problem by dissolving itself, by excreting self-dissolving acid. The pain was sharp and burning and did not pass. I may have slept a moment. Then I bought three large bottles of water and got back on the road. The night was unseasonably warm, the roads dry and empty. Past Innsbruck, as the road began to descend, the landscape changed. Rows of grapevines now lined the base of the hills. They were propped on crutches like legions of the stooped and gnarled, eternally lined up for some pitiless, middle-of-the-night roll call. Amid them someone had built an escape road for out-of-control trucks, a steep uphill dead-end off the shoulder of the road. Lit from above by spotlights, the ramp jutted up into the glowing fog like an ugly concrete ramp to heaven, abandoned midconstruction: it was the Third Reich as architectural joke.

Austria had been the straightest route out of Italy, and Germany had come without warning. Between Austria and Germany there was no checkpoint to warn you of the border. But the driving changed. Here the cars were bearing down, their angry brights flashing six feet behind your bumper the minute their progress was impeded. I wanted to get off the road, off this aorta of efficiency and rage, but the last thing would be to leave the Savant in Germany, to drop it to sink in the sea of furniture and silver and paintings and houses, of tapestries and factories, bought with hard-earned money in *perfectly legal transactions*— things relabeled, reengraved, reembroidered, reframed, recertified, reincorporated, repossessed. *(Ssh! the children!)* Innocent children, children settling more or less comfortably now into late middle age, children who along with their children live decent, classical-music-loving, American-movie-watching lives. God in heaven! Can that be an efficient use of time? One could hardly imagine anything less productive than obsessing on the provenance of one's linen or silver or paintings. Nor could it be of value in the area of travel to dawdle behind someone who lacked the wherewithal to purchase even your basic Mercedes, a sensible highway car, because of course all Mercedes are sensible, they last forever, unlike—

There was something wrong with my ears. I tried to call up the sound of Clayton's humming, of Marie-Antoinette's sobbing, anything to drown out the voices that had lodged there. Then stars floated across my eyes. My depth perception was unraveling: I could not tell the hills I was seeing from those I had already seen, either on this road or elsewhere, nor what was large and far from what was small and near. Also I was soaking wet. The thing to do was to get out of Germany, to turn towards the east. I had missed the turnoff for the Czech Republic at Nürnburg; now I was nearly past Chemnitz. An exit was approaching.

I veered off onto the shoulder, then swerved back onto the road and nearly lost control of the car.

A spectral glow began collecting on the horizon. On smaller and smaller roads, I tried Dubi, then Teplice, but at each border crossing a line of cars sat waiting, even at this ungodly hour. One by one, the cars were being stopped at the Czech border. Of course, exiting Germany would be tougher than entering. There was nothing I could do to make myself look nice: pale and sweating, my faced clenched from pain, my hair filthy, I was bound to get stopped.

On the German side, parallel to the border, I veered over the oncoming lane onto a mucky dirt track that ran through a field, parallel to the border. Potholes sent searing jolts of pain up through me. I was hoping to find some place where I could drive across a field to the other side of the border and run into a forest. In the survivors' books I had read in Milwaukee, people had talked a lot about the forests being good places to hide. But a knee-high iron railing ran along the border, dividing the Czech dust from German: it looked maddeningly, Sovietishly sturdy. Probably it would hold even if I rammed it with the magnificent rubber bumpers of Giulio's Alfa. And I could not make it on foot, with the Savant, without attracting attention. And I had to go to the bathroom again, badly. Finally I came upon another tiny road, another border station, with about ten cars before me. Why was I surprised that, to get out of Germany, I would have to get in line? Then I remembered my hair, that all I had was Clayton's passport. I reached down to Giulio's medical bag and groped around until I found a scissors, and adjusted the rearview mirror, and as the cars edged forward, I cut it off at the scalp.

The pimply adolescent guard at the border looked nauseatingly proud of himself. His uniform had little corner-creases at the nipples from where he'd ironed and folded it. I slowed to the booth, easing the car into first.

He sniffed at the car disdainfully. I had not bathed. He glanced at the passport, then at me, then paged through the passport again.

He straightened up.

—This passport is not valid, he said in English.

I sat up straighter. —*Doch,* I insisted in German, though I had a snowball's chance in hell of being taken for a sixteen-year-old boy.

—*Ne, ne,* he reiterated.

I reached for my purse, to find Giulio's wallet. The guard put a hand on the holster of his gun. I sat back up and gripped the steering wheel.

—It doesn't have the proper seal, he said. It's not valid without the seal.

A deep breath kept me from bursting into laughter. My little friend swaggered, angling his hips towards the car.

—I've used it a hundred times, I said.

Again he paged through it. —You only have one stamp.

—I filled up the old one, and had to get a new one. They must have screwed it up.

—Vehicle registration?

I hesitated a bit too long.

—Whose car is it?

—It's borrowed. If he thought I was rich, I'd surely have to bribe him.

—Papers, he said, his hand still on his gun.

I reached over into the glove compartment. Giulio's rubber gloves tumbled out on the floor. —They're here somewhere, I said.

—Pull over, he said, lowering the metal gate. —No cars are allowed over the border without papers. They get stolen. You'll have to turn around.

—It's borrowed from a friend who's in Prague, I said, pulling the registration card from Giulio's wallet.

The boy looked at me, looked at the registration, then looked back up again. —This car wouldn't be stolen, would it?

I shook my head. —Giulio wouldn't steal. He's a doctor.

—Pull over.

I nodded. He glanced back at the cars beginning to honk behind us. If I got out, he would search the car and find the Savant, and that would be that. Slowly, the decision came to me, that I would save myself, the only way I could. The pain, combined with the long release after drinking three large bottles of water, was indescribable. When I was done I told him I couldn't get the car into reverse. He grumbled that he would do it, and opened my door. Slowly I crawled out. He stared at the puddle of urine on my seat, the pile of hair on the passenger seat. His nostrils flared in disgust.

—Get the hell out of here, he said, shoving the papers into my gut.

The heavy traffic crept through the border zone like a slow procession into hell. The air acrid and sweet on my tongue from the exhaust of the mile-long convoy of German trucks, idling on the shoulder. In front and between them, packs of teenage prostitutes with dyed, too-bright hair stood in ratty clothes, sucking on kiddie boxes of juice with straws. After a time the roadside brothel thinned out to clusters of boys straddling bikes, who were smoking and kicking dirt. We were crawling into the heart of the brown coal region, our road snaking beside a smaller one that snaked beside a muddy river. On the little road, pairs of children wearing gas masks were carrying their satchels to school. As distant hills emerged an intense déjà vu overtook me; for a moment I wondered whether I was trapped upon the despoiled remains of the beautiful landscape on the Theresienstadt stamp, with its lush trees in the foreground, the brook winding back towards hills, the huge cumulus clouds in the distance, the strolling travelers completing the pastorale. At least these children now, I thought to myself, would arrive with gas masks in hand.

I tried to shake off the past, to shake myself back into the present. The sun was trying to break through the smog, and the traffic was making its way—I could see it—towards a bright green patch of the Bohemian forest. Then the snake of brake lights lit up red again, and we sat idling, waiting for a rickety train to pass. The cloudy air lit up. Soon I would be in the forest. But the ground ahead looked surreal, too green and even, like a flat, unnatural carpet stretching out for miles. The trees' bright green leaves and bark were the same fake green. Some toxic human-poison, I saw now, had dyed the place a creepy glowing emerald. The trees were not wintering or lichened, but encrusted in environmental blight.

A tea-stained drizzle began to fall, relieving the claustrophobia of the deadly human slag left on the landscape. I turned on the wipers, grateful for their steady click-clack. The wipers' rhythm began to make me drowsy. I reached up for my chignon, to wiggle my scalp, but all that was left of my hair was stubble. I rooted in my purse for the earrings Giulio had given me, hoping to pinch my ears awake, but I had forgotten them. On the radio I skimmed by the *Lachrymosa*, a medley of holy music, and a BBC news broadcast about two Turkish refugees who had been set on fire with gasoline by Dresden skinheads. The news turned to soccer. I fiddled the dial again, looking for some standard-issue pop music to flatten the roiling in my gut. Into a tiny vacuum of silence wandered the haunting opening motif of the cello solo from the *Quartet for the End of Time.* Messiaen wrote it while interned in a camp in Silesia, for the only four instruments in that camp. His was the Christian end of time from the Book of Revelation, conceived of not as death but beyond death, beyond time, the moment of revelation when the Sabbath in its repose prolongs itself into eternity. Yuri had seethed when I'd chosen the piece for my debut; whenever we'd pass a church he'd mutter, *Irrelevant!* meaning New Testament values, post-Shoah, which he felt had enabled evil to flourish. But it was this same stretching, a stretching towards the impossible, that gave rise to the four separate prisoners' orchestras in Theresienstadt, to the hundreds of recitals and lieder concerts, to the seventeen operas and operettas performed in a little over three years, to the fifty-five performances of *Brundibar* alone, to the staying up for two straight nights after working all day on dishwater rations to rush the premiere of a Czech opera to Wednesday, because the Nazis had pronounced, at noon Monday, that starting Thursday all public utterances should be only in German. It was this same impulse elsewhere, that same stretching to a *beyond*, that had inspired the living dead, had saved the lives of the survivors and the lives of the dead while they remained among the living.

Messiaen said that the work was never again listened to with such attentiveness and focus as at that first performance for those prisoners in Silesia. But this radio performance was gripping, the opening motif rising up again like the last curl of smoke from a conflagration, the melody both scorched by the inferno and soaring wildly beyond its captivity. It couldn't be someone who'd actually been in a camp—I knew the recordings before my debut, and this wasn't one of them—yet whoever it was had been there, was spiraling down to the music's quiet bottom, wending towards Messiaen's moment of revelation as if there were only one moment left in the world, the notes falling out from a place beyond time, beyond its one-way tyranny. This was the whole content of history, felt as a single touch of bow and string.

There was the sign for Lovosice. I was close. A door in my gut opened at the prospect of entering the walled fortress where my grandfather had died of starvation, my grandmother of typhus. A tiny, neon-red square, the fuel light, bled up from the dashboard—a silent alarm reminding me not to help him track me. I could not stop. The music on the radio, rushing out from a timeless center, forbade digression. I would find someone who would take the cash in Giulio's wallet and take me to Terezin. Would set down Hitler's *gift*, the Theresienstadt I carried, and merge it with the town of Terezin, and leave them both behind.

A sign. Lovosice. Swooning with pain, I plodded along for a half kilometer against a steady stream of oncoming traffic. Finally I saw a red cross sign for a pharmacy and pulled in. I scribbled some illegible scratches on the blank prescription pad I'd found in Giulio's glove compartment. When the metal gate rolled up, I made my way to the back counter by holding on to the shelves. English? He shook his head. In my best German I announced to the old pharmacist that an Italian doctor had given me this prescription for a urine infection, that I was sure he would know what it meant. He sniffled, his face puckering at my smell. I pulled out Giulio's wallet and spread the various currencies in it like an open hand of cards. He took ten American dollars.

—For this you don't need a prescription, he said, handing me a bottle. I took two pills there. He followed me to the doorway. I got in the car and drove.

When Giulio's car finally sputtered empty, I pulled over to the shoulder and got out the Savant. I left the leather binder of Giulio's documents in the glove compartment. By the time the Czech authorities called Giulio, I'd be long gone.

My brain began skipping on its new problem, the problem of what to do with Giulio's phone. I wanted to ditch it; but chances were some law-abiding lemming would find it and turn it in to the authorities. I shoved it in the duffel and pulled out the trunk's last item, the canister of gas. Lined up aside the ditch, the Savant and the duffel and the canister looked like a pathetic little family about to be interned in a camp. The car I eased into neutral and rolled, pushing from the open door, into a shallow ditch. Then with a piece of Giulio's laundry I wiped my fingerprints from the upholstery and the wheel, the handles of the door.

The cold drizzle damped down the odor-cloud of stench that clung to my body. I was walking down a potholed road towards a grim little industrial town, my body still weak, but no longer screaming. The pills were working. Truck after truck sprayed by. After a while a dilapidated train chugged by across a field in my direction. I trudged through the squishy mud. The tracks would lead to the train station. I stepped up between the rails and walked towards the receding train, counting wooden ties, grateful not to have to navigate. Somewhere close to a thousand, a train chugged up behind me. I jumped out of its way. The ground around me, I noticed now, was striped with tracks and littered with rusted freight cars, with cargo cars, with rusty chemical drums. The train ground to a halt. As I passed it I found myself facing a circle of workers in grimy blue jumpsuits. They were passing a good-sized bottle of Becherovka. With a ceremonial belch one of them began poking at the tracks with an iron pole. Then the one about to guzzle noticed me, held up the bottle, and yelled, *Medizin!* I hurried between them.

I climbed the steep set of rusty metal stairs that led onto the platform. A little ways away, a mother and two small infants were sitting on a bench. The name on the board did not say Terezin. I approached the mother and asked in English where the train was headed. She snatched up her infants and hurried away. I turned towards two middle-aged ladies waiting on the platform. They shook their heads at me to keep me away. It occurred to me that I was used to my own smell. The worker stepped aside, and the train shuddered into the station. At the other end of my platform, the mother was pointing at me to a man in a uniform. I needed to try to blend into the confusion, but there was no confusion. The train's doors clattered open; no passengers got off; the three women I'd approached got on; and then I was alone on the platform. I knew I should get on to get away from the uniformed guard. At the same time I didn't want to risk getting on unless I knew where it was going. The train pulled away. On the other side of where it had been, a scattering of people walked over the broken cement and gravel between the sets of tracks. I ran across the tracks behind them. The little uniformed man shouted something at me. I followed them around the side of the station building to another platform, on the other side, where another, smaller train was waiting. The board above it said Litomerice. It was the Litomerice gate, Yuri had said, where the train entered Terezin. This was my lucky day.

No conductor passed by during the short half-hour ride. At our first stop I asked some teenagers, *Litomerice?* They signaled a few more stops. I dozed off. Then one tapped me on the shoulder. We were stopped. He pointed out the door to an unlabeled building the size of a public bathroom. I thanked them and waved, to let them know I was staying on until Terezin. But then I looked out and saw that this was where the tracks ended.

Through the low, ugly, beige buildings, three roads wandered away from the station. A stout, balding elderly woman clutched bunches of plastic shopping bags around her elephantine legs. I picked up one she had dropped, waited as she shifted her burdens, and asked the way to Terezin in English. She shouted back a dense, incomprehensible wad of Czech. I tried Italian, then French: nothing. Finally I had to speak German, to say the word *Theresienstadt.* She jerked her chin towards the center road.

I wandered around the town for what seemed like hours. Litomerice looked as if it had aspired to charm for fifteen minutes sometime during the Hapsburg reign, then gotten drunk and let its face go to hell. Most of the buildings were decrepit and peeling; a few had been refaced in gooey apricot. There was not one tree in the town. It was late afternoon; I needed to find a bank to get Czech money, to bribe someone to take me to Terezin. After a while I stumbled on the only one in the town. Though tellers sat around listlessly gossiping, the windows were all closed. They told me to come back tomorrow and went back to their conversation. I asked about Terezin. They chattered back and forth. The tourist trade was not exactly burgeoning.

On the street I asked two women for the train to Terezin. One pointed me up a hill, the other down. At the end of a cobbled road I came to a fenced-in pen of rusted machinery. Down a side street, two women chatted over a fence. I hurried towards them. They hurried away as if I were a thief or a prostitute. An old man pointed me down a road that looped out over the hillside and towards the bottom of town. I started walking. Sometime later I spotted a narrow zigzagging alleyway, loosely paved with cobblestones, that led down. On top of the next hill, on the horizon, I saw a big square tower. That would be the center of town.

The alley was flanked by tiny thatched-roof trailers set on dry plots of dirt. The only relief in the flat sequence of rubble was a dilapidated chapel whose ravaged, patched stone facade ornament was chewed and broken. Birds perched on the ledges of its missing upper windows. One of its doors was off the hinges and leaned against the cracked and half-eroded plaster. A strip of yellow plastic hazard tape was draped around the padlock on the rusted-iron gate. Staring at it, I misstepped. The paving, I saw, was giving way to sand. The few cobblestones left were now stuck in at angles or dislodged entirely. I went slowly. This was not the place to sprain my ankle. When I next looked up, I was standing in front of a lean-to with a plastic tarp roof. A grizzled man with dirty toenails stared at me from a plastic patio chair. Somewhere, dogs were barking. Then I regained sight of the square tower and headed up towards it. Two filthy workmen in overalls shouted a question, over and over, louder and louder. I hurried up a huge set of stairs. There was bound to be someone in the center of town.

What I came upon, though, was a deserted courtyard. Two diagonal dirt paths crisscrossed the overgrown brown grass. It was a churchyard, nothing more, flanked on either side by low tan plaster buildings. A stopped clock adorned the tower. Not a soul was in sight. If I collapsed and died there, I thought, no one would know or care. My next thought was that Giulio would never find me. Somewhere in the distance some school-children were singing a patriotic hymn. It occurred to me that this was a weekday. The fresh, sweet air smelled maddeningly like Clayton. I looked down the staircase I'd come up. At the bottom the two workmen who'd been yelling at me were leaning against buildings on either side of it, arms folded, waiting. I turned and hurried across the courtyard to an opening between the church and the small church house beside it.

This dirt alley, its matted mud gouged from rainwater, was even more rugged than the first one. At the end of it I saw the exposed butt-crack of a man hammering beneath the hood of his three-wheeled truck. I ran down the hill and begged him to tell me where the center of town was. He looked me up and down as if considering whether to ignore the interruption, then pointed to a footpath up the side of the hill. It was under construction. I had to walk across loose boards covering a gaping hole with huge, hissing pipes. I looked back. Again the workmen were following me. I ducked through the long beads in the doorway of a dark little grocery store. The women standing around backed away from my overwhelming stench. I offered them about fifty dollars, worth of Swiss francs. The grocer took one of the bills and held it up to the light; then she nodded. I shoved a wedge of cheese and a hunk of bread in my mouth. By the time I was done, the workmen outside had gathered up two more friends; they were leaning against the building across the street, smoking. I sprinted up the zigzag walkway. Finally, I reached a cobblestone piazza. Considerately, in the center of town a map had been provided telling you how to reach the center of town. There was a visitor information center. It was closed. I noticed the clean glass windows of a little hotel across the square that was refaced in a sickly bubble-gum pink. I went in to ask where the station was. The clerk said there were two and asked where I wanted to go. I told him Terezin. He gave me a look that said, *Not there.* Then he quietly said that there was only a bus, that the train ended here, at Litomerice. Though there was definitely a train from Litomerice to Terezin—Yuri had ridden it right through Terezin's walls—I let it pass. Did he know the bus schedule? He said the last bus had left. I asked the room rates. He quoted an exorbitant price and asked for my passport. When he saw it was American, and not German, he lowered the rate by half.

I had avoided using Giulio's credit cards, in case he had reported them lost or stolen. Now I had no choice. I picked one and handed it to the attendant, and began to pray. The clerk smiled broadly at the sight of a Visa, punched in the amount, and swiped the card. Hours passed. Some trouble with our machine, the clerk said. He held up an index finger and began dialing in the credit card charge by hand. I started backing out the door. He held up his hand in a stop sign. Just a moment, he said insistently. He shouted the credit card number, then listened, then said some things I didn't understand. Then he hung up. He held his index finger up again, tapping his pencil off-beat between the incessant ticks of the tacky clock on the wall. Then the phone rang again. The man listened, but then unleashed a burst of Czech. At first I breathed, thinking it wasn't Giulio. But as the clerk hung up, I wondered whether Czech was one of the eight languages that Giulio half-spoke.

—Now, all fine, he said, pushing the slip at me to sign.

My room upstairs was a tired, earth-toned attempt at industrial glamour. There were huge mirrors on the wall above the bed. I took another pill, ran a bath full of brown water, and washed my clothes with soap in the sink. After an hour of soaking in the tub, the pain down below retreated. I dried off and took another pill, and lay down. It was four o'clock; I would rest for a few moments, I thought, then go out to the visitors' center and find the train schedule. I was sure that the bus clerk had been lying, that there would be trains to Terezin leaving at the end of the workday. I had forgotten my wet clothes. When I opened my eyes a few minutes later, it was still light, but the clock said ten after three. It had been four when I lay down. For a moment I had the creepy sense that I would never get to Terezin, that I was trapped in a place where time moved backward. Then I realized I had slept through the night and most of the next day. I knew I had to get up. But for some reason an almost deathly leisure now settled over me. It was as if my body had collapsed after years of strain. Yuri had taught me to drag around his past like a boulder, to keep it from rolling back down onto me. Leaving Giulio's car behind, my things in it, had been like stepping out of the way of the boulder, watching it slowly roll downhill. I felt as if each moment now could stretch as long as I wanted it to last, as if I had more time than I would ever need. As if I would never need to move again.

Sitting on the edge of the tub, I ate the rest of the cheese and stale bread over the sink, washing it down by bending my mouth down under the stream from the faucet. Then I took another hot bath and went to bed. Sometime in the night I started. Someone was knocking on the door. I lay still. Either it was the man at the desk, or Giulio's credit card company had tracked him down. Then there was silence. I pulled the covers over my head, thinking it was the man at the desk, that he would go away. Then I heard the short saw of a key in the lock, the tumbler falling, the uneasy sigh of hinges. The door thudded into place against the frame. The slice of the metal chain, sliding into its tiny track. I lay facing the wall, listening to the clink of change on the table, the buckle of the belt, the zipper, the latch on the bathroom door, the muffled sound of water sloshing from the ancient faucet. The staccato light switch click. In blackness I felt the cool draft on my back of the covers lifting. The mattress dipped, and there he was.

An arm slipped under, cradling my breast, the other clutching my belly. His body spooned in behind me, his breath gathering force. As he drank my scent in sharp, violent gulps, his almondy smell—it could only be Giulio—wrapped me in its promise of rest. It was Giulio; he had come this far to find me. Still I could not turn to him. The sorrow on his face would be too much. We had both let Clayton die, and now we were prisoners of each other, of what we had let happen. From behind, his flesh completed mine.

We lay still, taking in the terrible joy. Then his cheek grazed the thatch on my scalp. His hand groped my head, taking in what I had done to my hair, that it was gone. I saw myself through Giulio's eyes, my trip backward in time, my shaved head, the little march I had put myself through. I held myself still. If I spoke I would break, and if I broke I would never make it to Terezin. Giulio asked what I thought would await me. Again I held myself still. His breathing steadied, and I thought he was asleep. Then he told me what Rabbi Luzzatto wrote, that only when the soul was stripped bare could it witness the divine.

At dawn, while Giulio was sleeping, I gathered my things and slipped downstairs. At the desk I rang the bell; the clerk came out and told me it was Sunday, that the banks were closed. I asked for the station. He held up a finger, to ask me to wait a moment, and got on the phone. I left the credit card and ran, ran down a street and around a corner. I set down the Savant and caught my breath. I was standing next to a horse cart with some cheese. The smell was maddening, each breath of it impossibly *not* in my stomach. At the station, after a twenty-minute consultation with a dirty, dog-eared catalog of schedules, the woman behind the little glass window concluded that there was no train to Terezin. On a piece of scrap paper, she drew a little bus. I pointed to the clock on the wall. Again she buried herself in the huge schedule book. After an excruciating wait she concluded that on Sundays the bus left once a day, that I had missed it. I asked how far Terezin was. She wrote down 1,6 k. A mile away. I picked up the Savant and the duffel and my purse and asked her which way. She shrugged and shook her head. In the parking lot was an old ice-cream vendor. When he saw me he stared, then pointed to the display picture of his frozen ices. I stared at them. He opened his freezer and pulled out a multicolored rocket. I shook my head. He insisted. I pulled a bill from Giulio's wallet. Gently, the man pushed it away. He brought his stool around to the front of the freezer and set it down. I sat. He unwrapped the ice cream and handed it to me, and I ate. When I was done eating, he wiped the tears from my face with a napkin, said, *Terezín?* and pointed me the way.

The sky pressed down with clouds, and the heavy air clung to my skin. Terezin had been an Austrian military garrison, a walled-in town along with its smaller prison-fortress. I looked for the large fortress walls, but after an hour all that had appeared on the horizon were some ugly quadrangular buildings. Except for a boy and a girl listlessly kicking a pink ball back and forth, I would have taken the place for abandoned.

On those long library days in Milwaukee, hiding from my aunt, I had read about Theresienstadt. But I had no idea what had become of the town of Terezin after the war. I was not sure I even knew what a garrison looked like. But surely it would look strong, fortified, not like a handful of empty three-story buildings whose peeling plaster facades sat in advanced states of leprosy. Most of the windows, guarded by absurd sets of rusted bars, were broken or missing. In a courtyard, a little cement mixer stood near a heap of construction rubble. Perhaps I was still on the outskirts of Terezin. Perhaps the ice-cream man had sent me on the wrong road. A steady stream of traffic crawled along beside me. Following it, I made my way through a grid of ugly buildings. An old woman scurried by wearing a filthy skirt and jacket that had the prim, outdated look of a suit she'd worn as a debutante. Bright pink lipstick swerved wildly outside the lines of her lips. With a tiny clutch purse, she was swatting a swarm of invisible flies in front of her face.

A little farther down the road, half a dozen elderly men wandered randomly around a park, each talking to himself. I wandered into an insane zone, or some sort of mental institution. Cold entered my bones. For a moment I stood frozen, wondering if the people here were survivors, were people who had lost their minds as the result of wartime medical experiments on their parents. For a moment my legs would not move. Then I stumbled forward and rushed past their chatter down to the archway at the end of the road and hurried under it, expecting to come into the camp. But on the other side of the arch an empty road wound over a bridge and away from the town. Now I was more confused. Had I missed Terezin? Or had the town I had walked through been it? I shifted the Savant and the gas can and followed the road over a small man-made waterfall. Coming around a curve, I saw a house and a run-down tennis court with a sagging net, and then a parking lot full of school buses. Then a cemetery, then a fortress.

The Savant felt heavier, heavier, but I would not struggle much longer under the weight of it. I had not chosen my monstrous gift, Yuri's gnarled husbandry of it, the viney guilt that strangle-choked its boughs; but I could choose to stop carrying it, could perform my own *schleuse,* and strip myself of my burden. I passed the parking lot; clusters of German schoolchildren in white sweat socks and rubber flip-flops stood around a soda vendor in the parking lot, laughing hysterically, punching each other, drinking Coke. Shouting. On my way out, I thought,

I would buy a Coke to celebrate like them. On my way out I would be an American tourist.

The perfect cemetery was dominated by a huge modern crucifix. It had a fresh wreath tacked way up at its intersection. A perfectly straight pathway led through the graves. The flat, immaculate emerald lawn looked as unreal and dyed as the toxic forest. It was ordered by a perfect grid of uniform gravestones, each with its own manicured red rosebush coming into bloom, set out in dizzyingly geometric rows, their infinite diagonals cohering, the lines dissolving, then reassembling into other lines. A group of British tourists came up behind me. Their guide celebrated the six hundred Czech soldiers who had been dug up after the war and *properly reburied* here. The tone of his voice was as brisk and cheery, as professional as if we were touring Disneyland. Next we would approach the little fortress, he said, or *Kleine Festung*, which was built as a political prison next to the garrison town of Terezin in the late eighteenth century. Its most famous tenant was Gavrilo Princip. Princip had shot the Hapsburg heir to the throne, Archduke Franz Ferdinand, in Sarajevo, thus precipating World War I. He was held here in isolation until his death. At the little fortress, the guide said, we could look forward to hidden chambers. Mysterious passageways. And fascinating instruments of torture. The guide went on citing statistics and dimensions. The pride in the clipped, measured peaks in his voice made me want to scream. After a moment I realized that where we were was not Terezin, that I had walked through it, that the walls of the garrison town were so grown over that, without any marker, I had failed to notice when I had entered the town. No one wanted to live there after the war, the guide explained. As a result the residents were all very grateful to the Czech government for deciding to locate a significant mental health facility here.

All at once an army formation of sprinklers embedded into the ground began swishing up synchronous rhythmic arcs. The group walked on. I hurried to catch up and blend in with them. Even with the Savant and the duffel I melded in unobtrusively. We walked towards the first courtyard, passed under the entryway into the fortress, and slipped into what seemed to be called a courtyard of rooms, which had been the Germans' administration building. A curved, painted archway surprised me with a cheerfully repainted ARBEIT MACHT FREI. I supposed it was the least Terezin could do, to lend my project its evil epitaph. Tourists swarmed everywhere, posing for photos under the arch. A German guide pointed to the solitary confinement cells. I crossed through an archway into a courtyard punctuated by a series of low doorways. In one of them I heard a teacher lecturing. Then a bloodcurdling scream issued from the one closest to me. As I peeked into the tiny windowless cell, the shrieks broke into giggling. As my eyes hit the darkness a flash blinded me. A boy was writhing on the ground, his wrists slipped through the rusted shackles embedded into the wall, while a second held up a cheap plastic camera. Again its flash blinded my eyes. In the moment of blankness, of blindness, I thought of what it must have been to see nothing in that cell, day after day, and felt the blood drain from my head. That blankness, that blindness was what they saw of Yuri's past. For them the survivors existed as a field trip, as specks of the past to make fun of. I pulled my head out and ran. Then I heard kids' voices, imitating the staccato reports of machine guns. A ways down the wall, two teenagers were jerking back from hits into their best death-roll spirals as a third sprayed them with bullets with an invisible machine gun. I felt a shudder coming on, told my body to quiet, at least until I could get out of the fortress. Once past the perfect graveyard I walked back over the bridge, over the river I guessed was the Eger, to Terezin.

Even at its main entrance, the grown-over hillocks that covered the thick brick chamber-filled walls—*Kasematten,* they were called—made them hardly recognizable. Except for a few scattered and nearly hidden weapons windows, they looked benign. It was hard to imagine these mounds, with thickets of grass sprouting on top, constraining anyone. My error, I could see now, was expecting Terezin's star-shaped walls to be as high as the Great Wall of China. I stared at the drawbridge over the wild, overgrown moat, trying to imagine my Masurovsky grandparents arriving, jeweled and dressed in resort wear, to take possession of the lake-view villa they'd paid their fortune for. I tried to walk softly, to not disturb the ground, for if they could see what I was about to do, they'd roll over in their graves. *Der Führer Schenkt den Juden eine Stadt. Hitler Gives the Jews a City*—this was the title of the Nazi propaganda film, its look-at-the-happy-Jews-gardening scenes shot right here, in this moat. The problem now, these decades later, was how to give it back.

Of the fifteen thousand children who knew the ugliness, the dull terror of Theresienstadt, about a hundred passed through alive. Yuri had lasted among those hundred because he knew not to try to escape through the secret passageway in the chambers of the walls, knew there was no one to harbor him outside the walls; because the tragicomic sight of his father, hauling his wheelbarrow of corpses in a top hat and evening wear, had made Yuri laugh every day; because all three heads of the Jewish Elder

Council forced to draw up transport lists, Edelstein, Eppstein, and Murmelstein, had listened to Yuri perform—*(as if suspended, as if anything were possible)*—; because, after his father dropped dead, Yuri stole his work order off his body and assigned himself for hearse duty, so was able to give his father's body a proper burial; because Viktor Ullman, who had conducted the Prague Opera at twenty-two, persuaded him to get over his haughty snobbism about playing the only piano in the camp, a two-legged junker propped up by boxes left by the former residents of Terezin; because a sympathetic Czech guard managed to get Yuri transferred off hearse duty before the next transport, which habitually included all the wheelbarrowers—*(as if lancing the boils of festering eyes)*—; because the *Obersturmführer* had an urge to hear the Beethoven sonata Yuri was performing one evening; because even at six feet and eighty-nine pounds, Yuri's habitual arrogance made him glare out into the audience as he sat down to play, to see who was there; because a wild adrenaline made him give the performance of his life. Because, after a bunkmate sawed a copper wire with a spoon he had sharpened and cut the electricity for the entire camp, Yuri fainted a split second before the machine gun running down the line of random boys got to him, fainted for the only time in his entire proud life, and was taken for dead; because in the middle of the night when the corpses' heat seeped out, he woke before he froze, crawled out, and ran back to the barracks. Because when they began shooting *Hitler's Gift,* Yuri had horrible dysentery, so that later when they found themselves *forced* to deport its other screen stars—*(as if gulping, swallowing)*—he was spared. Because he had never worked his way up to the third, most desirable tier of bunks, and so was not deported in preparation for the Red Cross inspection when they sawed off the top layer of bunks, along with their eighteen thousand sleepers, to make the camp look less overcrowded. Because two days before the Red Cross visit, when the *Obersturmführer* was looking for him, Yuri heard the rumor and stole the papers of somebody who had died of typhus. So that instead of starring in that hoax and giving the poor officials no choice but to deport him afterwards, he got to be one of the supporting actors, one of the "healthy" people forced to crawl under the sheets of the infested infirmary now that all the deathly ill had been deported. Because his mother had died of typhus the night before she was to be put on a transport to Auschwitz, with Yuri voluntarily accompanying her. Because, a few months before liberation, when prisoners were forced to form a human chain stringing out from the repository at the Litomerice gate, through the town, and out the wall to the banks of the Eger River, forced then to pass thirty-three thousand wooden boxes and brown paper bags, each meticulously labeled with name and number—*(staccato, as if pinning butterflies on a board)*—and forced, finally, to dump their contents in the Eger, Yuri kept himself from crying out when his neighbor passed him the remains of his mother, forced himself to laugh when his neighbor, reading Yuri's hesitation and a guard's notice of it, joked, *They're drinking our dead!* because the Eger flowed into the Elbe, which was where the Germans drew their drinking water. Because, when the Russian army liberated them, Yuri knew that, as an émigré, he would have been sent straight to Siberia, and had the presence of mind, though starving and hallucinatory, to speak French. Because he'd had the will to get off the continent, to come to Brooklyn, to make himself a carpenter, to try and forget.

Survivors recognize each other, as if by the scent of their own. I always knew what it meant, wherever we were, when Yuri's sudden vice-grip steered me away. He couldn't bear the self-centered narratives—and these from the sane ones—stitching the inevitable yarn of miraculous reprieves into a needlepoint of God, a personally monogrammed God concerned with saving one life, and one life alone. Couldn't bear the faith they carried in their bitter quests for justice. The first one we tracked down was an old woman near London who'd taken one look at him through the screen door and hobbled away shouting. She returned clutching a letter from the German Reparations Bureau. Though her husband, a music teacher named Schmidt, had been shot in 1934, they'd denied her pension on the grounds that her husband had died an accidental death: it had been determined, the letter said, that they'd intended to shoot some other Jewish Schmidt. Another, in Jerusalem, had been denied compensation for her sterilization, the letter signed by the same Nazi doctor who had signed off on the euthanasia of her retarded son. The third, a man, found Yuri. On the subway in New York he seized his arm and begged him for a witness affidavit. For decades, the bureau had sent back letters saying they needed more documentation before there could be any question of compensation. The man's parents, his sister and brother had all died of typhoid on a train to Auschwitz, but only those killed *in* the camps were automatically eligible. Could it be proven, the Reparations Bureau wanted to know, that the family were healthy when they boarded? At the sight of this tiny, round man who still believed he'd get justice, Yuri's grip tightened to a tourniquet, and he steered me away, unable to hear more. After that we simply snuck up to a house, looked in the window, and left; at most, I'd ring the bell and ask directions while he watched from the bushes. He couldn't stand to meet them.

In the Shoah *Totenbucher*, the books of the dead, the Yuris are never listed. No record of the loss of his third and fourth fingers, bludgeoned with a plank three days before liberation by the talentless guard Yuri'd gone to conservatory with, for the wrong note Yuri hit when he heard the grumble-strafe of approaching American bombers. How to calculate a restitution—not that any was offered—for the arc of the plank swinging, the curved slur from Yuri's final notes to the lifelong rest that followed? For the loss of a continent? For a sleep that, without a wife to cling to, knew only the peace of a guard's whistle?

Yuri was a nonbeliever. He had nothing but bitterness for forgiveness, for martyrdom and other-cheekism, its shoddy Jesus-dreams of salvation. His scale of justice was the eye-for-an-eye, Old Testament balance. When his dreams got bad, the night cries too searing, Yuri's only relief was to count, to prove to himself that some of ours had outlived some of theirs. But it never worked. Because what Yuri lost was not two parents, or two fingers, not a musical community or a continent. What Yuri lost was a way of trusting the world, the ability to imagine that the world's immense silence contained any sort of listening. What Yuri lost was the possibility of God.

Hell Yuri could bear, but not a godless universe. That void, he could not bear. However often he pronounced himself a nonbeliever, his iron Russian idealism had to latch on somewhere, and I was what was left. Husbanding my talent was his way of making order out of chaos. But in tying the knots of the safety net that held us, in never forgetting, Yuri had tied us to the murderers. The loss of God had never healed. And when I broke down his prescriptions, the night of my debut, he surely stormed out, and my mother followed, and he crashed them in a rage. I had not killed Yuri, but I had wanted to, to kill the killed, to kill the part of him that was dead, the part that spent years force-feeding me the danger, and carving me into his musical phantom limb. At home, after my debut, I took the whistle I'd blown at Yuri in his sleep, and hid it inside my cello, knowing I would carry it with me, forever. But I had known a peace.

On a bench next to me, two tourists looking at a zigzag of postcards were critiquing the cheap sixties imitation Bauhaus furniture that decorated the former Gestapo headquarters. That was what the place had come to: a shabby tourist attraction. I heard a grumble of distant thunder. My head was pounding. I had to be done with it.

I stood up and headed towards the grassy turf next to the wall, towards where I thought a good place might be. A large section of the camp was fenced off, and I had to wander off through the rows of barracks to get back around to the wall. The light was beginning to fade. I passed another tiny cemetery whose gravestones here were haphazard, grown-over, unidentifiable, their illegible inscriptions eroded or thick with lichens. This would be the prewar one. I hurried away down a street between a set of barracks and came upon a little square park. A husband and wife were arguing in German about the tall trees swaying, leafless, against the early spring wind.

—There were none then, said the husband.

—Look at their height, insisted his wife. These trees are over fifty years old.

—Well, they must have been fenced off, said the husband, turning to me. Because I never saw them.

—*Bitte,* I said, for the crematorium?

They both pointed to an opening in the thick wall where a road passed through where three people, two tall, one very short, stood peering through gates into a dark chamber built into the thick cross section of the wall.

—Where those people are is the Litomerice gate, said the wife, taking my elbow. He was pointing, I realized, to the place where I had first entered the town.

—That was the mortuary, said the husband. Where the bodies were kept.

—Go out there, said the wife, and then turn left down the road.

—About one-half kilometer, said the husband.

I thanked them for their kindness.

—These streets were always so packed, the wife added as an afterthought. We had only two hours, you know, to see some family or get something to eat. Never were they empty.

I nodded and left them behind. At the Litomerice gate, on the ground in plain sight were train tracks. I had walked by them, not ten feet away. Missed them completely.

The air was darkening. The enormous poplars flanking the road swayed in the gathering storm. I hurried down the long walkway towards a huge, ugly menorah with thick, square, modern prongs that rose up on the other side of a field. A ravaged-faced woman scuttled past me, weeping, clutching tissues against her face. I came onto a vast, roughly cropped field. Twenty or thirty knee-high triangular gravestones were scattered across a field of brown, unmowed grass. To the left was a one-story building with a flat roof that looked like a garage or a shed.

The cheerful Czech guide was a tiny man in polyester slacks with a battered leather shoulder bag. In confident broken English he was explaining that the Jewish cemetery contained a mass grave where nine thousand people were buried. I tried to concentrate on remaining silent. At the same time I heard my voice ask why there were only thirty gravestones. The guide replied that they had run out of money. *They.* He pointed to the field on the other side of the garagelike building where waist-high grass grew freely. Money was why in that field there were no gravestones at all. I thought of the cemetery for the Christian soldiers, the sprinklers on the rosebushes, the fancy country-club lawn. I burst out laughing. No wonder they had run out of money. This was the best they could do? This pathetic sham was a neat attempt at contraction, the inverse of Jesus' turning one fish into an ocean of fishes and one loaf into oceans of bread. It was a landscape of the lie, the lie still happening. Then I thought of my parents' ashes, lost by the shipping company on the way to Milwaukee, because I had not taken them with me. Probably it didn't matter.

The three men moved away from me and into the tan school-house. Two elderly women were crawling around in brown grass outside its base. Behind it, a smoke snake slithered up into the sky. I thought I must be hallucinating.

—Nowhere do I find *Topf und Sonne,* one of the old ladies yelled in German as I approached.

—So this would be the only one not made by Topf of Erfurt? the other yelled skeptically. She crawled a little further aside the building, brushing away the long grass.

Though I intended simply to ask where the crematorium was—it would be too surreal that it would be this building, issuing the smoke—my voice again blurted out without intent.

—What is Topf? I asked, at their behinds.

—They make breweries and crematoria, said the one on the left, a widow dressed all in black, without looking up.

—They developed the use of body fats for soaps, yelled the second, further down the wall.

—In Erfurt, I said, to get her not to say any more.

—Not now of Erfurt. Of Wiesbaden, said the first. They have moved to Wiesbaden in March or April of forty-five.

—*Ja*, said the other, they are suing now the German government for compensation because they had to flee when the Russians came.

—The old man and top manager had the good grace to commit suicide, added the first, but now the sons have the nerve to sue for compensation.

She looked at me helplessly from her hands and knees. I dropped the Savant and the duffel, and gripped her elbow and helped her.

Upright, she was a plumpish Italian widow, dressed in black, with a thick, wiry gray bun. I stared into the shiny blackberry eyes that bore out from the labyrinth of wrinkles on her tanned, leathery face. She was the vision of what my mother would have looked like had she lived to grow old. I could not look away. She had my mother's full body, her defiant, stagy posture. Even the way this woman's throat twitched when she swallowed was my mother. This was my mother, in a body older even than if she were alive. She glanced at the Savant behind me, opened her mouth, then closed it again.

—Manfreda Levante, she said, offering her hand.

I had spoken my short remarks in German, but she approached me in English. My throat locked. I held out my left hand. She shook it. Hers was warm and dry and pillowy.

My eyes came to rest on the large, vertical scar that cleft her left eyebrow into two thick, fuzzy half-rests.

—A guard kicked me there, she said, smiling.

—I wasn't—

She took my hand and held it in hers. —Helga speaks English, she said.

Helga was standing in the doorway. A last patch of sun fell upon her, lighting up her green dress.

—And who is this? Helga asked. A relation?

—She is, Manfreda said, still holding my hand. She is a decent human being. I am related to all decent human beings.

—I also was a musician, Helga said, her eye falling again on the Savant. Imagine, a little girl like me playing the double bass. Too bad I don't play the cello.

—She was quite gifted, said Manfreda. I played the French horn, but not so good.

—You stopped?

—Once we got out, Helga said, we were so happy to be living that—

Manfreda shrugged. —We forgot our gifts.

I nodded and smiled politely, and went to pick up my belongings. To the left, behind glass, was an unlit white-tiled room with opaque glass windows and empty glass display cases. Facing us was a long cream-colored stone table with a wooden block at one end. The block looked like the bottom half of a gallows, had a semicircular depression cut out in the center of it. Attached to the table at this end was a stone sink, with a little metal post sticking up that looked like a water spritzer, and a red rubber tube leading out from the bottom. Other than the three glass jars of red, yellow, and blue powders that sat in one of the display cases, the tube was the only color in the shadowy, off-white room.

In the glass, I saw the father and son from before and the perky little guide peering in behind me. The son asked what the colored powders were.

—Just decoration! the guide proclaimed cheerfully. There were no medical experiments in Terezin. No medical experiments!

I turned and looked at him. He smiled. I smiled.

—What's this table for?

—That was just a worktable.

There followed a silence. They moved away.

Manfreda came up behind me and clutched my elbow. —That sink was where they broke out the gold teeth, she said quietly. They put your neck on that block. The red tube was so that blood could go down.

I could not bear any more. I felt certain they would know of Yuri. At the time of his arrest Yuri had played all over Europe. He and his father had been known as the only Russian prisoners in the camp. I tried to wriggle free, to get away. But Manfreda clenched my elbow with her ropy hand and would not let me go.

—Why did you come?

—We were here, in L-418, she said. And you? You are too young and bright to have known this inferno.

—Where's your number, I said.

Manfreda unbuttoned her cardigan and starched blouse to reveal the top of her small breasts, hanging down, the skin like bark. She stretched the skin apart to reveal a tiny, crinkled tattoo.

—This was from Auschwitz. I was there for two days before my husband, who was a Christian and a Czech government minister, got me transferred back here. I was one of only two people who went in the reverse direction. It saved my life.

—And the one from here?

—I had a number here, Helga said, twelve-three-nine. Ninth member of the third transport from Frankfurt, which was twelve. But not on my body.

—You were special, that they didn't tattoo you?

—There were none here, Helga replied.

—There must have been, I insisted.

Manfreda shook her head. —Here they didn't do that, she said.

My brain's desperate calculations fell still.

—I need somebody's number, I insisted. He died before I wrote it down.

—Why do you need it? asked Helga.

—To know what it was.

—Somebody who was interned only here and nowhere else?

I nodded.

—He wouldn't have had one, Helga said.

A numbness began spreading in my body, a dumb, numb rage. The place was not a fortress, but a place filled with mental patients; its walls had flowers growing; and the crematorium looked like a schoolhouse. Now I could not even call up a vision of Yuri's tattoo on his arm. It was an overlay of memory. My years of useless calculations were dissolving like smoke into air.

—He had to, I said, trying not to cry. I wanted a sum to hold on to, an equation to define and contain years of stupid sacrifice.

—This is ridiculous, Helga erupted. She rummaged into her purse and pulled out a green-and-gold-flecked fountain pen. —Rolled into this pen I smuggled into Theresienstadt the money that saved my life. Without this pen, these are my bones, she said, dislodging a chalky white clod from the trodden dirt with her toe. Come here, she said. It's water-based. She held out my forearm and pushed up my sleeve and slowly wrote out seven characters, SSS7777, and said, —There. This is more than we were ever given. Before you leave Terezin, wash it from your skin. And do not any more disfigure yourself with any more of your Ilse Koch obsessions.

—Who's Ilse Koch?

—The one at Buchenwald, said Manfreda. Who had people killed for their fancy tattoos. She made them into lamp shades.

—Let's go, said Helga.

The women stepped outside. Then Helga turned back and looked at me and waved me towards her. The darkening air was thick and heavy, the artillery bursts of thunder closing in. The dusty field was deserted except for a scraggly stray cat with patchy charcoal fur. Manfreda looked down as the skin-and-bones feline scraped its ribs against her shin. She looked down and laughed.

—You we would have eaten, she said.

I told them I needed a minute. Tactfully, they stepped away from the door. I went back through the anteroom and stepped down the short stairs to the four huge pitch-black furnaces. Each was clutched by a charred network of arteries and veins, pipes running everywhere and nowhere. An absurd crop of tiny Israeli flags had been planted in the pitch-black beasts. Yuri had fed me these ashes like bread, I thought, and yet practically all I knew of being Jewish was these ovens. I stepped back behind the first two ovens to one of the two in the back, set down the Savant, and opened its case. The oven's low door was open flat and littered with ashes. Were these *decorative* ashes, I wondered, or had the place never been cleaned? I pulled out the instrument. With absurd care I laid it on one of the horizontal dollies sticking out from the crematoria doors. I unscrewed the canister and sprinkled gasoline over the Savant. The paintings of piety and justice in its varnish began to disappear. I heard someone coming. There was no time. I got out the box of wooden matches I had stolen from the hotel.

—Aren't you coming? Manfreda called, appearing in the doorway as I struck a match. At the top of the stairs she stopped dead in her tracks. We stood there, staring, the flame's tiny heat pressing towards my fingernails. I refused to look down at the Savant. Giulio knew where I was going, and was sure to show up at any moment, and then I would never have another chance to leave the Savant behind.

All that was left was to drop the match.

Manfreda planted a hand on her hip. —We're waiting, she said, as if my holding a match over my cello were the most normal scene in the world.

—For what?

—Aren't you the music? she asked.

I stared at her, blankly. —The music?

—They promised us music for our reunion, she said.

—I'm not it, I said.

She glanced at the Savant. —You couldn't fill in?

She had taken me for a musical nobody, shrouded me in a mantle of ordinariness for the first time in my life. It felt so light I thought I might float off the earth. The match searing my finger and thumb burnt out. I heard a steady tapping, a gentle *pizzicato* of pitches. It was the language of rain. I shut my eyes and listened to the porous hum of drops on grass, the flat rhythmic ting from the metal spout over the doorway. I listened to nature's music, to how it threw the world into relief like an audible cloak, giving each object a voice, each invisible beast a safe, known shape. If I stepped out into it I would be one of those things, a thing in the present, no more, no less. Like Helga, I could forget my gift.

The wash of a car on a road swelled, then faded away. As quickly as it came, the rain had vanished. In the fresh silence I crushed the match's ember and let it drop. Manfreda snapped open her pocketbook and handed me a handkerchief. The gasoline had stripped the residue of pigment from the paintings on the Savant's belly. As I wiped it down, the Savant began to look like an ordinary cello. The old woman disappeared out the doorway. I picked it up and followed.

Around the back of the crematorium, about a dozen people were gathered. A bonfire was hissing and snapping and a sickly sweet stench hung in the air. At the podium a priest and a rabbi were taking turns reading names and dates from the Theresienstadt *Totenbuch*. At each name spoken, someone picked a lily out of a huge pile on the back of a farmer's truck, stepped forward, and dropped it onto the pyre. A few yards away, in the overgrown cemetery, there was Giulio, arms folded, leaning against a gravestone. His face, a ravaged landscape, begged me to take him in.

—We had a friend, Manfreda whispered, a boy whose job it was to go outside the camp to bring back the dairy products from the farmers. We were not allowed to plant anything. He sneaked in a tiny sapling, tucked inside his sock, and planted it. That is the tree. Every few years we get together and speak the names of anybody anybody remembers.

I sat down on the footstep to the truck and tightened my bow. A stout amputee in lederhosen and a green loden jacket, with a small accordion strapped to his chest, hobbled over on his wooden leg.

—May I be of help? he asked in German.

—Are you the hired musician?

—I am an accordionist at a beer-garden in Chemnitz. As a boy I was taught piano here by Gideon Klein. I just brought this along because the German government promised music. And with their promises. . . Well. You know how that goes. You know Bloch's *Jewish Song*?

He played a chord. Suddenly I heard the Kreutzer Sonata, as it had been performed during the war, by prisoners, on violin and accordion. Then, layered over it, the Verdi *Requiem*. Then a huge cacophonous cloud of noise, the hundreds of concerts performed at Theresienstadt, broke out all at once in my ear's attic. I could not unspool the staff of a single melody from the thousands screaming there. The idea of a lullaby to soothe all these souls seemed hopelessly small.

I asked if he knew the *Hebraic Suite*. It was the only piece of Jewish music I knew.

—For *viola*? he asked skeptically. I lowered my eyes and said I'd transpose down a fifth.

He lay a hand on my back to quiet my shuddering. —What about the solo from the *Quartet for the End of Time*?

With his question's end my mind dropped into silence.

I stared at the curl of smoke darkening the dusk. My moment of revelation had happened days ago, in the car, but in true Yuri fashion I'd been too driven by my mission to see it. The recording I'd heard on the radio, of course, had been my one unbreachable performance at Carnegie Hall, when my labored alloy of illusion and Eros, of art and love, poured out as molten ore. Yet even that performance had not saved Yuri, had not turned back time and undone the done. Even if cremating the

Savant could have burned off the dead weight of *special,* the act would not, could not ever, burn Yuri's stamp from my flesh. Music was the tangled love I was given; it was what I had. I would never perform the way I had again; never again could I dwell in Yuri's bunker; but music was still my logos, still my meaning and the structure of it; its perfect present still the best form my time on earth could take. I was made of it, and all things I made would be made in its time. Unless I threw myself in the pyre, no conflagration could singe the breath of a note.

The accordionist cleared his throat. Twilight was falling; the mourners were tossing the last of their lilies off the truck. I picked up a flower that had fallen short of the fire. Silently I sang the names of my Masurovsky grandparents, of Yuri and my mother and Clayton, and tossed the lily in. The silence that followed contained a breath, a pulse, the quiet joy of Giulio alive. I poised my bow, gasping for its air. The storm had passed, and now stars were dangling from the charcoal sky. I spread the opening motif out into them, into the thickening dark. The accordionist joined under, gently cradling my voice. This small shared sweetness undammed my underground river, my mother tongue, which was still the only grieving I would know.

About the Author

JOYCE HACKETT studied at Wellesley, the University of Milan, and Harvard, and she holds an MFA in fiction from Columbia. Her work has appeared in a variety of publications in the U.S. and abroad, including the *Paris Review, London Magazine,* the *Chicago Tribune,* the *Boston Review,* Salon.com, and the Berlin daily *Der Tagespiegel.* She lives in New York and Berlin.